To

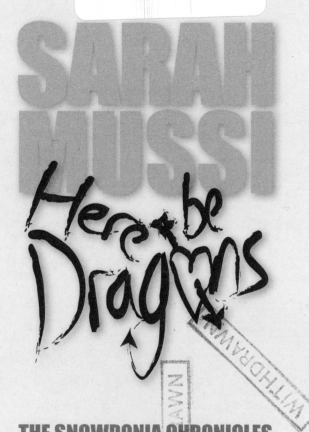

SARAH MUSSI

Here be Dragons

THE SNOWDONIA CHRONICLES
BOOK ONE

Best. wishes Sarah Mussi

SARAH MUSSI

Here be Dragons

THE SNOWDONIA CHRONICLES
BOOK ONE

VERTEBRATE PUBLISHING

Here Be Dragons
Sarah Mussi

First published in 2015 by Vertebrate Publishing

Vertebrate Publishing
Crescent House, 228 Psalter Lane, Sheffield, S11 8UT, UK
www.v-publishing.co.uk

Cover design by Nathan Ryder
Cover photo by Keld Bach, www.keldbach.com
Typesetting and production by Jane Beagley
Author photograph © Roger Bool

This book is a work of fiction. The names, characters, places, events and
incidents are products of the author's imagination. Any resemblance to
actual persons, living or dead, or actual events is purely coincidental.

A CIP catalogue record for this book is available from the British Library.

ISBN 978-1-910240-34-2 (Paperback)
ISBN 978-1-910240-35-9 (ebook)

10 9 8 7 6 5 4 3 2 1

Production by Vertebrate Graphics Ltd.
www.v-graphics.co.uk

Printed and bound in Great Britain by
Clays Ltd, St Ives plc

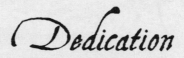
Dedication

To Y DDRAIG GOCH,
The Red Dragon of Wales

It is said that Y DDRAIG GOCH protects and
defends those who truly love and cherish the ancient,
beautiful land of Wales. It is said that He bestows a
Blessing on them. And upon his enemies He lets loose
the ancient Dragon's Curse. This is what is said.

From Welsh Tradition

Here be
Dragons

Their side

Y Lliwedd

Crib
Goch

Glyder Fawr

Snowdon

e mountain

Yr Aran

Dinas
Emrys

**Snowdon
Yr Wyddfa**

rnedd
gain

Clogwyn Du'r Arddu/
The Black Cliff

The Devil's
Bridge

Ranger Path

Llyn

Moel
Cynghorion

Our side of the mountain

Upper Pastures

N

Llanberis Pass

Halfway
House

Snowdon Railway

George's cottage

Ellie's farmhouse

Llanberis Path

Llyn Padarn

Pen-y-mynydd-gwryd
Hotel

Llanberis

to Caernarfon

So It Was

The girl turns her face to the summit. Above her the air shudders. Just thirty paces. If she can only reach the safety of the rocks. Heart pounding, blood hammering, she poises herself.

Run.

She races forward. She leaps from the ground, stumbles past the stony crags of the lair, bursts through the drifts of dark snow. The air shivers around her; she tears through it, swerves past the cliff edge above the llyn[1].

That dark fearful cliff edge.

An appalling shriek rents the air. The sound of teeth crashing, talons scraping. She imagines the yellow eyes searching for her. Soon they will know she's gone. They will nose the air, catch her scent. Soon they will come for her.

---

1. Welsh for lake.

Get to the rocks.

Steps crash behind her, mighty footfalls. She hears ragged breath at her back. A fetid stench slams into the dawn. They are coming.

Up ahead the rocky cave opens. Ten metres away. Ten metres of cliff edge. She weaves in between the clumps of snow-bound heather, ducking, leaping, twisting. The ground is icy, smooth, treacherous. She slips, rights herself. A booming, a shrieking tears at her ears.

They know she's gone.

Just one chance now.

Just run.

Just pray.

Just make it away from the old fortress of Dinas Emrys.

A deafening roar splits the dawn.

Hurry.

She sprints. The path turns. She skids out of control. She's falling. She screams, her arms outstretched. She hits the ground, tumbles forward.

'Help!' she cries weakly, 'Oh somebody help me!'

And the earth beneath her feet gives way. Heart bursting, body falling, twisting, turning; down she plummets over the cliff edge. Down into the gully beneath.

So It Is

Act One

Aduwyn gaer yssyd ae kyffrwy kedeu

Oed meu y rydeu a dewisswn

Ny lafaraf i deith reith ryscatwn

Ny dyly kelenic ny wyppo hwn

Yscriuen brydein bryder briffwn

Yn yt wna tonneu eu hymgyffrwn

Pereit hyt pell y gell a treidwn.[1]

From *Etmic Dinbych ~ The Book of Taliesin*
The Mabinogion (AD 1275)

---

1. Translated from the Welsh:
   A pleasant caer [stronghold] there is, which princely ones adorn
   There were liberties there which none human could desire
   I will not speak of its privilege, which I observed
   For he who knows not these forms of royal precedence has no right to a bard's fee
   In the writings of Pryderi, supreme one of Prydain
   There at the slope's end where the waves make a roar about it
   Long may it last, for there is the mountain chamber which I dared visit.

One

Infinite love is the only truth.
Everything else is illusion.[1]

It was Christmas. Although, you'd hardly have known it. I was at home pinging my friends in front of the telly. The telly wasn't actually working, of course. Nothing was. The only entertainment that morning was the snow. Since 5 a.m., the whole of North Wales had been issued with a severe weather alert.

You need to know what a severe weather alert means when you're me, Arabella (Ellie) Morgan, living in a remote farmhouse on the slopes of Mount Snowdon with only your mum. It means life comes to a standstill.

Totally.

---

1. David Icke.

Yes, that's right. Nothing. Actually. Happens.

There is no electricity. No fairy lights. No heating. No way to charge your phone. No hot water. No COMPUTER. No hope of watching Dr Who. No hope of a Christmas dinner. In fact, There is No Hope.

What kind of sad Christmas is that?

Sorry. Correction: There was one hope – the generator might fire up.

The generator had not fired up.

Mum and I had spent two hours in the barn trying to coax it into life, and failed, miserably. Plus that Christmas morning, it wasn't only the snow and the electricity. An hour or so after the severe weather alert had pinged up on our phone apps, the emergency services rang, closely followed by a call from the Llanberis Mountain Search and Rescue coordinator. That meant there was some *stoopid* hiker, who'd planned on spending Christmas morning on the summit of Snowdon (like you do).

And hadn't made it.

It also meant my mum (support member for the rescue team) was going to have to get out on to the mountain and do a sweep of all our top pastures and the slopes behind our farmhouse, as soon as it was daylight, to see if she could eliminate those areas from the main search.

4

And of course, she couldn't go alone (LMRT Handbook. Section 32: *'Emergency rescue searches in Severe Weather Alerts must be manned by a minimum of eight.'*)

Great.

I wonder who the seven others were going to be.

Ha ha.

Since the farm failed, (for obvious reasons, like, um, yes, would that be snow? Not to mention being halfway up the highest peak in Wales, plus all those new restrictions on where your sheep can graze/can't graze/might not be able to graze in future …), being a mountain guide, and servicing campers, is how Mum keeps us going. I don't know why we can't just leave, and go back and live in that nice little flat in central London (we were so happy there). But I guess that's another story, and probably something to do with Dad and the accident, and how he loved Snowdon, and how Mum has to help rescue everyone, because nobody rescued him.

Anyway there I was, 25th December, crouched with Mum in front of a log fire, sipping tea, feeling sorry for myself.

'You'll come with me, won't you?' said Mum.

Of course I would. Apart from Section 32, if we were lucky enough to find the hiker, Mum couldn't cope alone.

'It's just that, what with it being Christmas, Terry's gone to his mum's and Rhys's got his kids over, and I think Owen drank too much last night, and it'll take ages for them to even get up here to give me a hand and … '

'It's ok,' I said.

'And I just never expected … '

'I'll come,' I said.

'There's a full team out over on the Ranger Path with a medic, and the RAF helicopter's out too, but the visibility … and it's just to eliminate this side and … '

'I'll come,' I repeated.

'Thanks Elles,' she said.

As soon as we could, we got ourselves sorted: ice axes, crampons, whistles, compass, head torches, blizzard bags, thermal mat, space blankets and all the usual daysack stuff. We put away the fluffy slippers, new iPad, box set of series 6 of *Merlin & Morgana* – which we couldn't watch anyway. Sob. We called the rescue team back and told them we'd search the Llanberis Path from our farmhouse up towards Clogwyn Du'r Arddu, (FYI – that's Welsh for Arthur's Black Cliff). They said they'd get another team out to catch us up and take over; that their information led them to believe she took the Ranger Path anyway.

I re-read my pings and wrote my last message to the girls. *'Gotta go now, babes XXXX.'* But before I could click the phone off, my mate Rhiannon pinged me straight back.

Mum was at the door impatient to go. I slipped the phone in my pocket. Pinging Rhi back would have to wait. Who knows what the day held?

We left Ceri – our border collie – to guard the house, and set out. She wasn't very thrilled about that and neither was I, but she wasn't fully trained yet as a search and rescue dog and the weather, you know. The sky was still dark and the snow was driving down. Mum led and I trod in the path she cleared. Soon my fingers were numb, and I swear there were icicles on my eyelashes. The farmhouse disappeared behind us like it was part of a vanishing trick, and we were left marooned in a sea of white. If not for our head torches, compass and maps we'd have been as lost as the hiker.

The wind was rough too, gale force. It didn't blow at a constant velocity. You couldn't lean into it as you climbed and make steady distance. It broke at you suddenly in violent fits with such gusts of high speed that it sent snow flurrying into your face and knocked you clean off your feet.

Mum was great though. She kept turning round and

smiling her thanks and encouraging me. I guess she knew other teenagers were waking up to Christmas stockings and sparkly lights – or better still, not waking up till afternoon. I guess she knew I wished I were one of them.

My phone pinged again. Rhiannon? I dug it out my pocket. But it wasn't her.

Recent updates between Ellie and Sheila:

Sheila

Rhiannon's cousin is lush. Hands off.

I rolled my eyes, annoyed, and pinged her right back.

Ellie

Look no hands.

I shook my head. Sheila always does that. If there's ever any new face, anywhere within a zillion miles of Llanberis, she tries to bag him first. Like, was I even interested in Rhiannon's whatever cousin from wherevers-ville, anyway?

But what if he'd been nice? Was nice? Did that mean I'd have to wait until Sheila'd finished pawing him over and announcing him not fit for human consumption? Right there and then I wished I could meet someone that nobody else in the village knew about, someone they'd *never* know about … someone that Sheila couldn't get her claws into first, anyway. I turned my head towards the ancient craggy summit and sent up a silent prayer. *By the powers hidden in the mountain send me someone Sheila's never heard of*.

Mum turned and saw I'd fallen behind. She beckoned me to hurry up. I shoved my phone back in my pocket. First no electricity, then the call out – and now Sheila.

It was only 7 a.m. and already Christmas sucked.

It was as we broke out of the cloud bank above the valleys, that I first saw him. I think. I couldn't be sure. Everywhere was thick with driving snow. But through the dawn, I'm sure I saw a figure. There he stood, in front of Garnedd Ugain on the very rim of the great knife-edge way above the Llanberis Pass, in a dangerous place that Mum and I call the Devil's Bridge. I rubbed my eyes, but by the time I'd looked again, new banks of mist had swirled down.

'Did you see that?' I shouted. 'Up there … by Devil's Bridge.' Mum turned to make her way in that direction. She pulled out a high-beam torch and shone it into the blizzard towards the Devil's Bridge. Light bounced back from the cloud and dazzled us.

'A boy!' I shouted.

Mum shook her head. 'You must be seeing things!' she yelled. 'Remember we're not looking for a boy.' She retraced her steps. 'Keep your eyes peeled for a girl!' she yelled across the storm. 'Remember ... description ... alone ... 17 ... didn't make it to the top ... no information since ... around here maybe ... her phone battery's probably dead ... if she had equipment, she may still be alive ... maybe.'

I dragged the binoculars out and scanned everywhere. It was tough. The clouds had closed in again behind us and covered everything except the very peak of Snowdon. Sometimes when they rolled back for a split second I could see the café on the summit, but of course that was no help. It's always closed during winter. Only people who don't know the mountain think up stupid stuff like: 'Meet you at the café, on the summit, for a mince pie, on Christmas morning.'

We trudged on, keeping to the path. I never thought, not even for a minute, about the coincidence – about Christmas, and me wishing, and then the figure by Devil's Bridge. I just carried on feeling mad at Sheila and stamping down the snow. The uphill gradient was steep enough to ward off the biting cold though, and by the time we'd scoured the upper pastures I was puffed and glowing with the effort.

But we didn't find her. We debated what to do. Mum was worried that by the time they got a proper mountain rescue team up here, the girl might be dead.

'Let's go a bit further then,' I said, 'it's not like we've left anything cooking, is it?'

So we headed out for the mountain proper. I kept my head down, searching for any tracks that might show where the girl had lost her way. It was a pretty difficult job, and up ahead was Clogwyn Du'r Arddu, the Black Cliff. I was praying she hadn't strayed too close to that. There's something about those cliffs that sends shivers into your chest. I tried to drag my mind away from them, but now I'd banished Sheila from my thoughts there was a curious space left behind. A space I didn't want their gloom to fill up. I felt the coldness of their shadows reaching out towards us, then the image of that boy slipped uninvited right into my imagination to fill up the gap.

There he was, in my mind, as clear as if he was right in front of me. Standing by Devil's Bridge, his face turned in my direction. And somehow, miraculously, he zoomed in closer. All the little details about him stood out. It didn't look like he was wearing much of a jacket for a start, and he was smiling. He was handsome, with fine clear-cut features. He had thick tousled reddish hair, and his smile seemed inexplicably to be directed at me. Dark eyebrows framed his face, and even though I couldn't have seen it, I got the impression they were knitted together in a frown.

A shiver ran over me. There was something forbidding in the way he was standing there, smiling and not-smiling. I felt I should look away; I should be scared of him, but instead a thrill ran through me, almost like an electric shock. And it seemed like our eyes met. And his were smouldering and filled with something I couldn't quite place; something urgent, I think.

Suddenly he realised I'd seen him. (Although how he could have, I don't know.) For a moment his smile broke, gorgeous, incredible, bright like the sun. Then he seemed to catch himself and grow angry. A gloom replaced all the radiance and, quick as lightning, he whirled away and vanished.

The vision faded.

'There!' said Mum unexpectedly.

I blinked.

'Come on Ellie, stop daydreaming! Look!'

She turned and ran off the path at such speed that my stomach shot into my throat.

'By the white rocks.'

To this day, I don't know how she does it; how she can make out the tiny curled-up shape of a human being amongst snow drifts and boulders.

'Call the team or anyone on duty,' said Mum. 'Sighting on the upper pastures, north side below the llyn. Quick! Give me your compass, mine's at the bottom of my pack. I'll plot our position and I'll light up a flare.'

I unwound my scarf, looped the compass off my neck, gave it her, got on the mobile and called the Mountain Rescue Team. They were already half-way up the Ranger Path, and too far away to help, but the RAF helicopter was en route. If the weather allowed, they could land in minutes.

I gave them the general location while Mum tried to hold on to the map and shout coordinates off the compass. Then she set off a handheld ground flare, so they would know exactly where we were and be able to assess wind speed. (Mum doesn't trust GPS. She reckons it was due to GPS inaccuracy that Dad wasn't saved.) I vaguely wondered why Mum was letting the flare off before attending to the girl.

As soon as I'd alerted the team, I chased after Mum. When I caught up, I immediately saw the problem: the girl had wandered off the path and fallen down a gully. The gully was icy and it needed two of us to get down safely.

'You're the lightest, can you go?' shouted Mum.

I nodded and got out the rope and harness, grabbed the crampons and made sure I could reach the ice axe easily. Mum found a boulder to anchor the rope around.

'Hold ready?'

I held on and readied myself. Then I started my descent, heart pounding. Poor hiker. Suddenly I felt so shamefaced. She wasn't 'stoopid' at all, she was just a sad girl in a desperate state. I felt guilty too, because I was afraid. Afraid of what I might find. Afraid there might be frozen blood, broken bones.

Afraid she'd be dead.

For all my sixteen years, I've seen more dead bodies than I should. It never gets easier. Your heart flares up and beats against your throat, and then you don't believe it and you try everything, CPR, mouth to mouth, pleading, shaking, screaming – as if you could call their souls back out of the darkness. And the press of frozen lips against yours haunts you, jolts you, just when you think you've forgotten.

I'm aching for the day when I can leave this place. Get back to that nice suburban street where people never fall off cliffs and howling winds never rattle you to sleep; where the sound of helicopters landing on stony plateaus is only heard in nightmares. I'm very selfish really. I just want a nice little four-by-four life. Four walls around me, four wheels under me, all designed to keep me safe.

Anyway, I hacked and slid and picked my way down the gully, wind blasting at my back. You know, the very stones under my feet didn't even move. They were frozen completely into the cliff.

First, get the thermal space blanket over her. I knew that. I knew the routine. And dreaded it.

Once down the gully, I rushed to the huddled shape. I didn't know if she was dead or alive. I didn't stop to check. I crouched beside her. I flung the blanket over her first. Everywhere was misty grey. The snow was thick and she was half sunk in a drift. I started to say 'It'll be all right. This is Ellie Morgan, I've found you now – the Llanberis Mountain Rescue Team are on their way.' My words hung in the air like an icy haze. 'You'll be fine. We'll get you home. Try not to worry. Stay very still, until we can get you to the helicopter. Listen, that's the helicopter now, right above us.'

I shifted from one leg to the other. I carried on chattering out words of encouragement.

I knew I had to examine her. I held my breath, bit my lip. Then I knelt. I tore my glove off. I felt for a pulse. I searched and found nothing. Her skin inside her jacket was icy. I tried again. There it was: faint and thready, but a pulse. The girl was alive! I breathed a rush of relief. I hadn't realised how much I was praying she'd be alive.

Next, I checked her airways. I didn't try to move her. She could've broken a leg, maybe worse. We'd have to wait for the helicopter. Mum yelled. I turned. I gave her the thumbs up. I gestured: *What am I supposed to do now?*

Above, the helicopter tried to land. There was enough space, quite a clear, level patch, but a gust of wind tossed the Sea King back into the air, as if it were a sweet wrapper. I was going to have to wait with the girl until they got down.

Mum shouted words of encouragement, but I was worried; sometimes it can take up to five tries and thirty minutes to get a helicopter down. *What should I do?* The girl was barely alive.

I tucked a second space blanket around her, and very carefully tried to prise a thermal mat under her head and shoulders. You lose a lot of heat through contact with the ground, you know. As I tucked the thermal in I noticed that the stones beneath her felt oddly warm. She couldn't possibly have heated them herself. Must be some trick of the cold. I suddenly realised I might need to watch out. Cold can do that, you know. Make you think things are warm when they're not.

Anyway, I tried to huddle in beside her, give her the best chance I could. If I could rouse her, maybe I could get some high-energy food into her.

I rubbed her cold hands between mine. She stirred a little. I rubbed more briskly. Suddenly she opened her eyes.

She looked at me. I started the reassuring routine again, although I hadn't got a clue how seriously hurt she was, or how long it was going to take them to get her out.

'You're going to be all right. You've just hurt your leg. Try to stay still. Llanberis Mountain … '

'There were monsters,' she said. 'I was so cold … there was a boy … *told me to follow him … somewhere warm … *'

She was rambling. Shock can affect you like that. Extreme cold can make you hallucinate.

'So cold.' Suddenly she clutched at me, her eyes rolling wildly. '*Monsters!*' she cried. '*Inside the mountain!*' Her face seemed to shrink in terror. '*Had to run … had to escape from the den … *'

Her eyes fluttered shut.

I tried to press a small piece of glucose cake between her lips. I carried on with the reassuring; mumbling words out, trying to rub some warmth into her with numb fingers. The girl started to shiver uncontrollably. She raised her head and whispered, '*They were chasing me … *'

'You're safe now,' I said. It's better not to directly contradict anyone who's in shock. It just adds to their distress. 'The rescue team are here.'

The helicopter tried to land again and failed. Mum kept shouting for me to Hang On In There. Finally, the helicopter ducked under the gale and, in a short window of calm, it landed. The crew descended and set to work helping the girl. At last they got her into the huge yellow RAF Search and Rescue Sea King.

One crew member was a local man, Cecil Howard, a flight lieutenant. Before he got back into the helicopter he thanked us. He shook his head, a look of disbelief all over his face. '*Rydych chi wedi gwneud yn dda.* Hats off to you,' he said, cupping his hands against the blizzard. 'It's a miracle she's lasted out here on the mountain – must've found somewhere to shelter before she fell.'

'Said – she went down into some kind of monsters' den. Under Snowdon!' I shouted back.

Cecil Howard didn't laugh. He went a nasty dishwater grey.

I raised my eyebrows.

'Legends,' he said, shaking his head. '*Dim ond mewn chwedlau.* Only. In. Legends.'

'What?' I said.

'There was a girl too, she was lost at night. *Roedd merch hefyd; aeth hi ar goll yn y nos.* Upon The Yuletide … burn marks … bites … ' He shook his head like he didn't want to believe it.

The wind whipped his words away.

Upon The Yuletide? Sounded like something from the

flipping *Mabinogion*[2]!

'What girl?' I yelled.

'She was half crazed with terror – *Ofnus*! So they say.'

I couldn't figure out if he was repeating some old story or referring to a rescue.

'There was an evil place under Snowdon and a handsome boy who lured her …' his voice trailed off. He looked hurriedly around as if the very stones of the mountain might be listening. 'Old stories, old as the mountain. *Mor hen ag yr Wyddfa*. Old as Dinas Emrys …' And then he twisted up his lips and said something I didn't catch.

The two paramedics had finally got the girl into the helicopter. They'd have given us a lift too, but those Sea Kings are only really designed for four people, plus they needed to get the girl to hospital urgently.

So we saw them off and left. I rescaled the gully. Mum and I hugged each other. 'Thanks supergirl,' she said into my hair. We waved goodbye. We'd done our bit. We linked arms for a while before the path divided us. Every now and then I couldn't help breaking out into a huge grin. We'd rescued her! We'd beaten the mountain! Rescuing someone like that gives you such a buzz. You want to jump up and down and visit them in hospital and have

2. The *MABINOGION* is a collection of Celtic myths from medieval Welsh manuscripts.

all their family crowding round saying, 'Thank you, thank you, thank you!' while you nod and smile and act all cool.

Yep, we'd done it. But there wasn't going to be any hospital-visiting, of course. They'd probably fly her straight to Caernarfon and it was still Christmas Day. And we needed to go back to our No Telly and No Turkey cooking in the oven.

As we hiked homeward I said, 'The girl reckoned she'd been lured into some den or other under the mountain, she was terrified of something down there. Something weird ... said she'd been chased when she tried to escape.'

Mum didn't answer. She didn't need to. Her swallowed laughter told me everything. She shouted, 'That's hypothermia for you. She'd probably read about Dinas Emrys or watched too many episodes of *Merlin & Morgana*.'

I looked up towards the summit of Snowdon. The clouds above us parted. For a brief instant the peak shone in clear sunlight. Snowdon is so breathtaking. I flung my arms wide, happy we'd saved the girl, thrilled by the beauty of the mountain. And that's when a curious sensation rippled over me. It was almost tangible.

A feeling of being watched.

I stopped and swivelled on the spot. I'd definitely felt eyes on me again. I scoured the slopes, wondering who was out there.

My eyes settled on the peak. High above us, standing there on top of a pile of stones, right on the very summit, was a shape: just a blackened matchstick figure. Someone was watching us all right, probably watching the rescue. I yanked out my binoculars and squinted through them.

It was him! That boy. There he stood, the light playing on the mist at his back. He looked almost as if he could lean into it and swoop down. I blinked. Was it really him? How had he got there so quickly? From Devil's Bridge to the summit is a good two hours' climb, more even, in these conditions. I squinted again, seized for a second time by that curious shiver as it rippled down my spine.

But this time he didn't flinch or turn away. He looked directly back at me. He smiled slowly – as if he knew I was scoping him, as if he was challenging me in some inexplicable way. It made the blood rush to my face. I tried to zoom in on him, but, just as suddenly as he'd appeared, he was gone again, swallowed up in a gust of cloud.

I pulled off my glove and felt my cheeks. I *was* blushing. Hastily I put my glove back on; pulled my scarf tighter. Thank God Sheila wasn't here! I'd never hear the last of it. Plus she'd bag him first. A strange pain knotted itself into my chest at the thought of Sheila bagging him. She could have Rhiannon's cousin; she could have the whole of the

Mountain Marauders (Llanberis's local wannabe rugby team) – who *all* appreciated the virtues of a girl like Sheila – and YES, I know that was catty, but the *thought* of her bagging this strange mountain boy; I shook my head. It was impossible anyway. He wasn't a trophy *anyone* could have. He was in a league all of his own. Sheila was *not* going to get her claws into him. Not my mountain boy. I caught my breath. Why had I thought of him as *mine*? He was just a boy on a mountain. Not mine at all. I'd never even met him! Probably never would.

Not if he stayed up on that summit for much longer, anyway.

And that's when I started worrying: severe weather alerts, sub-zero temperatures, not much of a jacket, out all alone on the mountain. A sudden pang of guilt stabbed at me. We'd come all this way to rescue the girl and neither of us had even thought of checking if he was ok.

Correction: *I* hadn't thought of checking, Mum didn't have a clue he was even out there.

I ran to catch her up – to tell her – to ask her what we should do.

Then I stopped myself.

For some strange reason, this was something I wanted to keep all to myself.

Two

After the rescue we ended up at George's place. We wanted to say HAPPY CHRIMBO and all that, but I think both Mum and I also wanted to tell someone what had happened. It's like that when you save a life. I reckon we'd saved that girl. If we hadn't gone out straight away … if I hadn't gone too … if Mum hadn't spotted her. It's a big thing saving someone's life. Maybe I'll be a doctor someday. (When I've finished art college and been around the world, obviously.) Anyway, it's a feeling you want to share. So we took a small detour on our way back.

I thought I'd better let Rhiannon know I was going to see George, after all. So I pinged her.

ELLIE'S PHONE 25th December 10.30

Status: Available *except for Darren, apparently*

Sometimes I don't know why I bother trying to help Rhiannon with George. She professes to be totally 'crazy' about him, but I don't like her jokes. I think when you *really* like someone, it's kind of special and pure and important – not filled with Sheila-style, rugby-club humour. Maybe I'm just a bit old fashioned. Well, about that anyway.

Unlike George.

Anyway you'll want to know about George, won't you?

Well he's my age, and he's very straightforward (you know, sort of what-you-see-is-what-you-get). His real name is Siôr (John-George). But he says that sounds frilly (he's not at all frilly). So he's just George. And he's ok, for a boy. I guess. Thing is, he's always been nuts about me, right from the time when we were little and I came for my summer holidays to Snowdon. My gran, Mum's mam, owned the farm, before Mum and Dad moved here. Anyway we played Growing Up And Getting Married (don't laugh). George always used to say, 'You're going to marry me, Ellie.' And if I shrugged him off and imagined myself marrying A Royal Prince – so that we could play I Am The Queen And You Are So My Servant – he'd say: 'It's not allowed for you to marry anyone else.' And then he'd get so sad that I'd have to give in and agree to marry him one day, in order to play any kind of game at all.

Needless to say, these days I don't give in to him (although he doesn't seem to have quite got the message). Anyway George and his gran are our only neighbours. They live in a tiny cottage high on the slopes of Snowdon, even further away from Llanberis than us. They've lived in that cottage, like since forever. Mum says there's always been a Jones family living there, right from the time of the Celts (Mum actually grew up on Snowdon. I only half did. We moved into the farm when I was nine).

Anyway, we thought we'd stop and say We Wish You A Merry, and see if they were doing ok. For sure, their electricity would be down too.

But we needn't have worried. Granny Jones is just about

the most capable person ever. She'd got their generator going, built a huge log fire and everywhere was so warm and cosy. Christmas lights festooned everything (not on of course, because when you're on a generator, that is wasteful), but the tree looked so beautiful it didn't need electricity. And it was great to defrost inside their tiny cottage. George greeted me with his usual bear hug, his arms flung wide in welcome, his smile almost big enough to swallow me down, his crush like a prize fighter. 'Hey, Ellie, Most Beautiful Girl in Gwynedd Who Knows Maybe Even Conwy Too,' he said, 'Will You Marry Me TODAY?'

Which made Mum really laugh and Granny cast despairing looks at her rafters.

'Not today,' I returned, 'Wouldn't want to spoil Rhiannon's Christmas.'

Which made Granny laugh and Mum roll her eyes.

'Stupid,' he said.

George hates it when I tease him about Rhiannon. Long story.

Short version?

Right: He fancies me. She fancies him. He's too nice to tell her there's Not A Chance. She makes me act as go-between. I try to refuse, but then feel rotten because it's like I'm being Dog In The Manger. So I help her. He tries to misunderstand and acts So You Really Do Love Me, But You Are Too Shy To Admit It's You, So You Are Pretending It's Rhiannon. She buys him expensive things, because she's got lots of cash, because her folks own the big hotel. He groans and gives them to me. I have to pretend I don't know they're from Rhiannon. Of course she sees them at my place, and then it all goes Nuts. I think George may have to emigrate to escape. Or I may.

Needless to say, I never pass on any messages about big bangs or size or anything like that. And that's not just because they are in bad taste and scummy, but because, actually, I'm beginning to think that Rhiannon may not really be the right person for George after all.

And speaking of Rhiannon, my phone promptly pinged and her name flashed up on the screen. Isn't *that* weird, when you think of someone and then the phone goes? Like telepathy really works.

Recent updates between Ellie and Rhiannon:

Rhiannon

Tell George Merry Xmas and Darren's here, and we gotta do something to welcome Darren into the clan. He's lonely.

I pinged her back.

> **Ellie**
>
> OK. Like what?
>
> **Rhiannon**
>
> Like something which gets me in a dark corner with G.
>
> **Ellie**
>
> Like hide 'n seek?
>
> **Rhiannon**
>
> No, like find and eek!

See what I mean? She's definitely not the right person. George deserves someone a lot more sensitive and serious. But all I said was, 'Rhiannon says Merry Christmas and her cousin Darren's in town and would like a friend to hang out with.'

'Oh, Ok,' said George. 'I'll get over to their place and meet up with him.'

See what I mean? That's George all over for you. He's just A Really Nice Guy. He never thinks, even for one minute, that it might all be a Rhiannon ploy.

Much too nice for her.

And that morning he looked really handsome as well, all washed and brushed and in his best (bless), even though there was no way he could get to chapel. Granny Jones had put on one of her beautiful homespun shawls in honour of Christmas Day. Although underneath that she had a Peruvian knit jumper and a tie-dye T-shirt with a cringe, hippy sort of skirt in purple velvet – you've gotta smile.

As she busied about, congratulating us on finding and saving the girl, she looked more like a funky fairy god-mother than a granny!

But she fed us all right. And wow, her food was good. I polished off eggs and bacon and sausage, along with homemade bread and wild mountain honey.

So there I was stuffing my face, when Granny Jones announced, 'The Pendragons are back.'

George grinned and shook his head. 'Nan doesn't miss a trick when it comes to royalty.' he said.

What Granny Jones meant was the Royal Family, or at least some of their relatives, were down in Caernarfon Castle for Christmas. Snowdonia is practically all theirs. It's like some kind of imperial back yard they have, that stretches inland from their seaboard castle. Anyway they think they own it (they probably do) along with every soul who lives there. Sigh. Feudal times and all that.

'I suppose that means a formal dinner and evening wear at some sort of a reception,' sighed Mum.

Granny Jones nodded and pushed more toast towards her.

'I'd better not,' continued Mum, 'or I won't fit into anything.'

'I shall go in that,' said Nan indicating her Welsh outfit hanging up by the door. 'It keeps them at their distance.'

I looked at George and rolled my eyes.

'It's the day after Boxing Day at the Pen-y-mynydd-gwryd,' said Granny Jones 'And I'll be glad if you'll take me in your car, if the weather breaks.'

George groaned. 'Do we have to?'

I was thinking: the Pen-y-mynydd-gwryd Hotel equals Rhiannon. There Will Be No Escape For You, George.

'It'll be the worse for us all, if we don't,' said Granny Jones waggling a pointy finger at George.

Mum smiled. 'Mrs Jones,' she said, 'this is the twenty-first century. We no longer have to tug our forelocks in order to wrestle a living off the slopes of Snowdonia.'

Granny Jones shook her head. 'Things are stirring,' she said, ''tis no coincidence that the Pendragons are home and you rescued a girl this morning. And then there's the old stories. If the Pendragons come at midwinter, you know what they say … 'tis best you tug your forelock along of always.'

I raised an eyebrow at George, then crossed my eyes for good measure. I, for one, didn't have a clue what the old stories said.

'Y Ddraig Goch is flying over Caernarfon Castle for a reason,' finished Granny Jones with an enigmatic twist of her lips.

'Just a flag,' I said.

'Still a Red Dragon,' said Granny Jones.

George shoved two mince pies into his big gob all in one go. I think he was trying to gag himself.

'And what's more I heard the Beast is abroad,' added Gran.

'The Beast?' I said.

'I actually heard a report of a cougar up by Yr Aran,' said Mum, 'And Owen says he found two of his sheep ripped to shreds only yesterday.'

'Probably dogs,' muttered George, covering his mouth.

FYI sometimes we get reports of big cats living wild in the hills, panthers and the like, and there's one creature that supposedly lives on Snowdon called the Beast of Dinas Emrys, which apparently emerges once in a century and kills on sight.

'The Worms of Dinas Affaraon,' said Gran.

George grinned and made a She-Is-Just-A-Mad-Old-Woman face.

I tried to choke back my laughter, hiccupped on my tea, and sent a spray over the tablecloth.

Mum did that exasperated thing with one side of her mouth. George made scary-monster hands and clawed them in the air towards his nan, then pulled a We-Are-All-Welsh-Nutters face at everyone.

I got the giggles and had to rush out of the room. Rushing out of Granny Jones's room means rushing out of the entire cottage. So I wrenched open the front door and stood in the porch, doubled up, trying not to choke.

Outside the wind howled around the cottage walls, tearing at the slate roof, battering the few shrubs that managed to grow. My laughter died in my throat. *Why on Earth would anyone want to live here?* I looked up in the direction of the summit, suddenly disturbed. And for some stupid, weird reason I felt as if the eyes of that strange boy on the mountain were still boring down through the snow and mist, through the wild wind, and were staring directly at me. But now he was looking straight into my brain, and his smile was fading. My heart started pounding. *He was still out there wasn't he?*

Out there all alone.

All the rest of that morning I was twitchy. Even though we got home and managed to fire up the generator, meaning Christmas wouldn't be a complete disaster, I was still restless.

Mum noticed.

'I'm worried about that boy,' I said. 'The one I saw up by Devil's Bridge. He was out, without a proper jacket.'

'Well there's been no fresh call-out,' said Mum. 'If some-one was in trouble, we'd know.'

'But the weather forecast says it's getting worse.' I stressed, imagining him there, alone, freezing.

'Hon, we can't go chasing out after everyone who decides to go climbing in winter. We have to wait until there's a call. And even then we're only volunteers for our patch of mountain.' Mum smiled at me as if to say, *You're imagining things, Ellie, that's what happens after a serious rescue, you get paranoid, feel you can never relax.*

I sighed. I hate it when she talks to me as if I'm six. I know all about post-traumatic stress disorders and responsibility management, and it's not like I've ever stressed about people out on the mountain in general. But sometimes I think she doesn't want me to grow up. She knows that I can't stay up here on Snowdon forever. I'm going to have to move sooner or later. The nearest sixth-form college is in Caernarfon, and even if I could make the trek there and back every day, that'd only be for two years. My friend, Meryl, has the same problem, and she lives right in the centre of Llanberis. Her mum actually put her college prospectuses in the recycle bin! It's only girls like Sheila that'll stay and get a job at the corner shop – on the checkout till. (Mia-ow! You can see I still haven't forgiven her.)

But nothing Mum said could settle me. I paced from room to room in our old farmhouse, really restless, the dark eyes of that boy haunting me. Maybe he'd lost his phone or it'd gone flat, and I was the only one who believed he was in danger up there …

I didn't know what I could say to convince Mum we should *do* something. And when I thought about it sensibly, it was quite ridiculous for us to set out and look for him anyway. Snowdon is *huge*. He could be anywhere. We'd have no back up and no designated search area.

But by two o'clock that afternoon I was *really* jumpy. I couldn't contain myself. I *had* to do something. 'I'm going up to the train track,' I told her. 'I'll take all my gear and my phone. I'll be ok.'

Mum sighed. She knew I'd be fine. I'm a well-trained mountain girl. Moreover, the train track is really near. What I didn't tell her was I intended to follow the Snowdon Mountain Railway up to the Devil's Bridge. It's ok. It's not as dangerous as it sounds. You can't get lost on the track, going up or down, however misty it gets.

But still she wasn't happy: 'Hon, I promised Jeff I'd go into the village for a drink or something … ' Her voice trailed away. Jeff's her new boyfriend. It's all very fresh. Fresh and intense. Don't ask me how I feel about it, because I'm trying very hard to be supportive.

'It's quite a walk. If you're not back, shall I go without you? You know you're welcome to come.'

About as welcome as a snowball down your neck.

'Thanks,' I said, 'I just need to check out if that boy went that way. As soon as I see footprints and stuff, I'll come back. I know it's Christmas Day ... '

Mum shrugged.

I went to get my daysack. I checked I had fresh high-energy food, a foil blanket, ice axe, flares, torch, the whole nine yards. That boy might be in trouble. He might be out there freezing to death. Then I pulled on a dry Arctic Extreme down jacket, hat, boots, gloves.

'Take care,' Mum called. 'If anything, just call me, and don't go anywhere near the Devil's Bridge; the snow can shift.'

'Hey Mum!' I said sharply, 'I know!'

I left, before she could fuss any further. I slammed the farmhouse door behind me. Outside, the afternoon was bitter. Cold, deep blue shadows already curled across the valleys. It had stopped snowing, but a piercing wind, laced with ice, was blowing.

I made my way up to the top pasture, where we sometimes put the lambs if the spring comes early. Beneath my feet the snow crunched and where I hit a soft hollow, I sank thigh deep into drifts. It was supernaturally quiet. All I could hear was the slight crack of snow snapping somewhere beneath the slopes, and the sharp call of a solitary bird. Soon my nose was numb. I pulled my scarf over it and breathed soft, moist, warm air through its woolly knit. Keep moving Ellie, I told myself, keep the blood pumping and you'll stay warm.

Climbing uphill is the best exercise for staying warm, I can tell you. Soon I was nearly sweating, except that you can't really build up a total sweat in sub-zero temperatures. It's also not a good idea to either, because when you cool down so does the sweat, and it cools a lot faster than you.

So I slowed a bit as I saw the Devil's Bridge coming into view. If there really had been a boy up there this morning, snow or not, as sure as hell I was going to find his tracks.

By the time I got to the start of the causeway, the sun was edging fast toward the west. I thought I'd better touch base with Mum. I didn't want her to worry with me out on the mountain after dark.

I pulled out my mobile.

'Mum,' I said.

'Ellie?' said Mum.

'I'm ok.'

Sigh of relief.

36

'Just letting you know.'

'Ok, I'm going down to Jeff's, then.'

'I'm just going to check for tracks, then I'm heading home.'

Staying out on Snowdon after dark isn't a good idea, not in the middle of winter, even if, like me, you know every dell and brook, every cliff and boulder.

'Ellie, will you mind if I sleep over?'

I sighed. Then tried not to, in case Mum heard. I mean Jeff is 'O-kay'. Not all that. Not that I'd know, anyway. I haven't met the right boy yet. None of the ones in Llanberis make my heart even twitch, let alone flutter. And I'm not going to throw myself at one of the Mountain Marauders (obviously) just because they are the only boys around. I'm saving myself for something more than mud and smelly rugby socks. But since Dad died, Mum's been so sad. And the farm's been such hard work. And Jeff makes her happy. So I shouldn't mind, should I?

'It's just that it's a long walk back, and the weather ...'

'You stay,' I said. 'It's Christmas. If you don't, Jeff'll think he's not important.'

'Thanks, Hon,' she said.

I could hear the happiness in her voice. It was true anyway. If Jeff was going to be an important person in her life, he needed his share of important time slots.

And I truly *didn't* mind. It suited me actually. For suddenly I seemed to be drawn on – almost as if I'd been sucked into an enchanted force field. I decided, against all better judgement, that I was going to explore right up to the far side of the Devil's Bridge, I was going to follow that boy's tracks and see where he'd gone.

I found the tracks all right. There'd been a light dusting of fresh snow on them, but they were definitely there, deep indents on the far side of the causeway. At first they looked scuffed, as if he'd been dancing around, or had parachuted down, but a little beyond the scuffed up area, a straight line of footprints set out for the summit. I knew I should turn round then and head home. It was getting dark fast. But I thought, just a little further. When I get to the shadow of Garnedd Ugain, I'll turn back.

I guess I wanted to satisfy my curiosity. Had it really been him on the summit? And how *had* he got there so quickly? And then there were the tracks. All going one way and not coming back. That meant that unless he'd taken another route down, which was unlikely (and frankly unwise, for all the other routes were much more dangerous), he was still up there.

So I set out. I turned my head torch on, and I made sure a flare was in my pocket. I'd follow his tracks for another five minutes. And if I still couldn't see where they went, or if he'd come down – I'd call up the emergency services myself and explain everything.

Suddenly I got an unexpected rush of pleasure at the thought of rescuing him, of being the one to whisper reassuring words over his broken form: *This is Ellie Morgan, Llanberis Mountain Rescue sort-of-volunteer, I've found you now. I won't leave you. I'll stay by your side.* In my mind I planned it all. *I'd get the RAF helicopter back out, I'd tuck a space blanket gently round him. We'd sit huddled up together sharing our body warmth ...*

Only my plan didn't go much further than that. It was pretty stupid, anyway. The sensible side of me knew that. It was all, really, just an excuse to carry on. It was a way of silencing the voice in my head that was screaming, '*GO HOME NOW*, before *you* need the emergency services.'

But I didn't. I kept steadily on towards the summit. I was careful though. I stuck to the Snowdon Mountain Railway tracks, where I could get a grip on the steel sleepers. But every now and then I scrambled over the rough land that separated the train track from the hikers' route. Once over the rocks I dodged down to the pathway – just to make sure his tracks were still really there.

I suppose I was crazy. I should have listened to that screaming voice. It was trying to save me. But I just kept thinking about his dark eyes and him watching me and everything. And as I trudged ever on uphill, I kept imagining rubbing his cold hands and feeling for the throb of his heart. And then that shiver of excitement would go over me again, and the blood would rush to my face and I'd meet the challenge in that smile, and he'd know he'd met his match. (And of course, I couldn't leave him, because he'd need me, and I'd rescue him and …)

Sometimes I'm so pathetic!

Anyway, five minutes passed and still I kept going. The shadow of Garnedd Ugain fell across my path and yet I didn't stop. I was getting tired, and the cold bit into me. Still I continued. The blue shadows deepened and it became dark. And on I went. It was as if the mountain had cast a spell over me, and I could not help myself. The great spirit of Yr Wyddfa had told me to carry on searching, and I was doomed to obey.

It started snowing again. The clouds banked down on the mountainside. There was pretty much zero visibility. This is it, I told myself. You can't go any further. Just one last check. I scrambled over to the path again to look for his footprints.

And suddenly I couldn't find them.

They just weren't there.

I cast around in a great circle looking for even a tuft of snow-covered grass that was disturbed or flattened. Nothing. Even when there's been fresh snow you can still see the dints. After all, I'd seen them back down the track, and it hadn't been snowing again for very long. It was like he'd been plucked off the mountain. The prints just stopped. Nothing forward, nothing back.

Confused, I cast an even larger circle. All the time searching for some explanation. A wind started, icy raw, like it was blowing straight off the Arctic. I told myself I better stop looking for what wasn't there, and get myself back to the train track straight away.

Give up, I told myself, and I think I was probably ready to, but an unexpected mist descended and suddenly I couldn't find the train track either. I tried to retrace my steps, but it was so hard to see. The wind stung my eyes, the snow seemed to cling to me, every movement started to become painful.

I recognized worrying signs. My mind was numbing up, my lungs aching from the freezing wind …

I tried to struggle back through the snow in what I thought was the right direction, but I couldn't find anything familiar. I blundered about, beginning to panic. I must have gone off course. I couldn't believe it. Weirdly, I was going downhill now, when the train track was definitely uphill. I stopped.

When you don't know where you are on Snowdon, don't try to find your way. You'll end up going over a cliff. I know, believe me. I looked for my compass, then remembered I'd given it to Mum.

Oh shit. No compass.

I should call Mum. She was going to be so mad. She was going to think I'd done it on purpose, that I was jealous, that I wanted to spoil her evening with Jeff. But there was no other way.

I'd call her up. I'd dig myself a snow cave. I'd give her an exact time, then I'd set off a flare. It was going to be all right. I wasn't in any danger. I wasn't scared.

I didn't get scared until I pulled out my mobile.

And saw it was dead.

Completely dead.

Somehow, bizarrely, it'd turned itself on inside my pocket. The battery was totally flat.

And that's when I started to get really frightened. No phone. No compass. Shivering. Lost on Snowdon. Severe weather conditions. Mum wasn't even going to realise I was gone until morning. *I was out alone, at night, on the mountain.*

And then I saw him.

He just curled out of the mist. The boy I'd seen on the summit.

He looked at me, his eyes as dark as coal, his face as white as the snowfield behind him.

'Are you lost?' he called. His voice was smooth and warm and melodious.

Close up, he had an unearthly beauty, and I couldn't take my eyes off him.

He smiled at me. 'Are you lost?' he repeated.

I nodded, unable to believe what I was seeing.

'I can take you somewhere warm,' he said. 'If you like.'

Three

I just stood there staring. I didn't even say hello.

How come he was there? When just a minute ago, he wasn't?

I searched the snow. Only *my* tracks. Nothing else. (My boots have this swirl mark in their heels.)

How had he got here?

I pinched myself. Was I hallucinating already? It can happen, you know. Hypothermia can creep up on you, and before you know it, you're imagining yetis jumping out of glaciers and all sorts. Plus what did he mean by 'somewhere warm'? There Is Nowhere Warm Out On Snowdon In The Middle Of Winter.

I huddled deep into my jacket. I clapped my arms

around me. I shuffled on the spot. Through the mist and swirling snowflakes, I stared.

And he stared back.

He was taller than I'd first imagined and slim in an athletic way; broad shouldered, though. He had a carved look, a kind of sculpted feel that made you think of classical statues. And he was no hallucination.

And I *was* right. He *had* been out here.

And even though I was lost, and my phone was dead, something inside me burned with satisfaction.

Instantly, I wished I could ping Sheila.

> **IMAGINED ... Recent updates between Ellie and Sheila:**
>
> **Ellie**
>
> Mountain boy is mine. I bags him first.
>
> **Sheila**
>
> We'll c bout that bee-atch.

'You lost?' he shouted.

I stepped closer, my eyes met his. I found myself staring into the darkest orbs imaginable. In fact they were so dark that, for a second, I felt dizzy. My heart started to pound. Predictably blood rose to my cheeks.

'Are you?' he said searching my face.

And all around the snow closed in, huge whirling flakes driven almost horizontally. Something inside me shivered. There was this look in his eyes. It reminded me of a cat waiting at a mouse-hole. The hairs rose on the back of my neck. I'd seen that look before, but never in human eyes.

'Have you got a mobile?' I yelled. 'Mine's gone dead.'

'Sorry,' he shouted. 'No mobile … '

Shit.

I peered into the mist. Snow swirled faster. Everywhere was dark. 'Where did you come from?' I yelled. All that searching up the track, there had to be an explanation.

'Up there,' He pointed into the night, straight towards the summit.

'But you couldn't have … '

Suddenly my words were cut off. An eerie wail echoed through the darkness. Long, drawn-out notes that sent shivers up my spine.

What the hell was that?

Instantly I remembered Mum's report of the cougar, Gran's weird comment about the Beast of Dinas Emrys. The dead sheep over by the llyn. And it wasn't funny any more. Snowdonia is vast, full of mist and shadows. Anything could be out here.

The wail came again, prolonged, creepy. A cold chill prickled my neck. *What if there really was a big cat?*

I shivered.

Hungry, driven from its lair, sniffing our scent.

Right now.

Suddenly the boy staggered. It startled me. He reached a hand out towards me.

'*Help*,' he whispered. He was trembling all over.

Without thinking I grabbed hold of him. My heart thudding fast. 'It's gonna be OK,' I breathed, almost as if whatever was lurking in the darkness, might overhear me. 'I came out to look for you, I thought you might need help. It *was* you this morning, wasn't it? Up here on Devil's Bridge?'

Although, how could it have been? Out here all day?

A gust of icy wind blasted down. Snow flurried up into my face. The wind howled. The clouds rolled back. Just a little. Through a faint patch of sky, the moon tried to break through. The hairs on the back of my neck prickled again and a silence descended. Ominous. Threatening.

I looked behind me, peering into the mist. The boy stumbled forward and slipped. He was shivering badly. That pale marbled look wasn't natural. In fact he was so pale, he could easily be in the first stages of hypothermia.

And suddenly I felt *really* frightened. I grabbed his arm.

I shook him. He bit his lip. I noticed his lips were tinged blue. *I'd been right all along. It was him and he wasn't OK. And* there was some HORRIBLE thing out here, probably hunting him down.

What the hell was I going to do?

I stared out into the whiteness. *If only I could find a landmark.* My stomach tightened. The prickling on the back of my neck grew worse. There was a soft swishing noise. I jumped.

Holy Crap! There really was something!

I focused all my attention. The swishing continued. At first it seemed faint, just a quivering, a swirl of darkness travelling through the black air, an *impression* of nearness. But the more I tuned in, listening to the mountain, the more I knew I was right. Something was stalking us. It was heaving itself towards us through the coldness.

The mist rolled back. The sky opened up. I definitely heard rustling. '*Who's there?*' I hissed.

The boy gripped my arm. '*Shush!*' he said.

Another low, eerie howl.

The boy convulsed. A look of terror passed over his face. '*Down!*' he screamed. '*Lie flat!*' He flung himself down, dragging me with him.

The howling became a screeching. A screeching that

was definitely MUCH NEARER. It rose in pitch, filling the night around us, until it became a terrible shrieking.

I swear to God all the skin across my shoulders shrivelled up; my chest tightened and my throat stuck to the roof of my mouth. Lying there, half embedded in snow with that strange boy's grasp tight on my sleeve, I nearly Died Of Terror. I'd never heard anything like it. EVER. It split the air and tore into the storm, while the two of us lay there quivering.

At last it went silent.

'Quick,' said the boy. 'We must find shelter.'

'What *The Frick* was that?' I breathed.

'*Please*,' he said. 'I thought I could take you somewhere warm, but we can't go there now.'

'*Jesus*,' I said.

'*We must get away!*'

'*What was it?*' I said.

'*Please*, if you really mean to help me … ' he said. '*Anywhere* … '

'We're halfway up the highest peak in Wales,' I pointed out, 'there isn't just *anywhere* to go.'

He let out a groan.

'But,' I said, a sudden hope making my heart beat faster, 'if you've got a compass – there's a halfway house up here – somewhere – by the rail track. In summer they run a kind of refreshment stop from it.'

'Yes, *yes*,' he said as if he too knew of it. 'Can we get there?' His voice was urgent.

What on earth was that screaming?

He was shaking his head, trying to stand. The wind picked up again, sending a flurry of snow into my eyes.

'We've got to get there,' he said, 'believe me.'

I did. Not just because of the shrieking. We needed to get there fast or we were going to freeze to death.

'I know where they keep the key; my mum's a warden.' I said.

'How far?'

'Don't know,' I said, 'I don't know where we are. I need a compass.' The back of my neck was still crawling. If he didn't have a compass, how the hell could I find my way anywhere?

The wind blasted at us. The boy tried to rise again, but I could tell he found it hard. At last, after struggling to his knees, he unclasped his watch.

His watch with its digital compass!

I smiled then. I gave him the thumbs up, in what I hoped was an encouraging way. Because you see: I am Arabella Morgan, daughter of Mrs Jennifer Morgan, support member of the Llanberis Mountain Rescue Team. I am 'That Lovely Ellie Girl', mountain guide (for the old lady guests at the

Pen-y-mynydd-gwryd Hotel, who want to take the train for tea at the top in the summer) and part-time volunteer (when Mum needs me), I am The Original Teenager Who Knows Everything, and I mostly grew up on this mountain (when I wasn't growing up in London, obvs), like my mum and her mam did. So I can happily say I Am A General Encyclopaedia About Mountain Things (usually). And most importantly, I Know How To Use A Compass To Plot Absolutely Anywhere On Snowdon.

At least, I hoped I did. If I could find out exactly where we were.

But where were we?

Too near the Devil's Bridge for a start and too near the Black Cliff. One false move and we'd go over a sheer drop.

'Stay there!' I ordered (I tried to give him the space blanket but he wouldn't take it.) Gingerly, I counted ten steps away from him. I trod very carefully. Visibility was nearly zero.

Nothing.

I came back. 'Stay still!' I hissed 'or I'll lose my bearings.' The boy looked far too ill to answer, let alone move. Steeling myself, I headed off in exactly the opposite direction for another ten steps.

Still nothing. At least there were no cliffs.

On the third try (exactly at right angles to tries 1 and 2), I found a familiar stone. I felt like hugging it! I felt so proud of myself too. Like I said, I Know Every Stone On The Mountain.

'Thank you stone' I whispered on to its icy surface.

'Come on,' I said, pulling at the boy when I'd got back to him, 'let's get going.'

He seemed grateful. And so he should be! Halfway House was less than a mile away. And with the help of that compass, I knew exactly the right direction to take.

'Looks like we'll find your "somewhere warm".' I said. I etched a makeshift map in the snow and took my bearings. Gotcha! My self-esteem soared, my confidence returned. We'd get there before the creature found us too. Hopefully. With a determined grimace, I stepped out along the mountain.

It looked like I was going to have to rescue him after all.

Together we stood up against the wind. I supported him. He stumbled. I put his arm over my shoulder. Had to. He was shivering violently, falling all over the place. And I began to worry again. '*Rigours, muscle mis-coordination, movements slow and laboured, accompanied by a stumbling pace …* ' all symptoms of moderate hypothermia.

I stumbled too, and that worried me even more. Perhaps I was freezing up as well. If I couldn't function properly, how would we find Halfway House? Just when we needed to hurry and keep our blood moving, it seemed like we were going slower than ever.

Plus hypothermia is tricky, you know. You can feel quite warm while you're slowly shutting down. You have to watch out for paleness. *'Lips, ears, fingers and toes may become blue.'* I tried to peer at his lips again to see if they were any worse, but in the darkness I couldn't tell.

Stay calm, Ellie. Say something reassuring. I told myself: You're Arabella Morgan of Llanberis Mountain Rescue Team (sometime support volunteer). Encourage him; you know how to. But say what? We were out here with no hope of rescue. How Encouraging Is That?

Instead I held his arm tight, (as much to steady myself as him), and slipped my right arm round his waist as we walked. Underneath the thin cloth of his jacket, his muscles were as hard as stone.

'Talk to me!' I called, through the storm.

' ... anyone know you're out?' he tried to shout, but his words whipped away.

'Obviously,' I lied. 'Keep moving.'

'Will they be looking ... find you?'

Not quickly enough, I thought. Maybe tomorrow.

He lifted his arm off my shoulder. But he couldn't stand alone. Hypothermia is like that: *'mental confusion, although the victim may appear alert …'*

Engage him in conversation, I decided. Keep him thinking, Ellie. 'Tell me,' I shouted, 'Why were you on the mountain?'

He gritted his teeth and said something I couldn't catch.

I couldn't think of anything else to say, so we just struggled on, everywhere getting colder and quieter by the minute. And in that cold, quiet silence, punctuated only by the crunch of snow under our feet, I started thinking. Whatever *could* have made that noise? Fox? Dog? Eagle? Badger? Hardly.

Big cat, then?

But I wasn't convinced it was a big cat either. Believe me it didn't *sound* like any big cat I'd ever heard. They growl don't they? Or roar? This thing had SHRIEKED. Suddenly I wasn't so eager to find out. The only things that shrieked like that were devil dogs and werewolves in horror films.

And neither of those was too far-fetched to believe in right now.

Just like Snowdon, I thought. It has its secrets. It's a sly old place, you know. And although I reckon I know its sneaky ways better than anyone, no one can ever really *know* Snowdon. Yr Wyddfa, that's what it's called in Welsh. It doesn't quite mean the same as in English. It translates as 'den', as if the mountain itself is some huge icy lair entombing some gigantic, fiendish, mythical creature.

Nervously I glanced over my shoulder, half believing the Beast of Dinas Emrys *would* come roaring out of the storm. I tried putting the idea out of my mind. I tried humming *Good King Wenceslas*, but that made it worse. If there was something out there, it'd be listening, wouldn't it? And with every note I'd be giving us away.

'Please,' I said, 'Can't we go any faster?'

The wind howled. The snow whirled. My mind began to numb up. *Whatever was out there would find us, would tear down at us with razor claws, would slice through us, white snow stained red ...*

I shook my head. You must stop it, Ellie, I told myself. You must focus on logical things. 2+2 = 4. Good. Nothing will slash you open. Think of real things. Mountain rescues. Fallen hikers. *Ice fields smeared bright red with frozen blood ...*

Out here anything could happen.

Christmas night.

Blizzard.

*I was in some kind of story … under some kind of spell …
the Beast of Dinas Emrys … check the compass … keep
away from the right … keep away from the left …*

Huge cliffs.

Huge creatures.

Ice. Fire.

White. Snow.

Red. Blood.

Four

Thank God for that watch. Next Christmas I am *so* going to ask Santa for one. Together we staggered north by northeast. I checked and double checked the compass every time I passed a landmark I knew. I talked to myself: Keep your feet moving, Ellie. One foot then the next. Come on, girl. Brush the snow out of your eyes. That's it, keep checking the direction. Keep him upright. Try to keep him going. Save him. He's yours now. Forget about Sheila. She's a cow. And, step by step, I quite forgot how strange it was that I was out there with him, forgot that it was still Christmas Day, forgot that I'd only just met him, that he hadn't been with me forever.

And just when I thought we could go no further, I saw a dark shape moulding itself into the white blizzard. For a second my heart stopped. Then I recognised it:

The corner wall of Halfway House.

YAY!

I pulled on his arm. 'This way,' I shouted and steered him to the left. The sight of those walls seemed to revive him. He turned and flashed me the most amazing smile. 'Thank you,' he whispered.

And for some stupid reason my heart soared, and I felt like I'd won the lottery or something.

If you are ever stuck out on Snowdon on Christmas night, and you need a place to go, the key to Halfway House is hidden behind a loose stone above the door lintel (under the eaves, a little to the left). If you feel around and jiggle the old Welsh stones, you'll find it. Hopefully.

I found the right place in less than twenty seconds. (I was counting.)

But from then on things went downhill.

Like this:

1. Firstly, the stone didn't move. I tugged at it. I got both hands right round it and jerked, but No Joy. It wasn't loose any more. It was frozen solid into the wall.

2. Secondly it was dark. And I was worried that the stone might come away with a sharp crack, and then the key would spin out and find itself a snowy grave …

3. Thirdly, the boy didn't help. Half my mind was on him, and I needed every working brain cell to figure out what to do. Plus he'd double up, and look like he was going to fall over. I'd reach out to support him and he'd end up leaning on me to stay straight. I'd stand there shivering, unwilling to shift him off. And none of that was loosening the stone.

4. And finally, something *was* out there, heaving itself towards us like an avalanche. I could HEAR it. And I knew when it found us, the darkness of Snowdon would give up its secrets and we'd be Total Goners. (You can't imagine the super-paralysing effect that had.)

Anyway, I steered the boy to the wall and removed his arm from around me. Even though it was kind of nice (you know, all that hugging), it was handicapping me. I left him leaning up against the grey stones.

'Stay. There!' I yelled at him. Like he was Ceri.

Then I crouched down, took off my daysack and unzipped it. I scrambled around for my ice axe, found it, put the daysack back on, and stepped up to the doorway. *Please Snowdon, this is your little Ellie. Let me get the key.* Then I attacked the stone in a frenzy.

It did me good. It got my blood going. It did the stone

good too. Snowdon must have been pleased as well, because at last the stone started to wobble. And with my blood up, I thought nothing of pulling off my glove, yanking the stone out and sticking my bare hand into the icy wall to search for the key.

Let it be there, Oh Great Wyddfa!

My icy fingers closed around it.

Halleluiah!

But that's where Yr Wyddfa's goodwill ran out.

To open a lock you have to actually put the key in the keyhole, don't you? But the keyhole in the door to Halfway House was iced shut.

'DAMMIT,' I hissed. 'BLOODY, SODDING DAMMIT!'

The boy moaned by the wall. I started to feel desperate. He let out air through his teeth. I got out my torch. I shone it on the lock. It wasn't just the keyhole that was iced over, the whole stupid door was! I searched each whorl of timber, every crack of weathering, and not only was the whole thing frozen solid, but the wood of the door jambs was swollen AS WELL. That door was wedged in so tight, it seemed to bulge outwards under the pressure.

'Please … hurry!' yelled the boy.

'I *am* hurrying!' I yelled back. 'The bloody lock's frozen solid!'

I started to panic. I couldn't hold the damn torch straight and the damn key wouldn't go in.

I grabbed my ice axe and started trying to knock the ice loose around the keyhole – and then stopped in case I broke the whole bloody lock completely.

Even when I could get the key in, it wouldn't turn. I was afraid to twist it too hard. I kicked at the door in frustration. '*C'mon!*' I screamed. My foot skidded on the layer of ice. Desperately I scanned the walls. There was no way through them, *obviously*. The windows were shuttered tight with metal roller blinds (part of the stupid owner's new plan to rebuild the place). You'd never break through them.

Tears of frustration welled up.

Door iced shut. Windows locked against us. Temperature dropping. Storm howling. Something crazy out there …

No time left.

We'd Had It.

Five

The boy bent over shivering. He let out a sigh. He started to say something and stopped. I felt so sorry. If the damn door didn't open, he wasn't going to make it.

And neither was I.

I racked my brains. What did the *Mountain Search & Rescue Handbook* say about frozen locks?

Absolutely nothing.

But the Land Rover owner's handbook did. It said: ' ... *in extreme conditions if no suitable de-icer is available, use a dry source of heat. Do not breathe on locks as exhalations contain water vapour which will cause further icing* ... '

Body heat! That was my only dry heat source left.

And there wasn't much of that, either.

In desperation I took off my gloves again. My poor hands were nearly blue with cold, but I pressed them against the steel lock – praying and praying and praying there would be enough warmth left in them to unfreeze the thing.

Please Snowdon, I prayed. *Please. This is Ellie. You've really tried for me. Just this one last thing.*

I held my hand there as long as I could, twisting the key at the same time. To distract myself – to distract him, I yelled, 'I'm Ellie, who're you?'

'Henry,' he said. 'I'm Henry.'

(I was going to say, 'Like *Henry the Eighth*?' But that would be such a stupid thing to say. And he probably got that all the time.)

Then suddenly the lock turned.

I snatched back my poor hands. I twisted the handle. The door didn't shift. Tightening my grip I shoved my shoulder up against it and pushed. It didn't budge. I hurled my shoulder against it, flinging all my weight behind me. The ice merely cracked a little. The door held firm. I reached down for my ice axe.

'Let me!' shouted Henry. Pushing himself along the wall, he made his way to the door.

I reached out, worried he'd fall. But he didn't. Instead he straightened up. I stepped forward to hold his arm, but with one brush, he swept me aside.

I went spinning back into the snow as if struck by a

whirlwind. My back hit something. The contents of the day-sack flew in every direction. Pain spiralled into my chest. I let out a soft 'Ow' and screwed up my face. For someone in the mid-stages of hypothermia that was some strength.

'Hey!' I called, meaning to protest. But Henry wasn't looking at me. He didn't even turn his head. He just squared up in front of the door, and shoved it. I swear he just placed one hand on it and pushed.

Two things happened simultaneously: There was an almighty screech and the ice yielded. Like a glacier cracking open, the door buckled inwards. The hinges squealed – as if caught by the tail end of a hurricane – and the whole door banged open.

Un-be-lievable.

How On Earth had he done that? Even if I'd worked out in Llanberis gym, Like Forever, I'd never have been able to do that.

I clambered to my feet. A stab of pain jabbed into my left shoulder. I bent down. I grabbed my daysack, groped around, retrieved the torch, looked for everything else, but only found the space blanket and some chocolate. The rest of the stuff was lost. And I wasn't going to start looking for it.

Before he stumbled in, Henry turned. 'Ellie, you OK?'

I rubbed my shoulder. It hurt. I twisted my waist. It hurt too. But I was so euphoric the door was open, I just smiled. ' … OK!' I yelled. 'What. About. You?'

Henry laughed. 'I'll make it now,' he said, 'thanks to you.'

He flashed me such a smile that my heart, catapulted up into my throat. I forgot the pain and the snow and the Beast of Dinas Emrys and I think I fell in love with him right There And Then.

Stepping into Halfway House that Christmas night was like stepping through a portal into an enchanted world. We left behind the bitter cold, the howling wind, the snow, the danger. We closed the door on all of it. Henry closed the door, actually. And it didn't fit back properly. Still, he wedged it shut somehow. (Quite easily, in fact.) He just gave it another of his extraordinary pushes.

'How did you just do that?' I asked.

'What?' he said.

'Open the door.'

'What?'

'And shut it?'

'*Whaaat?*'

'How Did You Get The Door Open?' I asked more slowly

(maybe hypothermia was turning him into a moron). This time I shone the torch beam full in his face.

Henry looked back at me, his face blank. 'You did most of the work, didn't you?' he said, 'the ice was already cracked.'

I looked at him puzzled.

'You must be stronger than you know,' he said.

'The ice wasn't cracked,' I said. (I was quite sure of that.) 'I was going to use my axe on it – when you swept me aside.'

'Wasn't it?' he said as if that was all news to him.

I didn't answer. That ice had been two centimetres thick and set like solid steel all around the door. It would have taken supernatural strength to blast it open.

'No,' I muttered at last.

'Oh!' he replied as if it surprised him too.

I looked at him. Maybe he *was* confused. Maybe he couldn't remember even simple events properly. It must be hypothermia, mustn't it? It was a textbook case. In fact I even remembered the textbook:

The Mountain Search & Rescue Handbook

The symptoms of moderate hypothermia include:

- violent, uncontrollable shivering
- being unable to think or pay attention

- feeling confused (some people don't realise they're affected)
- loss of judgement and reasoning

I peered through the darkness at him. Were his nose or fingers blue? I needed my torch to make sure. I didn't like to ask if I could see his toes for obvious reasons.

'I think you better let me check you over,' I said, suddenly worried. Perhaps he didn't remember the door business, because he was in such a state. Who knows? maybe a swift surge of super strength was another symptom that the handbook had forgotten to include.

'Hypothermia's not something you mess around with', I said, gently steering him to a bench near the old fireplace. I needed to take his pulse urgently, to see if his systems were shutting down. 'Can you stop shivering – on your own?' I asked, as I got him to sit.

'I'm not sure,' he said, teeth chattering.

I reached to take his hands in mine, hold them still while I felt for his pulse.

'Would you mind if I just look to see if your pupils are dilated?'

'Ok,' he said. His pulse wasn't too bad, in fact it was quite strong and his hands seemed oddly warm.

I dug the torch out of my pocket again and angled its beam, so it didn't dazzle him too much. I looked into his eyes.

And those dark eyes looked back into mine.

I had the sensation of weightlessness, as if I might suddenly lose my balance. They were sooo dark that despite the torch it was impossible to tell if they were contracting properly or not.

I adjusted the beam (carefully of course). But he groaned. 'I'm ok,' he said, 'I don't need help.'

You *so* do, I thought. You are still doing '*violent, uncontrollable shivering*' for a start. And a tingly excited feeling glowed inside me at the thought of taking care of him: *I'd massage his hands; I'd gently feed him little flakes of glucose bar; I'd tuck the space blanket round us both and cuddle life back into him; I'd run my fingers across his brow, through his tousled hair, and smooth it back. And if he needed further help, I was absolutely ready to rush straight back out into that storm and find it …*

But all I said was, 'If I can get you a bit sorted, I can go for help. With the compass I'll be OK.'

'No.' he said. His voice suddenly sharp. 'You won't.'

He was totally right, of course. It was a stupid idea. My cheeks started to burn. Thank goodness it was dark. 'Fine,' I said, 'then we must try to get you *much* warmer.'

But how?

I swung the flashlight around. The beam jumped from ancient rafter to ancient rafter. It swung down cold stone walls, over a cold flagged floor and back to the cold open fireplace beside us.

A fireplace!

Eagerly I shone the light into the hearth. There was a grate and a poker, a pair of fire-tongs and a shovel. Above the grate, carved into the masonry in between two stone dragons, were the words: *Fight Fire With Fire*, which I mentally adjusted to read, Fight *Hypothermia* with Fire. (If you've got any fire.)

But better still, next to the hearth lay a pile of logs covered in dust and cobweb. Although they were probably too cold to get going, they were nevertheless fuel. Beside all that was a scuttle full of coal with enough lumps to sustain us through the night.

'Get a fire going, and we'll be fine,' I said as cheerfully as I could.

Like that was going to happen.

With the matches and strike buried somewhere in the dark outside, and both of us nearly dead of cold, going back out there to look (with or without some kind of horrendous predator on our trail) was as stupid an idea as going for help.

But I didn't give up. I hunted around with the torch. If there were logs and coal and we were lucky, there *might* be a light inside, plus (hopefully) a pile of old newspapers or some small bits of firewood – something anyway to get a flame kindled.

I searched with the torch. And its beam lit up a framed plaque above the fire place. I glanced up at it:

HALFWAY HOUSE

HALFWAY HOUSE, A PRIVATELY OWNED MOUNTAIN SHELTER, STANDS ON THE SITE OF THE LEGENDARY MEETING OF KING VORTIGERN WITH THE GREAT MAGICIAN MYRDDIN EMRYS (OR MERLIN, AS HE IS CALLED IN ENGLISH). IT WAS TO HALFWAY HOUSE THAT MERLIN WAS BROUGHT, FROM MOEL CYNGHORION (THE HILL OF THE COUNCILLORS), BY VORTIGERN'S ADVISORS TO RESOLVE THE CURSE HANGING OVER DINAS AFFARAON. MERLIN UNFOLDED THE MYSTERY OF THE WORMS OF DINAS AFFARAON TO VORTIGERN. THE MOUNTAIN ON WHICH HE PROVED HIS MIGHTY POWER WAS CALLED IN AFTERTIME DINAS EMRYS, INSTEAD OF DINAS AFFARAON, IN HONOUR OF MERLIN. HALFWAY HOUSE HAS LONG BEEN KNOWN AS A SAFE HOUSE, A PLACE WHERE TRAVELLERS CAN TAKE REFUGE FROM THE REAL AS WELL AS THE MAGICAL WORLD OF SNOWDONIA.

I couldn't remember ever having seen that plaque before, but then I hadn't actually been in the cottage for ages, not since its makeover anyway. Obviously it was a new addition to the place, along with the metal roller blinds. I hoped like hell a gas camping stove with a built-in electronic lighter might be another.

'I'm going to look in the kitchen,' I said, turning back to Henry, 'Just as soon as I've got the space blanket round you.' I opened up my daysack and pulled the space blanket out. I shook it clear of its packing. Even though he tried to shrug it away again, I put it round him. 'There,' I said, 'you'll be fine.' I'd suddenly found my old reassuring-wannabe-mountain-rescue-self again. 'Just hang on in there. I'll take care of you.'

'You shouldn't,' he said. There was a tone in his voice.

'I *will* take care of you,' I said, 'I'm not a beginner at this, my mum is …'

'You should stay away from me and take care of yourself,' he said quite coldly.

I felt his words like a blow in the face. 'But …' I said, 'I just saved you out there …' According to my logic, he should be like really grateful? I'd left my lovely warm house on Christmas night to tramp through a blizzard to find him. I'd got him here and found the key and everything. I could have just left him to his fate and gone into Llanberis with Mum. I should be his latest best friend by now.

'It would have been better, perhaps, if you'd left me alone,' he said, almost as if he could read my mind.

There was something about his voice that was so empty. It made me start and I dropped the torch. I groped around on the floor, trying to hide my bewilderment, my hands still achingly numb.

His voice continued through the blackness. 'I hope you're listening. I don't want you around.' A sudden loneliness laced his voice.

Tears sprang to my eyes and I bit my lip. Why had he just said that? I'd only been trying to help. I found the torch and flicked it back on. I shone it over towards him. There he was; his beautiful face screwed up into a scowl. 'I mean it,' he said. 'You should stay away from me.' He flung his arms out suddenly at the dark walls (as if they shouldn't be there either). His flying hands cast strange shadows in the torch light, shadows that flickered across the cold stone like huge flapping wings.

The mood in the cottage changed, suddenly became menacing. I realised I was alone with this strange boy and I didn't know a thing about him. I didn't know how he'd managed to push the door open, why he was out on the hill, or how he'd been able to survive all day, or *anything*. And for an instant I got a glimpse of something ancient, prehistoric, savage even, crouching there by the empty hearth.

'But … ' I started.

He warned me off with another look. The shadows condensed around him. I swung the torch away and turned into the darkness. My forehead knitted up. 'I'll go and look for matches, then,' I muttered.

I groped my way towards the kitchen feeling miserable, when almost as if by magic, I heard Mum's sane voice:

'He's a very sick boy, Ellie, of course he wouldn't rather have been left alone, but hypothermia muddles the brain. Some folks actually lay down in the snow to sleep and try to refuse all help.'

I glanced back towards him.

'Some try to fight you off when you approach, some get angry, others break down crying or laugh quite hysterically … don't forget the words of the manual: victims of hyperthermia **'lose their judgement and reasoning'***, have* **'uncontrollable mood swings'** *… '* Mum's imaginary voice carried on, soothing me, telling me not to lose my own good sense.

I reached the kitchen. My throat aching in a strange new way. Rescuing someone wasn't much fun, if they just got cross with you.

And I suddenly realised how much I'd wanted him to like me, to think of me as someone special. And (with a bit of a shock), how cold *I* was. My whole body was shivering. My teeth could hardly stop chattering. Maybe I was having 'uncontrollable mood swings' too.

Both of us needed to get that fire going. Pretty soon.

But how on earth could we with those stupid old logs? They were obviously frozen solid, and even if there were matches, they'd probably be soggy and wouldn't light. Plus we needed paper – every scrap in my pockets was wet and useless. As far as I could see there was nothing that was going to get those logs even thawed out, let alone lit. I vaguely wondered if sticking a flare into them might work. But stopped myself; that was *way* too dangerous, plus the flares were probably lost outside as well.

I shone the torch in front of me. God, the place smelt. Everywhere stank with cold and damp. Through a doorway at the back was a space, not really a room. You had to sort of bend your head and go through an arch of stone into a makeshift store room. At the end of this was a little panelled door – the loo. I groped in the darkness, swinging my torch around.

No camping stove.

No electricity (of course).

No matches.

There should be matches though – shouldn't there, or a lighter? The Snowdon Mountain Railway stopped nearby in the summer and delivered huge canisters of water to the place. I was sure that was for making tea and stuff. They must have had some way of boiling it. There *had* to be matches. I banged an old metal teapot down on the draining board.

'My head hurts,' I said crossly, 'And I can't find anything.'

'Sorry!' he called from the main room, his voice suddenly much nicer. 'I didn't mean to push you over out there. Is your head very bad? Do you feel dizzy?'

I managed a smile then, just a little one. I'd been feeling dizzy ever since I met him! My head did hurt though, and actually, maybe, I was just a little shaky.

'I'm ok,' I said. At least he'd said sorry.

'Maybe *I* need to check *you*?' A small laugh. 'A knock on the head can make you all muddled.'

Maybe that was it. I'd knocked my head, and got it all wrong about him pushing the door open. And anyway what was the point of letting it worry me? We were inside out of the cold. Away from the Beast of Dinas Emrys or whatever the hell it was, and getting a fire going was so much more important. With a fire we'd be in much better shape to last the night. With a fire we could begin to think straight.

A new determination to find matches seized me.

I heard Henry rummaging around in the main room and, strangely, the sounds of spitting and crackling. I found some candles, two tins, one metal plate and a spoon but no matches. I crashed around. I left the candles, for obviously they'd need lighting too, and with my little hoard of goodies, I stumbled back into the main room, ready to try and persuade him to eat – energy was important, especially if we couldn't light a fire – but my finds slipped from my grasp.

By some miracle he'd got a fire going.

There he was, warming his hands in front of it, as smug as a cat on a cushion. And what a fire! Logs blazing away like they'd been lit for hours, smoke curling in tendrils up the old chimney, warm orange flames chasing their shadows across the cold walls. The low bench was pulled up close, and it was as cosy as could be.

'Oh my God!' I said, astonished.

In the light of the dancing flames, Henry grinned 'You see before you, a Duke-of-Edinburgh-Award gold medallist, who can light a fire underwater.' He flung his hands around, twirled an imaginary cape, doffed an imaginary hat, flicked its imaginary feather, and swept down in front of me in an amazing bow.

And he looked so much better.

'I sincerely apologise for my ill humour,' he said, 'and politely request the company of the Lady of the Mountain.' He gestured gallantly towards the old bench.

'Oh,' I said still quite bewildered. And a lot happier.

'So, Lady Ellie, does this hotel have a restaurant?' He eyed the tins on the floor.

I nodded. *How strange that he should have recovered so quickly.*

'Excellent,' he said.

Still quite overcome, I bent down to retrieve the fallen cans.

'May I help?' He sprang forward.

Together we bent to the floor. Our hands touched. Instant electricity spiked through me. I lurched back as if punched.

'And the menu for this Yuletide Eve?' he laughed, springing up and bowing again.

I regained my balance, stood up, still in shock.

How had he got that fire going?

Somehow I managed to pull myself together. I even answered him in the same spirit, managed a curtsy to boot. 'Yer Duke-of-Edinburgh-ship, we have ye lovelee delicious corned beef on the menu with ye olde bakèd beans, warmed in the can, a speciality of Snowdon cuisine … ' I held aloft my trophies, then put the tins down on the hearth.

'There,' I said still reeling.

'Exquisite!' he said.

I took a deep breath. Shelter. Fire. Food. And this strange feeling that I'd somehow stepped into some kind of Narnia.

I fetched the candles from the kitchen. We sat down on the old bench in front of the roaring fire. The logs smelt of pine. The room filled with warmth. I adjusted the space blanket and wrapped it round both of us. Firelight sparkled off it in little dancing flickers. Together we huddled under it, until our shivering stopped. Then we opened the cans and stuck them in the embers. While the food defrosted, we carried on warming ourselves and breathing in the scent of burning pine, and shaking out the pins and needles. We dried our clothes. We lit the candles. And soon the beans sizzled and the corned beef fat melted. We banked up the fire. Golden shadows glowed from the old stone walls, and then we ate.

Both cans of food were burned on the outside and cold in the middle, but we didn't care. We tipped the beans and corned beef on to the solitary plate. We shared one spoon. We made it last, one spoonful at a time. It was the most delicious meal I've ever eaten. It tasted of cinder and salt, and of success. *We'd done it*. We'd beaten old Snowdon.

And it fed me in ways that I didn't even know I was hungry for. With every spoonful he offered, I'd look into his eyes and smile.

And he'd smile back and say, 'More caviar, my Lady of the Mountain?'

And I'd be unable to answer. (My mouth full of corned beef, which I could hardly chew, because I could hardly even swallow.)

And Henry found two old cracked mugs and filled them with fresh snow. And we stood them by the fire until they melted. Snow tastes funny, but we toasted each other with that melted snow as if it were the finest champagne.

'To you, Ellie, the Finder of Paths in the Darkness,' he said.

'To you, Henry, the Maker of Fires in the Coldness,' I replied.

'To us,' we laughed together.

'I'll always come to your rescue,' I said.

'And I'll always tell you not to,' he said

'And how come you pushed that door in?' I added.

'One day I'll explain,' he said.

'And?' I said.

'Don't … ' he said, 'Don't spoil it.'

So I didn't.

Six

We sat there for a long time, letting the warmth soak into us, listening to the howling wind, breathing in the scent from those old pine logs. And despite strange half-smothered noises, Halfway House was as good as its plaque, a safe haven from everything.

'So who exactly is Ellie Morgan?' Henry said after we'd eaten, after we'd toasted all our snow champagne away and were finishing up with squares of chocolate.

Telling him felt good. I told him about Mum, the farm – how she had inherited it from her mam – how Dad loved Snowdon, how we'd all come back to live there seven years ago, though I already knew the mountain like the back of my hand. How I dreamt of travelling, going to sixth form in Caernarfon (hopefully) and university in London, seeing my old school friends again. I told him about George (I didn't mention his infatuation with me, obviously) and Gran. I told him about my other friends – Rhiannon and how she was totally nuts about George and how it did your head in. I told him about Meryl, how serious she was and sensible and a little sad, but ambitious, and wanted to be a marine biologist and save the world by finding a million and one energy uses for algae, but how her mam was dead set she shouldn't leave the village. And Sheila, who was such a chav, and always flinging herself at boys until you wanted to strangle her, and how she was always wearing skimpy outfits and dying her hair pink, but such a laugh too, and would lend you her last penny and lie through her teeth to get you out of trouble. And I told him about the rescue, and how I was certain that I'd seen him that morning on Devil's Bridge.

All the time he nodded his head, listening, encouraging.

'Really, please tell me,' I said, 'It *was* you, wasn't it?'

He didn't answer straight away. Then he said with a slight laugh. 'Was it?' And I got the strangest feeling, a bit like déjà vu, or as if some weird time warp had wrapped itself around us.

'Yes, it was you,' I said stubbornly.

He shrugged.

'So tell me about *you*, anyway,' I countered. 'You don't live in Llanberis.' I was sure of that. I was certain. I'd have heard all about him from Sheila if he'd lived within a hundred miles of the place.

'Are you visiting? Where are you staying?'

'I haven't finished my questions yet,' he said, 'What about your dad?' he said. 'What does he do?'

'My dad's dead,' I said.

'Oh,' he said, 'I didn't mean … '

'It's ok,' I said. 'I don't mind. Talking about someone keeps them close.'

Henry shoved another log on the fire. 'How did he die?' he said, 'You don't have to – I'd like to know … if you want … '

Actually it was fine. At last someone who wanted to know. Mostly people don't. They clam up, change the subject. Death frightens them, I suppose. They don't realise how all the words burn inside, wanting to come out. But Henry was ready to listen. He was different – different in so many ways. And I wanted to tell him. I wanted him to know all about me.

So I started. And he listened, not just nodding his head, all bored and pretending not to be. He focused in on me with his strange dark eyes, as if everything I said was fascinating – and I felt grateful. That's so stupid isn't it? I felt like nobody had ever listened to me before, not *really* listened, and now I'd found him – I wanted to talk to him forever.

'Dad loved mountains,' I said. 'He loved climbing them, that's why we came to live here. This is where he met Mum during one of his first climbs. He died on Kangchenjunga, in the Himalaya. Nobody came to rescue him.' I guess my voice must have sounded very sad.

Henry immediately put his arm around me and said, 'Ellie, I'm so sorry.'

Tears sprang to my eyes. In all the trauma of losing dad and waiting and hoping and panicking, nobody had ever really asked me how *I* felt, how *I* was doing.

'It was two seasons before they found him.' My voice quavered and I stopped. I bit my lip, not trusting myself to continue. 'That's a long time, nearly six months.' I folded my arms over my chest, trying to hold in all the shakiness. Eventually I said. 'All that time he was there on the cliff face in Nepal, frozen against the mountain.'

Henry shivered as if he could actually feel those ice cliffs freezing around him. 'Wasn't there any chance of getting him down?' he said very gently.

I shook my head, feeling wobbly. I thought I was over it, but my eyes were full of unshed tears and a fresh ache had started somewhere inside my throat.

'It was the weather,' I whispered, 'an avalanche. He just didn't stand a chance. Everyone said it was too risky to try to get to him. They say he stayed alive for ... '

'Stop,' he said, 'you mustn't think like that.'

I dragged my arm across my eyes and swallowed. I looked up at him. He was trembling. He looked horribly disturbed. Suddenly I felt dreadful. I bit my lip harder. What was I thinking of? Dad had been dead a long time, but Henry was barely over freezing to death this evening and here I was talking about dying frozen up against an ice face. 'Oh,' I said, 'I didn't mean ... '

'It terrifies me,' he whispered, 'it really does, freezing against the mountain, being buried alive under an avalanche ... if I hadn't met you tonight ... ' He stood up and shuddered.

'Sorry,' I said.

He sat back down, squared up his shoulders and seemed to get a grip on himself. 'Sorry too,' he said, 'Christmas must be so hard for you.'

I nodded. Christmas was always the worst. I still remember the first one without Dad, when we didn't know anything for sure. The terror every time the phone rang. The relief when the lines went down.

'I think I understand,' he said.

I smiled. I doubted it. But at least he was trying to.

'But you've got your mum.'

I looked at him in the firelight. There was something in his voice. 'What about your parents?' I said. 'Won't they be going mental with worry?'

'I'm down in Caernarfon with my uncle,' Henry said. 'He's got business of his own. He won't worry about me.' Then suddenly he stopped, as if he'd said too much. 'You don't need to know all that,' he said.

'Why not?' I said. I'd just told him all about me, even the hardest bits.

'Because you don't need to,' he repeated, 'We're stuck here till first light – I'll get you home. After that I'm history.'

'History?' I said in bewilderment.

He said nothing but stared gloomily into the flames.

Slowly the penny dropped. History, like: *over, finished, no future*? Like right now – all our conversation, all our closeness was going nowhere. Something in me panicked. *I didn't want him to be history*. What did he mean?

'Let's not spoil it,' he said. 'There's still tonight.' He put his arm back round me. I allowed him to prop my head on his shoulder. 'There,' he said, 'Let me take care of you now. It's my turn.'

Confused, not knowing whether to relax, or snatch my head back, I sat there. Through the darkness, I could see the line of his jaw etched against the fire, the angles of his face.

I watched the blue centres of the flames flickering.

'But,' I said, pulling myself away, 'Why history? If you're only in Caernarfon … I can get into Caernarfon … '

He didn't say anything, but I got the feeling that he was holding himself back – but against what and why I had no idea. Everything about him contradicted his words, told me I'd made a friend, but he shook his head like he'd imposed some decision on himself and was not going to change it.

'You should get some sleep,' he said.

'And you,' I said.

He laughed. 'I don't sleep, alas.' He put his arm back round me.

What did he mean? He didn't sleep! And such bizarre language too. '*Alas!*' How weird! As if he came from a completely different era.

I mean, QUESTION: Who The Hell says 'ALAS' these days?

And, QUESTION 2: Who DOESN'T sleep (apart from EVIL, and Edward in TWILIGHT)?

I thought about shrugging his arm off, because a part of me was hurt. You know: OMG so I'm not ACTUALLY interesting enough to get even a trial 'future' rating. I thought about withdrawing to the other end of the bench in a childish sulk, but that seemed silly (and cold). And anyway I didn't really want to. Whatever he thought about me I liked him. And he was right. I should get some sleep – even if he wanted to stay awake all night. I'd been up a long time. I'd climbed the mountain twice. God, rescuing that girl seemed ages ago! Was it only just this morning? So I rested my head back on his shoulder. I closed my eyes. *How strange to be held by someone you don't even know!* Except that it felt as if I *did* know him, that I'd *always* known him and that it was the most natural thing in the world to sit here together … with my head on his shoulder … Tonight everything was such a muddle … I didn't even know how to think about any of it …

'Not history,' I murmured.

'There's no other way,' he said sadly.

'I can get Mum to give me a lift in, when she does the shopping.'

'It's not tomorrow yet,' he said.

And with the warmth of the fire and the buffeting of the wind and with Henry, I didn't want tomorrow to ever come.

'Rest,' he said.

'More like a mystery,' I mumbled.

'Sleep. I'll take first watch. If the Beast of Dinas Emrys shows up, I'll tell him to avaunt himself.'

There it was – that weird language again.

I laughed. 'Definitely not history.'

I think he laughed too.

I yawned.

And I think I must have fallen asleep.

Seven

Henry really must have stayed awake all night. And perhaps he was watching through the hours against whatever evil we'd left outside. I don't remember him moving, anyway. I don't remember much, except feeling safe and warm. When I stirred, a hand patted my shoulder and a voice shushed me back to sleep. And even though I struggled to wake up, to make the most of this strange night ... his words lulled me, and I sunk again into slumber.

What. A. Waste.

I could just imagine what the girls would say:

1. Rhiannon would swoon, going: 'Oooo! Ahh!' (Picturing herself out all night with George, obvs. Dot. Dot. Dot.)
2. Meryl would be all worried about a zillion consequences, I'd failed to see.

3. And Sheila? Sheila would know I'd wasted time.
I could just hear the conversation.

SHEILA: So you spent the *entire* night with a totally fit
         lush boy with *huge* muscles and a sexy smile
         and you *slept*?

ME: I was tired, it got so warm …

SHEILA: And you fancied the pants off him, and you
         didn't make even the teensiest move?

ME: It wasn't like that. He was special.

SHEILA: You didn't go on about how you needed a back
         rub, or how you were *soooo* cold only a hug could
         fix it – or flutter your eyes – or lean forward so
         your boobs pressed against him – or anything?

ME: I don't do all that kind of stuff.

SHEILA: Nothing? Not even the weeniest girly thing?

ME: I put my head on his shoulder.

SHEILA: I give up! I godamn frickin give up!

And so the morning came. The fire was still going. Henry
still had his arm around me. I opened my eyes. I raised my
head. I smiled at him, sort of embarrassed. He smiled right
back, a sweet kind of half-grin, like he knew we shouldn't

really have stayed out the entire night.

I was kind of shocked at myself. Maybe Sheila did this sort of thing all the time, but I didn't. I'd just spent *all night* with a strange boy. One I'd only *just* met.

Henry gave me a little squeeze and took his arm away. 'I think you slept well,' he said.

'Yep,' I said, surprised I had, remembering the terrors of the night before.

'We'd better get going,' he said.

'Must we?' I said.

He nodded and turned his face away.

Stupid question.

We tidied the fireplace. We hauled more logs in from the lean-to outside. We washed the cracked mugs, the plate and spoon in snow. Together we closed the door as best we could. At least we managed to lock it. We put the key back behind the loose stone. It was kind of sad to shut the door. My throat dried up. I couldn't swallow. I was leaving my little enchanted world behind. The place where Merlin met Vortigern, and Ellie spent the night with Henry. It was a world I'd only just discovered. And now I had to go.

And in the cold air outside I remembered the word: History.

Silently we tramped through the snow. I glanced up at

Henry, trying to fathom him. I longed to catch his arm, to point out all the crags and peaks I knew so well; the ones I'd climbed as a child, the ones still unconquered. I wanted to talk of everything and nothing.

Why didn't he say something?

I wanted to read his mind, ask him: *Why don't you want to see me again?*

And that Boxing Day morning was perfect. We could have chatted so easily. A clear, baby-blue sky arched above creamy snow clouds. The air was crisp, the mountainside smooth. Its coat of snow lay unbroken from peak to valley in every shade of white. High above the summit of Snowdon a lonely bird circled, cawing out its sharp cry across the valleys.

But as soon as we left the slopes where Halfway House stood, the magic disappeared. Every step was an effort. I kicked drearily at the icy tufts of yellowing grass. The snowy hills stood lifeless, like they were printed on cheap Christmas cards, the showy sky merely a painted backdrop.

Henry was a stranger.

There was no longer any doubt about it. His face was angled away from me. All The Time. With every step I felt the separation. And when eventually I plucked up courage and tried to say something, he blanked me completely.

And he kept his distance.

He walked at least three paces away, which was quite difficult given some of the banks we had to clamber down. When we got in sight of Llanberis, I stole a last side-long glance at him.

His profile was perfect. His forehead, nose, chin, all set with precision. I had to catch my breath. Somehow in the glow of last night's fire, he'd looked different. He'd been different too. A fellow survivor of Snowdon. A potential friend. Not this remote flawless face.

And I felt a sudden longing to be back there, sharing baked beans and warming our socks by the hissing fireside. A lump started to grow in my chest.

At last he turned towards me. 'I'm sorry, Ellie,' he said. 'You'd thank me if you knew.'

'What?' I said, 'knew what?' I turned to him, hoping for some explanation.

'Why last night must be consigned to history,' he said, gently.

My heart sank. The morning lost its sparkle. The sun was just a hollow eye, the hills, bleak wastelands.

At last I rallied. 'I'll show you George's place,' I said. 'His Gran does the wickedest breakfast.' My words fell flat. Why had I just said that? Why was I trying to impress him with Granny Jones' cooking? I looked down the slopes towards the cottage. Suddenly it looked very small and insignificant. He wouldn't like it. He'd hate George and he'd think Gran was mental.

Henry didn't answer. He pressed on, his footsteps crunching in the snow. Thank God, Mum had stayed at Jeff's. If she'd been home, she'd be doing her nut by now. I suddenly wondered: could I take him to our house? I framed the words, then shut my mouth. He wouldn't come. I didn't want him at my place anyway. Our farmhouse was old and chaotic and too rural for words. There'd probably still be no mains electricity, and Mum might come back. I cringed at the thought of him meeting Mum.

The strange thing was, in all that walk down the mountain, I never once thought how little I knew about him: his parents, school, friends, pastimes. It was as if he existed outside normal things like homes and family and breakfast and college. Anyway as we got nearer to George's place I started worrying. If George knew I'd just Spent The Night with Henry, he'd go ballistic. At least, I think he would. George is funny like that. He tries to act all open minded, but he thinks he owns me and my opinions about that don't count.

I squirmed around inside my mind, trying to avoid a voice in my head which asked: *Why are you taking him to*

George's place? Are you mad? What are you tying to prove?
*Why do you **want** to upset George? What has George ever done*
to deserve that?

And to tell you the truth, I didn't have any answers,
except a shadowy feeling that I was hurting, and therefore
others must hurt as well. It'll do George good to see I have
a life too, I rationalised. *See George*, I said to him in my
head, *there are other boys on the playing field. Don't think that*
being next door-ish neighbours automatically leads to marriage
and joint bank accounts. And then I felt guilty, because I love
George very much – but you know Not In *That* Way – and
I really didn't want to upset him.

George wouldn't say anything, of course, it'd just be that
look in his eyes, like he was a puppy and you'd locked
him out on a cold night. He wouldn't say anything nasty,
either. He'd do the opposite and, before I knew it, he'd
pal up with Henry and be off playing rugby with him. But
he'd be hurt all right. I knew George like I knew Snowdon.
He'd be so hurt he'd run off and join the Foreign Legion or
something equally improbable.

We crossed in front of the ridge of Moel Cynghorion,
the Hill of the Councillors, and made our way down the
steep gullies that sheltered Granny Jones' cottage from the
north wind. That's why we ended up arriving at her place

from the back. I didn't mean to startle her. Honest. I didn't know she'd be outside. We just rounded the corner and there she was.

She jumped and stood bolt upright. She dropped her bowl, the corn for the hens spread out in a shower. Each grain hit the snow, making its own little crater. I stopped abruptly. 'Sor-rree,' I said, all smiles.

Grandma Jones' face went pale. Then grew dark – almost purple. She looked at the two of us standing there. She backed up. Her mouth fell open. Her hands fluttered in front of her, as if she were drawing signs in the air.

'No … ' she stammered.

'Hey, Gran!' I said. I stepped forward.

Henry didn't move.

'No,' she said again.

I took another step. I didn't mean to make her jump. I reached out my hand. She grabbed it with a strength you'd never have guessed at. She yanked me forward. I slid, I tripped. I came crashing towards her. I banged into the wall of the cottage and held on to a drain pipe in an effort to right myself. Granny Jones stepped forward and stood between Henry and me.

Henry looked confused, hurt even. He stepped forward too, as if to grab me back.

But before he could reach me, Gran waved her hand in the air. 'Be gone!' she said, '*Ewch o ma!*' She waved her hand again. '*Bydd y gwyntoedd yn chwythu o gyfeiriad y de, bydd y lleuad yn codi o'r dwyrain, ni fydd ei chyflawnder yn para ac ni fydd eich cysgod ychwaith.*'

My Welsh isn't that good. In fact I'm totally rubbish at Welsh. I can't tell you the tears I shed in primary school, when we moved here.[1] But I think she said '*The winds will blow from the south, the moon will rise from the east, its fullness will not last and neither will your shadow,*' which seemed like a pretty weird thing to say to anyone – let alone a stranger who could be anyone and hadn't sworn at you or anything.

A look of death passed over Henry's face. His eyebrows drew together in one long low line. '*Byddaf yn gwneud fy ngorau; yr wyf yn gwneud fy ngorau,*' he said. Which I roughly translated as: '*I will do my best; I am doing my best.*' Or something.

'*Nid ydym am gael y rhai sydd wedi cael eu melltithio fel chi fan hyn,*' bellowed Gran. Which wasn't very nice of her because it actually meant, '*We do not want your cursed sort here.*'

'*Gwn. Dyna pam yr wyf wedi dod â hi yn ôl i chi,*' Henry said very sadly. Which was really sweet and made me want to cry,

---

1. Lots of schools in Wales deliver their education in Welsh. Children do not have to speak Welsh to attend – but they have to learn the language quickly.

because even after Gran had been so poisonous, he'd only answered, '*I know, that is why I have brought her back to you.*'

My heart missed a beat. An ache started again in my throat.

He turned. He held his jacket close. The snow swirled around him. He disappeared back around the corner of the cottage.

'Hey!' I yelled, 'Hey, wait!' I stepped forward to follow him, but Granny Jones grabbed hold of my wrist again and with a grip of iron yanked me back, 'Let him go, child. He's not one of us.'

I slipped over and looked up at her. I was So Not Believing this. Granny Jones had just been totally – I couldn't even put into any kind of language what she'd just been – so YUCK – and I'd fallen on my bum. I burst into tears.

Granny didn't let go of me. I struggled up, but by the time George came out to see what was going on, and she'd finally let go of my wrist, Henry had gone. And everything was spoiled.

I raced back around the corner of the cottage. All I could see was a small dark figure striding away in a flurry of snow.

'Henry!' I yelled.

But he didn't stop or turn or look back.

Eight

I was utterly inconsolable when Granny Jones dished up breakfast. The eggs, sausages, bacon and slices of toast didn't seem the tiniest bit wicked after all. I couldn't swallow anything. How can you possibly eat sunny-side-up with Tesco Value streaky bacon when your heart is broken?

And I didn't want to be there. I wanted to be anywhere *except* there. I wanted to run and hide and dig myself a hole in the ice and die. My hands were trembling. I couldn't even butter toast. How could Gran have done that?

He'd gone.

If only I could have explained, told him she was just a mad old woman. It was all my fault. I should have known better than to take him there.

I fiddled with a piece of kitchen roll. I plugged my phone in to recharge. I checked my phone messages.

And that made everything worse.

And more.

I already felt like DEAD MEAT.

So I updated my status.

(It didn't make me feel any better.)

And I checked my other messages.

Recent updates between Ellie and Rhiannon:

Rhiannon

Will u c George 2day?

Rhiannon

Can u tell him We're havin a party for Darren on
New Year's Eve. We want him to play his guitar.

Rhiannon

Ping me

George was peering weirdly at me over the ketchup.

I told myself: try to see it from Gran's point of view. She must have a reason. She's not horrid. I ordered myself to calm down, to work on making everything ok, pretend nothing had happened. That's the funniest yet, pretending everything was normal when all you want to do is disintegrate.

George tried to help out. (He really is the sweetest guy.) He looked at me puzzled. He got down my all-time favourite, chocolate-hazelnut spread, which Granny disapproves of. He put it by my plate, like I was a little kid. (Fat lot of help chocolate spread was going to be!) I didn't touch it. But I did flash him a smile, which I hope read: I Am Trying

Very Hard Not To Show How Upset I Feel.

Why had Gran behaved like that?

She can be so weird. Every now and then she does something that makes you think, she really needs a full check-up from the neck up. I mean, she bumbles about like a harmless dotty old lady, then she goes all rabid on you.

I wanted to ask her – up front – what the hell she'd got against Henry. Was there something she knew that I didn't? But I'm a big coward and I felt I'd messed things up enough, already, so I didn't need to make it worse.

And Gran, for her part, kept her lips sealed in a tight, hibiscus-red line. If she knew anything at all she wasn't saying.

So I sat very still and tried to work it all out. But with nothing to go on, I didn't get very far. I thought about saying something, but every time I opened my mouth, she shot me a look, as if to say: Don't You Dare. And that convinced me – more than anything – that there probably wasn't anything other than her bad temper. More than once I opened and closed my mouth. And while I was sitting there doing a poor imitation of a goldfish, George seemed to have gone completely catatonic. Instead of rolling his eyes and doing We-Are-All-Welsh-Nutters-But-Some-Of-Us-Are-More-Nutty-Than-Others, or *anything*, he just kept staring at his plate and pushing the tomatoes around with the bits of bacon.

Why on earth had I come here? I could have taken Henry *anywhere*. Now he was gone. I didn't even have his phone number. No pinging, no calling. I didn't know how old he was. I didn't know if or where he went to college. I didn't know where he lived. I didn't even know his surname. For Christ's sake! *I didn't even know his last name.*

I didn't know anything.

Full stop.

He was gone and I was never going to see him again.

Granny Jones put the teapot down on the pine table. She shoved the cosy (padded with pics of cats on) into George's hand, nodding at him to cover it up. George reached out. His shoulders slumped inward, which gave him a funny Neanderthal look.

Finally he said, 'Who is he?'

Good question.

I tossed my head. George might be my best friend, but he better not forget I had a choice about that. 'He's my fairytale prince, actually,' I said. 'A Christmas special from Santa on account of me being good all year.' And actually I thought that was pretty funny. In a not-funny kind of way.

'He's no good', Granny said. 'That's all you need to know.'

I don't know why, but suddenly I giggled, a half-mad,

insane kind of snort, born more of suppressed emotion than anything else. Maybe it was the thought of me spending the night with a boy who was No Good. (Quite an achievement.) When you live halfway up a mountain, any kind of boy is an achievement, let alone a really Bad One. Proper tracksuit-wearing, hooded-up Bad Ones probably never set foot outside Cardiff.

Anyway George jerked his head up, his eyes puzzled. Then he stood up and left the table. He crossed the room and stood by the fire, as if he'd suddenly got cold.

And that upset me even more. I'd been going to tell him *everything*. Ask him what he thought. See what he made of shoving open doors and magically lighting fires. Now he was acting all funny.

'George?' I said. But he didn't look at me. 'George?' I said again. He looked up then. His eyes as empty as black holes.

I'd messed up, hadn't I? In less than an hour I'd managed to lose Henry, annoy Gran and annihilate George. Nice going, Ellie, I thought.

I made to get up, to go to George, to try to make it better. Shake his arm, tease him back into cheerfulness. But instead I managed to knock over my tea.

Granny Jones reached for kitchen roll. The tea soaked into her special Christmas table cloth with holly sprigs on it.

Some of it splashed on to George's plate. I said sorry a zillion times. George said it didn't matter. Granny put on Rod Stewart's *Greatest Hits*. And everything just went terrible.

'I'm taking you back to your mother's,' announced Gran.

'Mum's not in,' I said. (And, hello, since when did I report to Granny Jones?)

'No matter. I'll get you home.'

Oh, and hello again, did I, Arabella Morgan, Helper of the Llanberis Mountain Rescue Team actually need escorting anywhere in broad daylight?

Granny Jones just buttered herself a crumpet.

'Thanks for breakfast,' I said stiffly, 'but I can get back on my own.'

'I know you can,' said Granny, 'but I'm still coming.'

And she meant it.

She pulled on her patchwork coat, her pashmina shawl with fringes, her boots and gloves. And George was ordered to come as well.

And I was frogmarched down the hill in another kind of stony silence.

'Get yourself inside, Ellie,' ordered Gran, waggling her ringed fingers at me, when we arrived.

Like I was going to hang around outside?

'And stay there.'

I took the key from under the mat and let myself in. Inside it was bloody freezing. Ceri, our little border collie, was elated to see me. She hurled herself at me. Then stopped. With a strange yelp she suddenly twisted in mid-air. She stopped short. Her tail dropped. She backed away, as if overnight I'd turned into Voldemort. Wonderful. I'd even upset Ceri!

Somehow I'd been expecting Granny Jones and George to follow me into the house, where there'd be more awkward silences and clumsiness over coffee, during which Mum would arrive, and we'd all try to pretend everything was normal. But after all the trouble of escorting me halfway down the mountain, they didn't. When I turned to shut the door – they weren't there.

And they weren't in the front porch either.

I ran into the living room and peered out of the window. There they were standing on the front lawn. Granny was sprinkling something across the side path. She'd hitched up her long velvet skirt and had one pointy black boot stuck into the border. So much for the azaleas. I pressed my nose up against the cold pane, wondering what the heck she was doing.

As usual it was something weird. She was drawing strange symbols in the air. First with her finger and then with what looked like a bunch of dried flowers. I let out my breath in a rush of air. The window misted over. I wiped it clean with my sleeve. Granny was drawing symbols in the snow on either side of the drive now. God! She was majorly mental. One of the symbols was a circle and the other looked like a sickle moon. I sighed again and succeeded in misting up the window further. George was just standing there. Head down. Shoulders slumped.

Granny crossed to the back of the house by the kitchen path. I ran into the kitchen to watch. She started all over again, the sprinkling and the signing and the full mumbo jumbo. George had followed and stood now with his hands thrust deep in his pockets, pushing a loose piece of paving stone with his toe.

Em.Barr.Ass.Ing.

Poor George. How was he ever going to introduce anyone to her? I imagined him bringing a girlfriend home. NOT Rhiannon of course. Someone small and fair-haired and very slim with sparkly blue eyes – a bit like me really.

GEORGE: Meet my Nan. She's taken care of me ever since my parents died.

GIRLFRIEND: Hi Nan. That's cool.

GRANNY JONES: Hi thee hither you wicked wench, you'll not bring evil curses upon this house.

GIRLFRIEND: Sorry I didn't quite get you. Say again?

GRANNY JONES: *Nid ydym am gael y rhai sydd wedi cael eu melltithio fel chi fan hyn!*

GEORGE: Oh, don't worry, she's just checking you out, to see if you are a witch or a hagbag, or likely to bring a thousand years of plague upon us.

GIRLFRIEND: Bye George.

That's what spending your entire life up a mountain does to you. You go mental. Gran must have gone whacko a few centuries ago. She was so full of myths and magic and traditions and conspiracy theories, she'd need the full anti-legendary, anti-virus, firewall treatment downloaded into her mental software every five minutes to sort her out.

You know, if you followed her advice – I swear – you'd never get out of bed.

Irritated, I pulled down the latch on the window and yanked it open. I yelled out across the frozen morning, 'You coming in or wot?'

George shrugged his shoulders. He stood there like a garden gnome or something. *Why did he stand for it?*

If my mum started going publicly loopy, I'd stop her. I swear I would. Still at least he lifted up his head. George can be really good looking sometimes, but just then wasn't one of those times. He looked like the living dead. He stared at me from hurt eyes. He nodded at Gran. 'Best to go along with it, Ellie,' he called.

Totally hopeless.

'She'll be done in a minute. Stay in till your mum comes. Gran says don't forget we'd like a lift to the reception at the hotel tomorrow.'

'Oh yeah,' I said, 'I forgot. Oh, and George, tune up your guitar for New Year's Eve: Rhiannon's having a do for Darren. She wants you to play.'

'Darren?'

'Her cousin, 'member?'

'Oh, ok.'

'What time tomorrow?' I yelled again, wishing he didn't look so down.

'Afternoon. Early reception. Two-ish?' he said wearily.

'Rhiannon might be there,' I called.

George looked at me as if he was trying to figure out what I meant.

'Don't be such a zombie,' I yelled, 'Rhi-ann-on. Your Official Fan Club Member. You can tell her yourself about New Year's.'

'More like my official stalker,' George replied.

'Cheer up. *She. Is. Pretty.*'

'Pretty scary.'

I could see that wasn't going to work either.

Granny Jones seemed to have finished first footing, or her archaic Snowdonian custom, or whatever it was she was doing. She turned towards me one last time, but I realised she wasn't looking at me at all. Her eyes seemed to have settled on the summit of Snowdon, way up there, behind the house.

'I … ' began George.

He didn't get to finish.

Granny's shrill voice took over.

'*Gadewch i chi ymladd am byth, am nad oes un diferyn o'n gwaed a fydd yn golchi ymaith y Drydedd Guddfan a'r Trydydd Datguddiad, oherwydd y bydd y dreigiau a gladdodd Lludd Llaw Eraint, mab Beli, yn Ninas Ffaraon yn Eryri yn aros o dan ddaear ac yn parhau i ryfela ar gyfer yr holl dragwyddoldeb.*'

Granny Jones addressed the mountain. And this time it must have been High Welsh with a bit of Lord of the Rings chucked in for good measure, because there wasn't one word of it I understood.[1]

---

1. *You'll want to know. It was something odd like this: 'May you fight forever, for not one drop of our blood will wash away the Third Concealment and Third Disclosure, for the Dragons which Lludd 'of the Silver Hand' son of Beli buried in Dinas Emrys in Eryri shall stay buried and be at war for all eternity.'*

Nine

ELLIE'S PHONE 26th December 10.30

Status: Definitely irrevocably AVAILABLE *sadder face than any sad DM face ever invented*

The rest of Boxing Day dragged by.

The dog was hopeless. She whimpered and ran away from me, her tail between her legs. She wouldn't eat the food I put down either. I paced from room to room, staring out of windows, hoping to see something, someone, anything. I don't know. And succeeded only in freaking Ceri out all the more. When Mum got in, Ceri was so pitifully glad to see her, it was pathetic.

Way to make me feel great.

And I got more divine messages from Sheila. Like:

Recent updates on Ellie phone:

Sheila

I am on your case now.

And:

Sheila

I know it's a boy-thing.

And:

Sheila

You'll have a fight on your hands.

And:

Sheila

Oh Ha Ha Ha. I get it you're having a phantom lover moment.

And:

Rhiannon

Are you Ok? Sheila seems to think you've met The (Imaginary) One? (I told her you are NOT insecure and needy)

But you would tell *me* – wouldn't you?

Hon?

And:

Meryl

Don't mind Sheila. Don't let her upset you. She bitches about everyone. You know that's just her way. She loves you really.

Fantastic!

So even though nobody knew anything (least of all me!) – and Ceri thought I was the reincarnation of the Abominable Snowman – I was now a needy, insecure creator of fake boyfriends to boot.

Even Mum gave me strange looks. Once she said, 'I do wish you'd stop moping around, looking out of windows as if you've lost something.'

I wished I'd stop. I didn't know what I was looking for. I saw the same vast expanse of white snow everywhere and it made me feel so sad.

Eventually I ran a hot bath, which was wasteful, I know. And I don't normally when the power's off. But believe me when you're on a generator everything is wasteful. So who cares? I put in every kind of bubble bath I'd had for

Christmas, as well as some special bath pearls left over from last Christmas. I lay down in it, half submerged in white froth, until only my nose was showing. As heat seeped into every joint, I tried to go over last night. But the more I thought about it, the more depressed I got. Why had he left me? Why couldn't we meet again, if he was only in Caernarfon? It was holiday time. I could go anywhere, pretty much. Why couldn't we even ping each other? Was I so unattractive, so horrible that even if I saved some-one's life, they'd still never want to see me again?

My phone pinged; my thoughts were interrupted by George.

Recent updates on Ellie phone:

George

R U really *that* AVAILABLE?

Ellie

Please George. NOT NOW. I'm not v happy

George

Sorry – Can I cheer you up – Can I come an hug U?

Ellie

Can I check something?

George

NEThing. NETime. NEWhere.

It was hopeless. George wasn't going to give me a proper answer; he never took anything seriously, plus my hands were all slippy and I nearly dropped the phone in the bath, so I gave up. I ordered myself not to think horrible things. Instead I went through my list of weirdo questions about Henry.

1. Where had he come from?
2. How had he managed to do the door thing?
3. How had he got the fire going?
4. What had Gran got against him?
5. Was I ever going to see him again?
6. Did he like me even the tiniest bit?
7. Where was he now?

And all the time I felt as if his dark eyes were searching me out. And to tell you the truth, when you're lying in a bath that is not such a good feeling. So I stared into the bubbles, until the bubbles all seemed like snow.

I squinted down the bath to where my knees rose out of the whiteness. I saw the snowfields of yesterday, with the faint moonlight on them, stark and bright. I heard the wild wind, and then I started feeling restless all over again. I had to get out and towel myself down and get dressed and start pacing around to calm down.

At least after I'd washed, the dog liked me a bit more. She came snuffling towards me on her belly with her tail thumping the floor. I ruffled her neck and everything was forgiven. Mum made a huge, amazing supper with everything that didn't manage to get cooked or eaten on Christmas Day along with stuff she obviously brought back from Jeff's, or perhaps even took to Jeff's in the first place. Anyway it was all cooked up and sliced and diced with grated cheese on it. Mum was trying to make up for being out all last night – that was obvious.

I didn't tell her I'd been out all night too.

I didn't tell her about Henry either.

For some strange reason I thought she'd be against him, like Gran. That was probably a mistake. But I'd made so many mistakes in the last twenty-four hours one more wasn't going to spoil anything.

Where was Henry anyway? Had he got back to Caernarfon? I imagined him walking off, feeling embarrassed and awful. And there obviously weren't going to be any buses on Boxing Day. And Caernarfon was miles away. And that was after you'd got off Snowdon. He'd have to walk all the way.

Dusk fell. The wind stopped and so did the snow. The sky was clear and cold. After supper I went and stood in the front porch, clutching a hot chocolate and looking up at the stars. They were so low and bright and beautiful. I couldn't look at them for long. Have you noticed that about stars? They shift and twinkle and you can't hang on to them.

Once again I was out there with Henry, climbing the slopes, battling the blizzard. I scanned the horizon, over and over, sweeping the snowfields for something, *anything*. My hot chocolate became cold chocolate. But still I stood there.

How the snow glittered. How calm it felt. I went out of the porch on to the front lawn, probably the only bit of totally flat land in the whole of Snowdonia. I know because Dad dug it out and rolled it even, and together one wet spring we stamped the soil flat. As I stepped out on to the lawn, the snow squeezed itself into soft crunches beneath my feet. The moon rose away in the east. It was very nearly full. Huge and round and yellow, it hung on the horizon, like some giant snooker ball threatening to roll away down the mountain.

As I stood there staring up at its vast face, I heard that creature again.

I swear I DID!

The same shrieking as last night!

Just like before, it started as a low howling, but despite the shivers running up my spine, I held my ground. I reached for my phone. *This time I was going to record it.* I fumbled around amazed at my own boldness. But somehow my glove got tangled up in my pocket, and by the time I was scrabbling to see the stupidly small buttons, the shrieking had become a screaming.

It was the most unnatural sound.

Awful.

Bloodcurdling.

My knees started shaking. I swear if I wasn't in North Wales, halfway up Snowdon, I'd have said a demon straight from hell was screeching out through fire and brimstone.

A shiver literally rippled over me, from my hair roots to the soles of my feet. It was so unnerving that instead of unlocking the phone and turning it on, I managed to hit the camera app. And then it took ages for that to come on before I could turn it off. And by then the shrieking sounded like it was getting nearer and I panicked. I nearly dropped my cold chocolate. A huge splash of it went shooting out on to the white snow of the lawn, staining it like a spurt of blood.

I turned back towards the safety of the house. A cloud sailed across the moon like a hand across a face. Like a great eye the moon blinked out. All that remained was the bright snow and the shrieking. And I couldn't see the phone apps at all.

I bolted indoors.

Breathlessly I raced to the kitchen. 'Hear that?' I shouted at Mum. But she was nodding along to *Rocking Around the Christmas Tree*, in some kind of mumsy seasonal heaven. She just stared at me.

I shook her arm. 'Did you hear it?' I said again.

She shrugged and held up her glass of sherry as if to say, sherry drinkers don't have ears, and did a little two-step around the table. Jeff makes her happy. I guess.

And I remembered something. It was odd. I'm not sure why it mattered. But *it was after the shrieking that Henry had got ill. Was it just hypothermia?* He'd been fine up until then, or at least had seemed fine. I tried to remember clearly. Yes, he'd been fine, he'd even offered to take me to somewhere warm. And then he'd got so ill, I'd had to rescue him! It was weird, wasn't it? (And what had he meant 'somewhere warm' anyway?)

Like there was anywhere warm out there on Snowdon.

Ten

All evening I was jumpy. The slightest noise set me off.
Set me roaming from hall to kitchen and back again,
peering out of windows and snapping the curtains shut
on any tiny cracks. When a strange humming noise came
from the front door, I nearly jumped out of my skin.

Oh My God!

It was a squeaky tuneless whining, along with some kind
of squealing that sounded like me doing a bad job on my
recorder in primary school. A shiver went over me, and I
froze. I grabbed the telly remote (I'd been pretending to
watch some festive show). 'Mum?' I called.

There was no reply, only that strange humming and
squeaking. 'Mum?' I called again. Already the little hairs
on my neck were on end. What the heck was it?

I turned the telly completely off and listened. It was

definitely coming from the front of the house. Carefully I stood up. I was really glad I'd pulled those curtains shut. What if something out there was circling the house, trying to look in?

The noise continued. What should I do? Turn on the telly again, loudly? Find Mum? Get Ceri? Go and check? I knew at once I should go and check. So I crept into the hall and tiptoed towards the front door. At the coat rack I stopped. The droning and wailing stopped too. I stood there poised, waiting.

Images of monsters risen fresh from their lairs at Dinas Emrys rose before me. Then I distinctly heard a racking cough. A moment later the silence of the front porch was shattered by a terrific rapping. I nearly jumped out of my skin. My mind raced over snowy hillscapes into terrifying places. I was out there again in the vast whiteout of the storm, struggling to hold Henry upright, hearing the swishing darkness, knowing something else was out there too …

Then I heard the raucous sound of laughter. I heard a unfamiliar male voice suddenly bellowing out 'Good King Wenceslas went out – in a drop-top Audi … ' And I raced to the door and in a rush of relief so huge it could have swept all the snow off Snowdon, I flung it open.

And there stood Rhiannon, Sheila, Meryl and a tall boy I didn't know.

'Meet Darren you goon!' yelled Rhiannon.

The others shouted over her. 'Merry Christmas! Told you I'd GET you! Happy New Year! Mince pies? Mulled wine? CAKE! What took you so long?' and, 'Don't you think we'd make it on *X Factor*?'

And Darren started in a tuneless tenor all over again '*Good King Wenceslas* ... ' and they literally fell into the house shaking off snow, hurling presents at me, laughing and screeching. And Rhiannon looked around and said, 'George not here, I suppose?'

And Mum appeared from somewhere, and their coats were thrown off, and there was a tug of war over the sherry bottle (we won), and the coffee cups were lined up in the kitchen and Sheila didn't wait to be offered cake or sherry, but flung her arms around Mum and said, 'Is there cake in your pockets?'

And when Mum gestured at the cupboard, she was there like a shot pulling out mince pies and crisps and fudge fingers and stuffing some in her mouth and others on a plate, until the whole kitchen was filled with shrieks of laughter and Christmas cheer.

'We've been tramping for *hours*!' yelled Sheila.

'Not really,' said Meryl.

'How can you bear to live in such a middle of nowheres-ville place?' yelled Sheila.

'How did you get here?' I cried.

'Moi,' said Darren, smirking all over his face.

I looked at him. He was quite attractive, with dark blond-ish hair, which at some point had been streaked; cute brown eyes and a thinness that was all athletic; a nose, a little too big, but it looked like he was growing into it just fine, and ... Sheila caught me looking. She slapped my wrists. 'Naughty, naughty,' she said, 'Don't look at what you can't have.'

I dropped my eyes. It wasn't even as if I wanted him! My mind was full of someone much more mysterious and handsome. Someone whose arched brows had a sculptural beauty found only in the work of Old Masters. (So there!) Someone who made all the Darrens in the universe look like toddlers' scribble.

'I got us here!' exploded Darren triumphantly. 'It was all ME!'

'How?' asked Mum. She could see he was dying to get all the attention and take all the credit for this wonderful surprise they'd sprung upon us.

'Well,' he said mysteriously, giving me Looks. 'When I heard of the mythical beauty of your daughter, Mam,' (he said the word 'Mam' like he was in the American cavalry from the southern states during the raid on Gettysburg) 'Well, Mam,' he continued, 'I could not rest until I saw her – nor foul fiend nor winter weather daunt my spirit!'

He switched from gallant soldier of the American civil war to pilgrim on the Canterbury Trail striving to reach the promised land. And I could see that he considered himself a bit of a showman, slash poet, slash actor sort of person and was extremely pleased with himself at that. (Ok, translate that as ~~What-A-Jerk~~, sorry I meant: Full-Of-Himself-And-Possibly-A-Prize-Prat.)

'Well I … '

He didn't finish. Rhiannon gave him a shove and said, 'He's got a new Range Rover. It can get through anything. I'm sure if he drove it up the Black Cliff it'd go, no sweat.'

'How clever of you!' said Mum. (She always knows what people want to hear, and is a total expert at stroking their egos.) Predictably Darren purred under her praise. I tried not to raise an eyebrow (or vomit). He couldn't be more that seventeen. How in the hell could he afford a new Range Rover?

Anyway, I jumped to the window and looked out. There it was though, a spanking new 4x4 all gleamy and black, and parked up on the drive with the front wheels slewed into a rakish angle. I tried not to feel resentful. Mum has been trying to get us a better 4x4 for years.

'The roads were fine anyway,' said Rhiannon.

Sheila saw me looking at the car and crept up behind me whispering, 'Ha ha ha, girl! You Wish.'

And I suppose I did. I wished we had a car like that. I wished I could drive. I wished Mum's life was a bit easier. A new 4x4 would save her such a lot of trouble.

I wished other things as well.

But none of them were about Darren.

Rhiannon, Sheila, Darren and Meryl stayed all evening. It was a bit cringe, because Sheila kept saying narky things like: So Who Is He? And: Did You Know Mrs Morgan That Ellie Has A Boyfriend? Luckily Mum thought she meant George, and Meryl fielded most of the cattier remarks.

Anyway we ate all of the Christmas cake, a plate of turkey'n'stuffing sandwiches (thanks Mum) and finished off the sherry (soz Mum).

Rhiannon gave me a gift box full of very expensive smellies. Meryl, who was being so sweet, gave me a lovely scarf she'd knitted herself, all stripy and student with a big card which read: *'For those evenings when you're coming home from sixth form and it's kind of nippy'*, which was a lovely way of telling me that she believed I'd get into St Xavier's Sixth Form College in Caernarfon. Sheila gave me a tin of rude chocolate things, which were all in the shape of boys' unmentionable body parts. I thought they were gross, but she laughed her head off at them. And Darren gave me a huge present all wrapped in scrunchy pink and shiny purple paper with BIG bows. I didn't quite know what to do with it. I didn't really want to open it there and then. Heck, I didn't want the present at all! I didn't know him and we weren't on present-giving terms, (and I hadn't got him one anyway), so it was all weird and embarrassing.

I was going to have to open it up though, wasn't I? And that was even more embarrassing, because what if I didn't like it? *What if I hated it!* I'd still have to give him a kiss and say thanks and admire it, like forever. *I was definitely going to hate it.*

Anyway I started out by just owning up to the fact that I hadn't got a present for him. 'I'm sorry,' I said. 'I didn't know you were coming,' as I gave Sheila and Meryl and Rhiannon my little wrapped gifts (huggy one-size slipper socks in alpaca – with charity status bonus to the Peru Mountain Rescue Fund and a gift voucher each for make up.)

126

'Hey Girlie,' he said (which was a bit creepy, because whoever says 'Hey Girlie' anyway?), 'don't worry. Open up the pressie I got you; come on – spit spot.'

Spit Spot! Now he was doing Mary Poppins!

I picked up the huge crispy thing and pulled at the silky ribbons. Everyone stopped and watched. It was horribly awkward. Beyond a shadow of a doubt I knew I was going to hate it. But I put on my best Auntie Betty Fan-club face and smiled like I was a hostess on a sparkly TV game show. I pulled off the wrapping paper. I built in dramatic pauses for oohing and ahhhing. Inside, I could tell from the squidgyness, whatever it was was all cushioned up in loads more tissue paper.

Sheet by sheet of puce and lilac was pulled away, until the last sliver rustled off and revealed Darren's present. I held the item up. I couldn't quite believe my eyes, at first. Obviously it was ~~something completely revolting~~ a nice kitchen apron with nice pictures of eggcups on it. I smiled a little, forcing the corners of my mouth up. I said 'Oh thank you Darren! How nice.'

In fact, when I looked at it more closely, it was not just completely revolting it was completely revoltingly sexist too. It had GIRLS LOOK GOOD IN THE KITCHEN written on it.

'Thanks,' I said again, as best I could. 'This'll be just great for … ' I couldn't quite finish the sentence. I couldn't quite bring myself to say 'great for doing the washing up in.'

'Practical too!' smirked Darren, 'I knew you'd appreciate something useful.' He put on an Aussie accent as if he owned a sheep station in the outback and was returning laden with treasures from his European tour. I didn't even raise one eyebrow. And I was mighty glad that Sheila had bagged him first.

'Well now,' he said, 'How lucky I am, the only guy with the four most beautiful ladies in Snowdonia. I am going to spend the rest of the evening flirting with you all until you can't stand it!'

And true to his word, until they all left at two in the morning, he did.

Eleven

ELLIE'S PHONE 27th December 01.00

Status: Still available *hopeful face*

Recent updates between Ellie and Meryl and Rhiannon:

Meryl

Just letting u no we got back safe, hon. Darren and Rhi dropped

Sheila first then me. OXOXOX

Ellie

Feeling much better – thank you guys – U R D best.

Meryl

Sleep tight.

Ellie

XXX

Rhiannon

Darren says U R hot.

I didn't sleep well. It wasn't because of the wind howling around the farmhouse or the creak of the old timbers, as the temperature dropped and dropped. I think it was the moonlight. It streamed in through the crack in my curtains and lay in long stripes across the floor. I got out of bed. I padded to the bathroom. The same silvery light spilt in there. It poured down the walls and pooled itself across the tiles.

I went in search of a cup of tea. I stood huddled against the kitchen stove, trying to drain its heat into me. While the blue flames struggled to boil the kettle, I hugged myself and shivered. I should have been totally exhausted, but I wasn't. I looked out of the kitchen window, through its leaded panes. I don't know if it was the moonlight or the old glass that distorted the lawn, but the snow outside seemed to rise and curve like a slow-moving, frozen sea.

I thought of last night in Halfway House, groping around with the torch, lighting candles, crouching in the dancing glow of the fire watching Henry's silhouette stretch and shrink, as if he was some mythical creature that could shape-shift and cast shadows wherever he chose. Henry. He'd cast a shadow over me. No, that was unfair – not a shadow, a moonbeam, a spell maybe. My life had never been brighter, never been darker. Yesterday night had been the best adventure ever.

Henry. I couldn't seem to think of anything else.

I poured the water on to the tea bag, dumped in two huge spoonfuls of sugar and a slug of milk. I carried my tea into the front room and curled up on the window seat and cupped the warm mug against my chest. I gazed out on to the silent mountain, kind of stupidly hoping Henry might suddenly appear. I know, don't say it.

The sky was inky black. The moon sailed across it, a halo of bluish silver shining around it. I looked up towards the summit of Snowdon.

There in the distance it stood.

A shadowy outline, huge against the world. I think something was moving over it. Something whitish. I peered closer.

At first I thought it was an aircraft, but what aircraft has no lights? Then I thought it was a bird, a huge sea bird maybe, or an owl out hunting. But what owl is so ginormous that it can be seen up there from the foothills of Llanberis?

As I watched, the thing wheeled into the dark sky. A coldness crept over me. My skin started to prickle. My heart beat faster. The bird, whatever it was, darted nearer. It flitted sometimes like a bat looping up and back on itself, sometimes like a flash of lightning. At an impossible speed, it swooped straight down towards the farmhouse. It zoomed in – right at me!

I strained to look at it through the darkness; was it an eagle?

Nothing like an eagle.

A pterodactyl?

Not a pterodactyl.

All talons – all leathery wings – all speed – all scales. I blinked – unable to believe my eyes. I swear to God, it looked just like a dragon straight out of some fairytale.

A dragon.

I mean it.

A huge white dragon.

I pressed my face against the cold pane. Its reptile eyes, ancient, fixed me with a look. A paralysis came over me. Then all of a moment, it seemed to hit an invisible barrier.

I watched as suddenly it was there, and just as suddenly it was only a gleaming shape again, swooping away over the snowfields.

It was a long while before I could draw back from the window. I sat there shaking, glued as if by some stupid, sickening, mental superglue. My hand trembled. I tried to sip my tea. I squinted up into the sky. A blur scudded across the moon. The lawn rippled in shadows.

A dragon?

It didn't look *anything* like that cute thing on the Welsh flag.

But I didn't try to tell myself that it was All Absolutely Nothing and Probably A Pet Vulture That Had Escaped. After all the Himalaya have a Yeti, and Loch Ness has Nessie, and America has Bigfoot so why couldn't Yr Wyddfa have a Dragon?

Plus I'd heard the shrieking.

And I'd seen it.

There *was* something out there on the mountain.

Something I'd never known about before, (and though my heart was going like the clappers, that annoyed me, because it was my mountain, and I should know).

So as I turned to go back up to bed, I promised myself: if there was a real dragon or some other undiscovered prehistoric creature up there, as sure as hell I was going to find it.

~

The next day the mains power came back on. I awoke to Mum bouncing into the bedroom, flicking on the lights, thumping herself down on my bed. 'We are officially back in the land of the civilised,' she said.

Thank God.

'I've put on the fairy lights. I've got the news on. We can hunker down to the telly this evening. We can play all your DVDs and make up for lost time!'

'Um,' I nodded.

She stood up and picked up my TV remote and slung it at me, as if to prove her point.

'So, masses to do. Better get in the supplies from the great big freezer.' She pointed to the garden shed, 'Got any washing?'

'Um,' I said again, trying to linger in the warmth of my bed.

'I'll put on the storage heating and: Amazing! You can have a proper hot shower!'

'Mum,' I said, 'we've managed ok with the generator – I even had a bath, remember?'

But nothing was going to spoil her mood. As she twirled

out of the room, she called, 'Don't forget we're taking George and Wynnie to the royal reception this aftie.'

I'd forgotten. And I wasn't ecstatic to be reminded.

I thumped over in bed and grunted out, 'Must we?' But Mum had gone, and I knew from experience it was easier to go than put up a fight.

Anyway she certainly meant it about making up for a Christmas with not much Christmassiness. Mum delivered The Full English with interesting additions like Turkish delight and, weirdly, crystallized ginger (?) while playing non-stop carols on YouTube.

Immediately after breakfast I decided to go for a walk. It was a lovely morning, but that wasn't the real reason. I'd decided that if I was going to be sharing my mountain with a dragon, I'd better educate myself on its habits. Plus I was going to go back up to Devil's Bridge – just to satisfy my curiosity about the tracks (I know), before I started dragon hunting.

I told Mum. 'I'm going for a walk.'

She immediately said, 'I'll come too!'

I sighed. Have you ever felt sort of doomed?

'A lovely walk in the fresh air will do us both the world of good!' she said, like we hadn't spent any of the last forty-eight hours trekking anywhere at all.

I didn't know what to do. I didn't want Mum to come. I tried saying, 'What if Mountain Rescue call?' But she said, 'Lewis and Owen and Nigel can handle it. The power's on and the roads are clear. Oh, and by the way, did I tell you? The girl we found made a full recovery.'

I'd forgotten about the girl. But as Mum mentioned her, I suddenly remembered. Her icy skin, her clutching me, saying, '*Monsters, inside the mountain!*' her face all shrunk in terror.

Inside the mountain, eh?

'Great,' I said. (I may have sounded bored. That was the effect I was trying for. But I was thinking fast. Monsters? Inside the mountain?)

'Mum, do you believe that something like – say, a dragon – could exist? If it was hidden away – say in a cave or something – deep under the mountain?'

'The Beast of Dinas Emrys?' she laughed.

'But what if one actually did exist?' I watched her, as she wrapped cling film over a bowl of baked beans.

'You mean a real live Y Ddraig Goch, Red Dragon of Wales?'

'No-oo, more whitish.'

'You've been listening to Granny Jones,' she said.

'But I think I saw something last night.' I wanted to tell her.

Convince her. Ask her to explain it.

'And watching too much *Merlin*.'

'But – '

She cut me off. 'And too much sherry. I shouldn't have let you have any.' She threw my bobble hat at me. 'Now, come on, back to reality, I think we should go and take a look at the place that girl fell, and assess whether Mountain Rescue should put up a warning plaque there.'

There was nothing I wanted to do less. Apart from the memory of her limp form, and the gully being in the opposite direction from Devil's Bridge, it'd be torture to be out on the mountain and not be Looking For A Handsome Boy Or A Dragon.

So I tried saying, 'But what about the reception?' And, 'Don't you want to touch up your roots?'

But she just tossed her head. 'Dark roots are so the fashion right now! Who knows, I may never do my roots again!'

And that was it.

I decided there and then that I'd get tired halfway across the upper pasture and insist on coming home.

Luckily I didn't need to.

As we were sorting out our scarves and gloves and deciding whether or not to take equipment with us, Jeff phoned.

GOD BLESS JEFF!

Mum pulled off her gloves. She took the phone with her over to the sofa. She pulled the patchwork blanket over her knees. She curled up by the fire and started talking in a soft sexy voice. I looked at her. I goggled my eyes at her. I waggled my head. She smiled and smiled and nodded and waved. I could see she wasn't paying any attention. So I thought: Good. Nice one. I'll go on my own then. Quick. And I'll blame it on her! So I bolted to the back door. I pulled on everything at top speed, and ran tripping out of the house as fast as I could.

I probably needn't have bothered with the total velocity. When Mum gets on the phone to Jeff the whole world might as well fall apart.

Funny, that used to annoy me. Now I was smiling all over my face! I had a good feeling. A happy, excited feeling – like something was waiting for me up by Devil's Bridge. Did I say Jeff was boring? Rewind. Jeff's the greatest! I just love Jeff!

I climbed up the top pasture and out on to the mountain as quickly as I could. You know, by the time Mum put that phone down and found her gloves again, I'd be long gone.

Twelve

Of course he was waiting for me. How did I know he'd be there? How did I know that if Mum had come with me, we might have trekked the whole of Snowdon only to find the wind howling down the slopes, and the mountain cold and empty. It was almost as if he could read my mind. As if he knew everything before it happened. You know, I wouldn't have been surprised if he had arranged that phone call from Jeff too!

There he stood, bareheaded, his thick chestnut hair specked with snow. I saw him from miles away. Oh My God, WAS I SEEING THINGS? I couldn't believe it.

Yet, I did believe it! I held my breath, and when I wasn't holding my breath I was running uphill until my lungs were bursting. So when I arrived and saw that it really was him, and he really was waiting for me, I couldn't breathe at all.

And up close he was even more amazing than I remembered.

I opened my mouth. Nothing came out.

'Hey, Ellie,' he said, 'You came.' He laughed like he'd been betting with himself and won.

I gasped, trying to breathe. Words came rushing out in a great splutter. 'How did you know?'

'Just did,' he said.

I stood there smiling. I took time to compose my breathing. I stuck my hands in my pocket. Inside I was screaming: *HE KNEW I'D COME! HE CAME UP HERE ALL THE WAY FROM CAERNAFON!*

'It's nice to see you.' I finally squeezed out.

NICE! I give up on myself sometimes.

He looked at me, looked at my tatty old jacket. (MY TATTY OLD JACKET???) Why hadn't I put on something better? Why had I just rushed out of the house? I hadn't even brushed my hair!

'You're so you,' he said, 'I like that.'

He liked that! He LIKED my tatty jacket, my unbrushed hair look! Hastily I pulled my stupid woolly hat off. I dragged my hair into a bunch and stuffed it under my collar.

'I'm sorry about yesterday,' I blurted out. 'Did you get home all right? Did you have to walk all the way? There weren't any buses were there?

Areyouoknow?IwassoworriedIfeltsobadIfI'dknown
GrannyJones wasgoing tobeso … '

Henry was laughing. 'Hey,' he held his hand up. 'It's OK.
She was just trying to protect you.'

Phew! Wow! He was OK. He wasn't dying up a cliff,
frozen, with his face against the ice …

'If you had any sense you'd listen to her, though.'

Whoa.

Why had he said that? *WHY HAD HE SAID THAT?*
Maybe he was waiting here to tell me he never wanted to
see me again. He was seeing me again though, wasn't he?
(Question: If you never want to see anyone again, do you
go and see them to tell them you never want to see them?)

'She thinks you should stay away from me. And I do too.'

'You want me to stay away?'

Oh *HELL*. Here it came.

Henry's face looked troubled. 'No,' he said, 'That's not
what I mean.'

What did he mean, then?

'What I *want* may not be what's good for you,' he said.

I breathed out slowly, telling myself, Just Breathe, Ellie,
Just Take In What He's Saying. Slowly. But my mind was
exploding, fireworking, high jumping.

'I don't think you really know,' I said slowly, 'what *is* good for me.'

I wanted then to tell him, all about losing people. Losing your dad, for a start, when you were just at the age to know you loved him; before you found out that he was obsessed with climbing icy rock faces, before you realised he didn't love you enough not to die on one of them. Believe me, losing people you love is never good for you.

'*Safe* for you, then,' he clarified.

Safe? Since when did being safe have any appeal? And with one toss of my head I dismissed all my dreams of a little four-by-four life.

'Then I decide to live dangerously!' I said.

He sighed. A gust skittered over the surface of the snow. A little shower of powdery whiteness eddied around my feet.

'You have no idea, do you?' he said.

I probably didn't.

'I waited here for you Ellie, to tell you to stop. To go home. To forget me.'

I looked at him. Now I was laughing.

'I thought I should give you the chance … '

'That's not logical,' I pointed out. 'If you want me to forget you, you wouldn't come and find me.'

He laughed as well. 'Maybe I want to see you too. Have

you thought of that?'

We both stood there then. Kind of embarrassed. Kind of excited. Kind of scared.

Henry sighed as if he'd just remembered something he'd rather forget. 'I tried yesterday, to stay away from you all day.' He threw his hands out in hopelessness. 'It was horrible. I can't face doing it again. So you'll just have to stay away from me.' He grinned at me in mock despair, but I could see in his eyes that he meant it, that he'd been through some kind of personal hell that had driven him nearly crazy (Oh YAY!), that had weakened his resolve, that had brought him back to me. THANK THE STARS!

I couldn't help rejoicing at it, but all I said was: 'Why?'

'There are things you don't know.'

'Then tell me.'

'I can't tell you.'

'Try me,' I said

'Nobody would understand,' he sighed.

'Is it the shrieking?' I said

'Don't try,' he said, 'You won't guess.'

'Then tell me,' I said, 'Trust me. Whatever it is, I'll help you.'

I wanted so much to be trusted. I wanted to be a part of whatever it was, whether it was safe or dangerous or anything.

'I wish.' he said.

'Come,' I said on a sudden impulse, 'Walk with me up to Garnedd Ugain.'

Together we started out across the narrow causeway, that I call the Devil's Bridge. On one side the mountain fell away hundreds of feet to the Llanberis Pass. On the other, it tumbled down a cruel slope of stone and rock to the icy waters of the llyn.

At the centre of the causeway, at the spot they call Lovers' Leap, I stopped.

'I asked you to trust me,' I said. 'Let's start here.'

I looked up into his dark eyes. Big mistake. A wild giddy feeling suddenly exploded inside me. I swallowed hard. If I was going to convince him to trust me, I'd better get a grip. I held his gaze and breathed in, resisting the rush it gave me. There behind the warnings and the smiles, behind the mystery, his eyes told another story. He was hoping for something. Hoping desperately. Not confident. Hoping yet despairing? I was on the right track.

Very much encouraged, I led him to the edge of the bridge and let him look over. Sheer cliffs. Rocks. Ice. You couldn't even see the bottom. It was shrouded in mist. It was impossible not to imagine falling, striking stone, twisting and spinning out into space. Falling and falling to a broken death far below.

Dizzy now from the thrill of vertigo, I turned to him. I looked beyond his smile to the pain in his eyes. 'Trust me,' I said.

That flicker of hope seemed to catch. His eyes lit up a fraction.

I led him to the furthest rock, which balanced precariously out over the abyss. 'Come,' I said. Together we climbed up on to it. The wind whistled at our backs, pushing us forward. Beneath us, in the chasm, mist rose upwards, bitter, cold. I beckoned to Henry. I held out my hand. Gingerly he took it. Together we stood on the very edge.

'Trust me,' I said. 'When I count to three we're going to step out.'

'You're crazy,' he said.

'No. Not crazy. Not suicidal, just close your eyes and trust me.'

Henry's grip tightened on me until my hand was crushed. 'No.' he said very firmly.

'Would it help, if I told you that this place is called Lovers' Leap?' I said. 'Guys come up here to impress their girls, they throw themselves off for love – but it's a trick. You can't see it, but directly below us is a ledge of rock and when we step out like this … ' I raised my foot and let it hover over the mist. 'We'll land quite safely on it.'

Henry hesitated. 'No Ellie, it doesn't help,' Henry whispered, 'for myself I'm not afraid, but you mustn't. I can't
… '

'Give me your hand, then. C'mon.'

Henry's hand found mine. 'Please Ellie … ' he started.

'Now close your eyes.'

He looked at me. Then reluctantly closed his eyes.

'Go on. Step out. Keep your eyes closed.'

He raised his foot. And stopped.

'Come *on*, Ellie,' he said, 'this is crazy.'

'Do you trust me?' I whispered.

Henry looked very uncertain. 'If I do it first, will you trust me then?' I asked.

Without waiting for him to answer, I stepped out into the mist. There was a moment of doubt, a moment when his hand tugged at mine. A moment when even I hardly trusted myself, hardly trusted the mountain, the rock could have moved, I could be in the wrong spot and then my foot hit the stone ledge and I breathed out a great rush of pleasure.

Henry's eyes flew wide open.

'Don't peek!' I said, 'Come on, trust me.'

He held out his hand.

Wild on adrenalin, I turned in the haze. Fingers interlaced, Henry stepped out. There was the briefest beat –

that moment – that pause – and then he too was there on the ledge beside me. And there we were on a pinnacle of rock, the clouds at our feet, the mist swirling up until I could hardly even see the ledge at all. We were flying out over a sea of whiteness, way above the world.

'Open your eyes.'

Aloft, sailing high on a bank of soft air, with the wind rushing up into our faces.

Henry let out a soft 'Oh!'

As far as the eye could see continents of clouds swirled, seething in smoky plumes, twisting away into wispy nothingness.

'It's beautiful,' he said. He turned to me 'You're beautiful.'

I think my heart must have burst right then, exploded in a Frenzy Of Happiness, ripped Clean Out Of My Chest and gone soaring Straight Up To Heaven!

He Thought I Was Beautiful.

A column of white swept up at us. Henry stepped back, then remembered not to. 'I'm not afraid of heights, anyway,' he said suddenly clinging on to me.

I started giggling and somehow the giggling became a step backwards too, and I slipped.

Again that moment. I swayed, scarcely balancing. Henry's hand tightened on mine. He slipped his arms around my waist. He pulled me back from the edge. He pressed me to him, and I was still giggling, and he was murmuring, 'How can I resist?' as he held me tighter and tighter.

He swung me off my feet, squashed my head to his chest, until I could hear the hammering of his heart.

'God help me,' he said. Then he bent his head and kissed me!

Oh My God!

I tried to breathe. I tried to regain my balance. Feebly I lifted my hand, but he crushed me to him, as suddenly and completely as if we were two parts of the same whole.

And I kissed him back.

Oh My Double God!

I laced my arms around his neck.

And I kissed him and kissed him!

We climbed back from the ledge, hearts thudding, blood thundering in every artery.

We Had Just Kissed!

'I believe you,' he said. 'I trust you.'

His hand was as warm as fire.

I had to catch my breath!

'Deal?' I gasped out.

'But the time may come, Ellie, when you'll need trust me.'

'Ok,' I said.

'I shouldn't be doing this.' He bit down hard on his lip. His eyes grew dark. 'But I will. Damn it. I will.' He threw his arm back towards Snowdon, as if he was cursing every rock of it. 'Do you hear me?' he screamed, as if he was defying some ancient curse. 'It's too late. I can no more stay away from her than …' he stopped.

'Fly?' I suggested.

He pulled me to him, kissed the top of my head. 'Flying would be so much easier!' he said.

'Well I'm ready for anything,' I said.

'Then together we'll live dangerously!' He squeezed my hand.

'And no more "history"?' I said.

'No more history.' He laughed as if a burden had rolled off him.

'This mountain's got secrets,' I waved my arms around. 'Things nobody would believe. Like hidden ledges and leaps of faith.' (And gorgeous mountain boys!)

'And you,' he said, suddenly holding me close, and then just as abruptly letting me go. His face clouded and he pressed his lips tight. 'I must master myself,' he said. And he took a step back and folded his arms over his chest, as if he no longer trusted them, as if once they encircled me again, there would be no letting go a third time.

'And steps into the unknown.' I carried on joking. (Note: I have no objection to a little loss of control.)

'But now, it's time to go on home.'

'And dragons, apparently.'

His mood suddenly changed. A cloud rolled down from Garnedd Ugain. 'What do you know of dragons?' he said.

'Just the usual,' I quipped. 'You know wings, big scary claws.'

'They're not funny,' he said. 'And it's time to go.'

'Not *Go*?' I said.

'Yes, home.'

'But?' I said.

'Trust me.'

I sighed. (I'd got myself into that one, hadn't I?) My mouth opened to frame all the questions, I'd promised to find answers to.

'Not now,' he said.

'When?'

'Soon.'

It couldn't be soon enough for me.

Act Two

'… Perhaps
I may love other hills yet more
Than this: the future and the maps
Hide something I was waiting for.

One thing I know, that love with chance
And use and time and necessity
Will grow, and louder the heart's dance
At parting than at meeting be.'

From: *When First I Came Here*
Edward Thomas

Thirteen

Recent updates between Ellie and Sheila:

Sheila

I knew it! I KNEW IT! U r up 2 sumting

Ellie

Climbing mountains ha ha ha

Sheila

And you didn't tell us – so we know it's a BOY

Ellie

R U going to Rhi's hotel 2day?

Sheila

Whoever he is, I bags him first

By the time I got back down the mountain, I was being as girly as Mum. Both of us showered for hours, twirled around the farmhouse, forgot to defrost anything for supper, had a lunch of microwaved leftovers and spent too long peering at ourselves in the mirror/doing our nail polish/straightening our hair.

I put on my prettiest little dress. It had tiny, faux freshwater pearls sewn into it, a daring low neck and the daintiest of waists. 'My gosh!' said Mum when she saw me. 'You look like a fairy princess.'

'Yuk, not all old fashioned?' I said suddenly worried.

'Course not,' said Mum. 'I mean you look beautiful, enchanting.'

I did a pirouette for her. I felt beautiful. I felt enchanted. After the miserable day I'd spent yesterday, it was good to be alive again, good to be young and sixteen, with all the rest of my life stretching in front of me.

Yay, it was so good to be me.

The ping from Sheila wasn't so good though.

As soon as I saw it, I felt annoyed. How dare she?!*! And I felt uneasy too. What if she went and found out about Henry? I knew her only too well. She'd bust heaven and hell to have him off me. (Why on earth was I friends with her?) I'd been going to tell Rhiannon all about him, but suddenly I was scared. I peered at myself in the mirror all over again. How could I compete with Sheila? Compete against those massive D cups and those legs that stretched right up to her armpits? (I mean I DID trust Henry. But there's TRUST and then there's SHEILA.) All she had to do was bend over him and give him a glimpse of her cleavage, and she'd have him in the palm of her hand, TOTAL putty, just like all the others.

With a groan I flung myself on my bed. How the Hello was I going to keep him away from Sheila?

At about one-thirty there was a knock on the door. I jumped to the window. Outside George was stamping the snow off his boots. Granny was prodding at something or other by the front gate. I raced Ceri to the door. I flung it open, flung my arms around George and dragged him in.

'Woo!' said George admiring me. 'You! Are! The! Bomb!'

'Come on Granny!' I yelled down the path. She stood up

and nodded to herself, as if she was very satisfied about something.

'We need to get changed now, George,' she ordered as soon as she was inside. Royalty expects a good show, so get upstairs and straighten yourself out.'

George waggled his eyes at me. 'First hot shower since Christmas,' he said. 'Want to come and scrub my back?'

'Ugh!' I said, pulling a towel off the radiator and chucking it at him.

'You don't know what you're missing,' hooted George as he picked up his rucksack and disappeared towards the bathroom.

I didn't want to either!

'Coffee, Wynnie?' said Mum brightly.

'Nothing at all, thanks,' said Granny. 'But put out a plateful of anything you've got handy for George.'

Mum laid out some slices of Christmas cake.

'I think he'll need more than that.' said Granny. She turned to me. 'Now wear these,' she pinned a tiny beautiful spray of dried flowers to my dress. 'It's traditional.'

Mum raised her eyebrows and added chocolate fingers, cold turkey breast, dates and smoked salmon to the plate.

'That's it. Let him fill up. I'll not have him following the waiters around at the reception as if he's never had a decent meal.'

And true to form, when George came out of the bathroom, all clean and brushed and actually looking very ~~gorgeous~~ respectable, he devoured the lot. I watched him shoving in marzipan icing, after a forkful of salmon, and decided that Granny was very wise to try and fill him up first. Although I wasn't sure how effective it would be. I had a feeling that when we got there, he was going to be helping himself to as many of the royal canapés as he could get.

Once we got out, off the mountain and down the lane a bit, the roads were fine, just like Rhiannon had said. They'd been gritted and salted and, beyond the bubble of our mountain existence, the whole world was ticking away.

The Land Rover didn't give us any problems either. At one point I thought we might end up in a drift, but to tell the truth, I didn't care much. I was wary of seeing Sheila, sure that Rhiannon wouldn't even notice me with George around, and Meryl wouldn't be there. I had no interest in seeing a bunch of city folks deigning to grace our small community, just because we happened to be sort-of neighbours. After all, did the Royal Family ever do a reception in Vauxhall to meet the residents there? (Believe me Vauxhall is a lot closer to Buckingham Palace than Caernarfon is to Llanberis.)

Granny kept stressing, 'Royalty expect Form, and Tradition is Tradition. That's why they are Royal and Top of the League.' I don't know quite what she meant by 'Top of the League,' as if the whole country was made up of rugby teams. Sometimes you know, I just think she's getting old. She's got that thing that old people get, when they go all rigid and set in their ways. George must have thought so too, because he didn't stop rolling his eyes in embarrassment from the moment we got into the Land Rover until the minute we stepped out by the red carpet over the steps of the Pen-y-mynydd-gwryd Hotel.

'Let's escape from her, as soon as we can?' he whispered in my ear.

I nodded.

'We could creep off into one of the rooms and watch the rugby.'

'Well you could,' I said. 'You could ask Rhiannon to open up the penthouse suite for you. She might enjoy a bit of rugby herself if you play your cards right.'

George frowned at me. And I giggled. Actually I don't know what he's got against her. Rhiannon is sweet and petite, dark haired, with rosy cheeks and china-white skin. She is absolutely potty about him and has written: I HEART GEORGE on the side of Llanberis Mountain Railway

Station ladies' in indelible red felt tip. If he is holding out on her for me, he is going to be disappointed.

And besides, what made him think I wanted to watch rugby?

But I didn't say any of that, of course.

'I'd rather stroll down to the ornamental lake,' I said, 'and feed profiteroles to the goldfish.'

'Boring,' whispered George.

By that time we were being shooed off the red carpet and told to enter the hotel by the steps at the side, like the commoners we were.

Granny Jones nodded her head in an obliging way, but poked the doorman with her sharp pointy finger at the same time. 'There's Royalty and being Royal, Llewellyn,' she said, 'And you're neither!' But she didn't step on the red carpet. Although I noticed she doubled back from the side steps, mumbled something and waved her hand, all mystically over the two stone dragons that guarded the main entrance.

Inside we were ushered into the Great Hall. It was very beautiful. There were two fantastic fireplaces at either end. Huge fires blazed in both. Above the fires, fighting salamanders battled for their lives in the same kind of carved stone work I'd seen in Halfway House. Apparently salamanders are the heraldic beasts of the Pen-y-mynydd-gwryd Hotel.

Over the salamanders were wide marble mantelpieces, and above all that, tall mirrors reflected flames from one end of the hall to the other.

Crowning everything, chandeliers sparkled and lit up the rafters which were hung with delicate snowflake crystals.

'Wow,' said George, 'this is where I'm going to bring you on our first date.'

It was pretty magical. I twirled twice across the foyer to a Victorian glass conservatory at the side of the Great Hall. Inside it a colossal Christmas tree stood, all shimmering white.

Guests spilled in through stone arches, milled over the polished floors, and chatted in groups by the tapestries, their faces lit up by flickering fairy lights.

As soon as we were inside, someone dragged our coats off us. I'd hardly got my arms free before mine was whipped away. I looked around for Rhiannon and saw her carrying two large silver platters full of canapés. I sidled nearer to her and blew her a kiss. She smiled back and mouthed through the crowd, 'George come?'

I nodded. 'Sheila couldn't make it,' she whispered. 'Whisked Darren off to Caernarfon.'

I pulled an I-am-sorry face, but secretly I was glad. I didn't want to see Sheila. She'd sniff out everything about Henry, and try to flirt with George – just to upset Rhiannon.

'Darren says he refuses to be a waiter.' She raised her eyebrows at the trays she was carrying. 'And Dad totally needed the extra help too. Darren's such a mollusc.'

Worse than a mollusc! Not to help his own uncle – with such a large reception going on. What a creep! And trust Sheila to scoop him off. The two of them deserved each other. I reached forward and gave Rhiannon's arm a squeeze. 'George's dying to see you,' I lied. Rhiannon flashed me a happy smile. (Oh dear.)

A crowd of guests surged forward and Rhiannon turned to serve them. A waiter thrust a flute of champagne into my hand (apparently underage drinking is perfectly ok at royal receptions), and I steered my way back to George. Rhiannon followed with the canapés held shoulder high. Trays of prawns, salami, cheese, egg, ham, tomatoes; juicy morsels on sticks, rolled in crispy batter, curled into bows, with dips, pickles and pastry.

Of course George didn't need prompting. He loaded up a napkin with skewers of spicy chicken, fish kebabs, mini veggie burgers, tiny parcels of cream cheese'n'spinach until his hands and his tissue were full. Pig. Then he proceeded to whisper in my ear with his mouth full: 'Ellie you're *way* the prettiest girl here. All the others look like horses – or maybe camels.'

Which wasn't fair, because Rhiannon was standing near and she's very pretty, and nothing like a camel; plus whenever she could, she kept bringing him lots of lovely nibbly things on silver doilies (plus she is my friend and was trusting me to put in a good word for her).

George pointed at one young woman who had on an Alice band above a long donkey fringe. Her hair seemed to sweep into her champagne glass every time she raised it. George pulled a horsey face and pretended to rear, paddling the air with imaginary hooves. ~~It was quite funny. She actually did look like she belonged in a gymkhana.~~ (Strike that out. I shouldn't encourage him.)

'Stop it,' I said. For all I knew he'd burst out laughing and snort duck liver paté all over my sparkly little dress.

As I drew back from him, something over the fireplace flickered and caught my eye. I pressed through the crowd to see it better. Over the stone mantelpiece was carved:

THE BLESSING
IF THE DRAGON BE THINE
BY FAIR MEANS AND TRUE
BRAVE HEART AND GOOD FORTUNE
WILL E'ER FOLLOW YOU

A shiver went over me. These were the words of *Y DDRAIG GOCH*, the Red Dragon of Wales. These were the words supposedly uttered by Merlin when he released the dragons from their lair under Snowdon. Impatiently I struggled to the far end of the hall. I pushed through the guests, trying to avoid their feet, (their glasses, their elbows and their egos), until I got to the twin fireplace at the other end of the Great Hall. There, carved into the stone of that fireplace was the last verse of Merlin's spell.

THE CURSE

IF YE TREAT A DRAGON

BY FOUL MEANS OR FORCE

ON THY OWN HEAD WILL FALL

THE FULL DRAGON'S CURSE

I thought of true hearts and blessings, of false hearts and curses, and wondered why those ancient words of Merlin's should be carved here in the hotel, and why I should be standing here reading them right now. I tried to shrug off the strange feeling they gave me. I mean, in Wales we get a lot of dragon stuff, and usually I just ignore it, but since I'd seen that dragon-thing yesterday, it felt weird – like Merlin's words were aimed directly at me.

I left the fire and went into the conservatory. Outside it had started to snow again. I stood by the silver Christmas tree. I watched huge snowflakes whirl through the sky. They settled on the glass roof above me. I caught my breath. (Can you imagine, even snowflakes reminded me of him!)

Anyway apparently royal people always arrive late. The Pendragons were no exception. But luckily, just when I couldn't bear the sight of another tray of mini, mini, mini mince pies passing under my nose, the oyez man stepped into the Great Hall and called out in his loud baritone:

'The Pen-y-mynydd-gwryd Hotel has the honour and the deepest pleasure in announcing the arrival of: His Excellencies; Baron Latimer of Hereford; Sir Stephen Edward Rudolph, Lord of Carlisle and Lady Elizabeth; Sir Bevan Cardiff; Sir Oswald Pendragon de Clare; Sir Henry Pendragon de Clare, Lord of Chandos and Viscount of Carnarvon and The Honourable Mrs Spencerford.'

There was a fanfare, and somehow the red carpet got rolled into the middle of the assembly (a bit askew). All the guests stepped away from it, so that it lay there looking weirdly random. A raised platform had been set up against one wall, and on it waited a row of plush chairs. Four security men stepped forward. They made it perfectly clear that no one was to crowd forward, or speak out of turn (or at all, apparently), or in any way get too close to the royals.

The double doors were thrown open. In swept the Baron, followed, I supposed, by Lord and Lady Carlisle. Behind them came an older gentleman: Sir Bevan Cardiff? Next came a tall pale man (I swear he was an albino, but Rhi said after, he wasn't, because albinos have red eyes and his weren't). Anyway he had silver flowing hair, a pinched angular face and thick white eyebrows, and there was something about him that was vaguely repulsive.

As he stepped through the archway, he hesitated. His eyes swivelled around the room, as if he was some huge bird of prey, scoping out the weakest and the most vulnerable amongst us. Instinctively I hung back. I tried to melt into the fronds of the Christmas tree, but his eyes alighted on me. They narrowed. A small smile, a thinning of eyelids, a barely imperceptible nod.

I have seen you. I have marked you out.

Then he turned abruptly, and began bowing coldly to the crowd. A shiver went down my spine. I stood there rigid, staring at him, his hooked nose, his long hands, his revoltingly thick eyebrows ... ugh!

The crowd fell quiet. I could almost feel time thaw. Like we'd just stepped out of the Tardis or something ...

and this wasn't a Royal Reception at all, but some ancient custom. Where the rich gathered and the peasants trembled and someone from among the crowd was selected and the hounds were loosed and the hunt begun ...

I actually felt so ill, I didn't even notice who walked in next. It was only when I heard the town crier, calling out his name that I turned. My heart stopped. My mouth fell open. My eyes. Oh my God! MY EYES!

'The Pen-y-mynydd-gwryd Hotel is delighted to announce the arrival of his Excellency, Lord Henry Pendragon de Clare.

A bolt of electricity blasted through me.

HENRY.

Lord Henry Pendragon de Clare, Baron Chandos and Viscount of Carnarvon.

My hand trembled. I gulped at my champagne. I didn't know what I was doing. It went straight to my head. I came over all faint. I reached out. George caught my arm. 'Steady on Elles,' he said. (Thank God for George!)

Henry was not so thrown. He smiled. His eyes twinkled. He bowed his head to the company. He bowed to the dignitaries. He bowed directly to me.

In an instant all heads turned. The tall albino man with the face like a hawk stepped forward. This time he fixed me openly with his eyes.

I tried not to FREAK OUT. Don't let Henry down, I told myself. I took a deep breath. I arranged my face. Butter wouldn't melt.

'*Trust me.*' That's what I'd said. I better be as good as my boast. I dipped my head. I did the prettiest curtsey I could (I'm not really the curtseying type). But as I curtsied, I remembered how Henry and I had bowed and curtsied to each other in Halfway House, so I added the same little toss of my head like before. Then not trusting myself any more, I kept my eyes firmly fixed on the floor.

Granny Jones helped. (She must have recognised Henry.) She unpinned a small bunch of flowers from her shawl; like the ones she'd given me. She quickly stepped forward, made a slight curtsey, and offered them to the tall albino man.

'*Blodau'r deri, y banadl a'r erwain a greuodd Blodeuwedd; ni allwch hela morwyn gyda'r blodau hyn,*'[1] she said.

Boy, that took the attention away from us!

Two things happened simultaneously: a security guard flew forward. He held his hand up warningly right in Gran's face. He needn't have bothered. For at exactly that same moment, the albino man stepped back. He too held

---

1. 'Oakblossom, broom, and meadowsweet; created Blodeuwedd, you cannot hunt any maiden with these flowers.'

up his hand, as if he were warding off something majorly unwelcome. I saw Granny Jones drop her curtsey even deeper. Then she refastened her flowers with a silent smile.

The moment passed. The oyez man made another announcement. Somebody made a speech. Somebody responded to it. The press crowded into the room. A few cameras flashed. George grabbed a handful of cocktail sausages. He made eyes at me. His eyes said: Isn't it about time we went to watch rugby? I didn't make eyes back.

I had to get out. I had to sit down. I had to think. My mind was spinning. My thoughts were bumping up against each other like dodgem cars. Some explosion had gone off inside my head. I needed to piece it all together.

Henry Pendragon de Clare.

I had to get out.

I left through the conservatory. I slipped around the Christmas tree, across the marble floor to the glass doors. Thank God they were open. I stepped outside into the bitter afternoon. I had no idea where I was going. The little freshwater pearls on my dress sparkled. I followed the flag-stone path down towards the lake. I didn't have my coat. I didn't have my gloves. I was wearing the tiniest, prettiest little shoes. They were not designed to be worn in subzero temperatures. Nor in two feet of snow. I didn't care. I had to GET OUT.

Lord Henry Pendragon de Clare, Baron Chandos and Viscount of Carnarvon.

Everything was nuts.

How come he was here? Less than five hours ago, I'd met him up the mountain.

How come he was allowed to wander around on mountains anyway?

How come he could spend nights with local girls, in halfway houses, in front of old log fires, with nothing rich or royal to eat or drink?

This was his secret!

No wonder he'd wanted us to be HISTORY.

I turned the corner past the folly. I stood by a stone bench, in front of the lake. I shook with cold. Shook with surprise. Shook with outrage!

In front of me the entire ornamental lake was frozen over. The twigs above me hung with a lattice of icicles. They sparkled in the low rays of the sun. The little bridge in the distance was frosted with shining silver – like in a fairytale.

'Don't be too mad,' said a voice behind me.

I wheeled round.

Henry. Just standing there.

All the blood in me drained away.

'Why so pale?' he said.

I didn't know what to say.

'I didn't know you'd be here', he whispered. 'Nothing is as it seems.'

The shining fairytale world around me started spinning.

'I didn't mean to have you find out like this.'

My breath stopped.

'I had to find you and tell you.' His voice was very low. 'You've changed everything.'

Silver spinning snowflakes.

'I can't stay.'

He caught hold of my elbow. 'Ellie?' he said.

I wanted to say something. I wanted to scream, punch my fists against the silk of his jacket, but my words were caught in my throat and all I could manage was a croak.

Henry put his arms around me. He was shaking. He bent his lips to my cheek and whispered, 'Please. Trust. Me.'

In the distance the conservatory doors opened. Out of them stepped two men: a security guard and a tall whitish figure.

'My uncle,' said Henry, quickly, urgently. 'Stay away from him … '

The figure loomed nearer. Another security guard stepped after him.

'Meet me tomorrow evening?' hissed Henry. 'Halfway House?'

I nodded.

'Make sure you come before nightfall. It's important.' Henry leant forward, took off his crimson silk scarf and draped it around my shoulders. (God, it smelt AMAZING).

'Before it gets dark, remember – your life may depend on it.'

I had no idea why he was being so melodramatic. I didn't care. I WAS GOING TO MEET HENRY TOMORROW. He took my hand. His uncle advanced. The security guard broke into a run.

Henry bowed to me. He raised my hand, kissed it and whispered. 'Tomorrow, promise?'

I tried to curtsey. I saw another figure step from the conservatory door. Granny Jones. The security guards closed in parting Henry and me. Granny Jones started shouting. *'Ewch o ma'r epil seirff. Ni fyddwch yn ei chael!'*[2]

Henry and his uncle promptly took the lavender walk and strode away. The guards rounded after them down the side of the hotel. I stood there completely bewildered and feeling like I was about to implode.

And that's how Granny Jones found me. She took my arm.

---

2. 'Be gone spawn of serpents. You shall not have her!'

She led me back to the huge fire in the Great Hall. She found me a goblet of spiced wine. (I think I will always remember the smell of cloves and cinnamon when I think of the Pen-y-mynydd-gwryd Hotel.) She pushed my hair back off my face. Before she found Mum, she said, 'It has gone far enough. Ellie. We must talk. As soon as your mother will let you, tomorrow, come to my cottage.'

I looked at her. It was a summons I dared not refuse.

Fourteen

ELLIE'S PHONE 27th December 21.05

Status: Puzzled

Going home in the car was difficult. I was in a state. Mum was driving, oblivious to everything and talking about the clothes The Honourable Whoever-She-Was had on … and wouldn't it have been better to have made all the canapés vegetarian? … because so many people these days just didn't eat meat … and fish might have been an acceptable alternative … George was scowling at me like he knew everything. And Granny Jones was steely eyed and steely lipped and steely everything. She just poked me with her pointy finger and said, 'Tomorrow.' Like I was going to be shot at dawn.

Once I got home and into bed, I forgot about Granny, though. I tucked Henry's scarf against my cheek. It smelt so lovely. I thought of the way he'd kissed me. A real prince (Ok a Viscount). I thought of standing with him on the pinnacle at Lovers' Leap. The clouds rushing in my face. His arms. His lips. He really had kissed me! Oh God, why wasn't it tomorrow already?

And then I slept. No sooner had I hit the pillow than my eyes closed. The mist rolled down from Garnedd Ugain and closed in tight around the farmhouse. No dark shadow flitted down from the mountain top to fix me with its evil glare. No shrieking monsters woke me.

I must have slept very deeply because by the time I bumbled downstairs the next morning, I found Mum and George sitting together, giggling in whispers, over Marmite toast.

'At last the princess has woken from her thousand-year nap,' greeted George.

It looked like a night's sleep had cheered him up. I was glad. A happy feeling started glowing under my ribs, like when you drink hot tea really quickly. George smiled at me and it was lovely. His face was all kind and pleased. I hadn't realised how horrid it was when we fell out.

I flumped down on a chair beside him. He grinned wider, put an arm over my shoulder and then shoved the remains of his Marmite toast in my face. 'Just for you,

O beautiful one,' he said.

There were two slices of toast actually. The one on his plate was intact. The one in my face had a bite out of it. That is *so* George, such A Boy. What other kind of creature would think of giving the girl it loves its leftover toast? But I wasn't fussy. In fact I was hungry, so I leant forward and crunched into it. George tried to snatch it back. He made as if to protect his plate. I slapped his hands away and growled, 'Mine' at him in a scary, big-nasty-beastie voice.

'Granny Jones has invited you up to hers,' said Mum, 'George's come to fetch you.'

'In a limo, I hope,' I stabbed a finger in his direction.

'Naturally,' George raised his eyebrows. (Have I told you George has exceptionally nice eyebrows?)

'She wants you to help her do something or other. What exactly does she want help with?' Mum turned a questioning face to George.

'Don't know,' said George, 'Acting normal? Maybe?'

Mum laughed.

What *did* Granny want me for? Suddenly my heart beat faster. Maybe she knew something horrible about Henry? She seemed to know so many things. When I got up there I'd ask her. Maybe. But asking her would somehow mean agreeing with her. Tricky. And then there was her own agenda. I had a nasty feeling she was going to get all bossy and tell me things I didn't want to hear.

'It's true,' said George, 'Ever since Ellie turned up with that boy yesterday, Gran's done nothing but brew herbs and climb into the attic in search of dusty old books.'

'What boy? When?' Mum said sharply.

'Oh, nothing and nobody,' I lied.

'Ellie?'

George raised his eyebrows at me, and mouthed, 'Liar.'

I reached for the coffee.

'What boy?' repeated Mum.

George raised his eyebrows again and mouthed, 'Shall. I. Tell. Her. The. Truth?'

I picked up the butter knife menacingly.

'Shall I Tell Her The Mystery Boy Was *ME*?'

'You wish,' I muttered.

'Ellie, stop winding him up,' said Mum getting hold of the wrong end of it.

George twisted his face up into Oops-I-Just-Put-My-Foot-In-It. I made sure I stamped on the said foot under the table. Hard.

'Ow!' said George.

'I'm going into Caernarfon while the roads are clear,' said Mum, (Yes, I did suddenly have a truly wonderfully mad idea.) 'So you can go and help Wynnie with her dusty books all morning, darling.' Mum went off into the scullery. She started checking through the contents of the chest freezer to see what we needed.

'Come on then,' said George.

'But I'm not even up yet,' I moaned.

'Do you want me to come upstairs and dress you?' George said, putting on an I-Am-A-Fledgling-Stalker-Of-Young-Girls face, and raising his eyebrows a zillion times, as well as licking his lip at the same time in a really gross way.

'Pervert!' I said and taking my coffee and shoving the last piece of toast into my mouth, I went upstairs to dress.

When I got up to George's cottage, Granny Jones was sitting by her fire, spinning. Round and round went the wheel. Round and round went the spindly thing. Up and down went the treadle. And Granny Jones just sat there, looking like she'd been hijacked straight out of a fairytale[1] and plonked down in the Here and Now, with no regard for modern technology at all.

I mean, who the heck spins wool these days?

---

1. One in which fairy godmothers wear funky fur body warmers (?) and bum bags – along with other strange fashion choices.

George took one look at her. 'You have to take pity on me, don't you?' he said and threatened to lark about and do a gorilla dance behind her back.

She put him in his place. 'We need more logs, Siôr.[2] This cold weather isn't going away until next spring which is in exactly three months' time. So get yourself outside and start chopping. Don't stop until the woodshed's full. I've got things I want to tell, Ellie.'

'Well you *should* take pity on me,' sighed George. 'She's not only mad, she's a slave driver.' He put on his old jacket and stomped off.

Granny Jones harrumphed as if George was just a troublesome puppy. Then she waved me over to the fireplace. 'Park yourself and fire away,' she said without looking up from her spinning.

'But I thought you wanted … '

'Ask me your questions.'

'OK, then! Why you don't like Henry?'

'Let's start there,' said Granny Jones. 'It's not him; it's *what* he is I don't like.'

'I didn't know he was a Pendragon.'

'For one of them, he's not the worst,' she continued.

'And neither did you,' I added.

---

2. That's what she always called George, because Siôr is George in Welsh.

'It's not his royalty that's the issue.' She hesitated. 'But then maybe it is.'

Sigh. Here she was, going all mysterious and enigmatic and conspiracy theory-ish again. (Was I truly going to be able to stand it?) I thought sadly of Mum motoring away. I'd never really rated Caernarfon before, now I just loooonged to be going there with her. Even if it was only to Iceland for groceries (and who knows, I might have caught a glimpse of the castle …).

'He's not good for you and there're things you don't know – very few people know – unless they've lived their lives up here on the mountain.'

'You can't help the family you're born into,' I said.

'Since Bedwyr died, maybe Siôr and I are the last ones to really know … ' Granny's hand stayed steady, but there was a twist of her mouth. A shadow darkened her face. Bedwyr was her son, George's dad. He and George's mum had died in Newport. (They were on the pavement. Drunk driver. Car mounted the kerb. George was flung out of his buggy into a garden. Never mentioned.)

'Tell me then,' I said.

'Old stories,' muttered Granny. She straightened up.

'You've called me up here, so you might as well explain,' I said.

'Ellie, the boy likes you, but his uncle doesn't, and he is not one to let the boy's feelings stay his hand. Do not underestimate Sir Oswald. He intends to harm you.' She cast her eyes at the fire and muttered, 'The Red one must always battle the White, and it always ends badly.'

I ignored her incomprehensible mutterings. 'Harm me?' I said. But I knew she was right: the malice in his face, that look in his eyes … *I have seen you, I have marked you out …*

'I've called you up here to warn you. There are lots of boys around. There's one right outside, taking out all his jealousy on a lump of wood.' She stopped and nodded meaningfully. The sound of George's axe hit the silence between us.

'You get my point?'

Like I'd have to be brain dead to miss it. But since when did *'his uncle doesn't like you'* ever warn any girl off?

'Let Henry go. He's a Pendragon. The likes of them are not for the likes of us.'

My heart sank. That was true. But I wasn't going to let that stop me, either. And it was no use saying there were loads of other boys. I didn't want *'loads of other boys'*. I wanted Henry. And I was not going to give him up.

'You're young' said Granny Jones. 'Feelings don't last. Nothing lasts.'

Nothing lasts? She was so wrong.

182

'Even love ends somewhere,' said Granny Jones.

OH GOD. TAKE ME INTO LLANBERIS AND BACK A LORRY OVER MY HEAD.

I mean, then what was the point of anything – of family, of friends, of being alive at all – if none of it mattered? Sometimes I just HATE old people. They're so NEGATIVE. I don't want to ever grow old, if that's what happens.

'Think about it.' Granny Jones carried on, as if by somehow repeating and repeating her point, she could convince me. 'He can't be with you. He may not even want to be with you.'

I looked her square in the face, felt my cheek grow hot. 'Didn't you ever love anyone?' I asked pointedly.

She stopped and raised her face from the spinning wheel. Her eyes seemed to be looking at me from a great distance, as if she remembered something, somewhere, way back in her girlhood.

Then she pressed her lips together in a straight line. 'He will destroy you,' she said. A coldness laced her voice. She turned back to the wheel and round it went.

'*What is it?*' I moved closer to her. 'You better tell me everything you know, if you want to convince me. All that stuff you were doing with the flowers. I know you know.'

She hesitated. Her spinning hand wavered. The thread ran slack.

'*Go on*,' I urged.

Granny Jones looked up at me. 'Imagine there was an old woman who'd lived all her life on a barren hillside,' she started. 'She could never leave the place. It held too many memories. And she'd promised someone she never would.'

I looked at her. Was this *her* story? Or was she being crafty, trying to find a way of telling me something else?

'Long, long ago this woman knew a girl, who fell in love with a mysterious boy she met on the mountain. It was the middle of winter. The boy was kind to the girl, and the girl planned a life where she could be with him, far away where winters were never harsh and life was not always uphill. But it never happened. The boy had a strange secret. He didn't tell the girl his secret, maybe he didn't love her.' Gran said this sadly as if it was an unhappy truth that had haunted her. 'Maybe he didn't trust the girl enough to believe him.'

'Yes,' I said eagerly. 'What was his secret? Was he really a Prince?'

'It was *his* secret, so I can't tell you,' said Granny, annoyingly.

I sighed. 'Well, continue with the story then,' I said.

'He didn't tell her that on that New Year's Eve his secret would overpower him. He didn't tell her he was going to have to make a terrible choice: either to sacrifice himself, or to lead her to certain death. There was no escape for him. So in the waxing of the thirteenth moon of the year, he told the girl to find certain flowers and wear them. He arranged to meet her at Halfway House. He taught her how to lay symbols around her door. She laughed at him. But he made her promise to do it and to wait for him at her house without going out once for three days.'

OK, bells were ringing. Dried flowers. Strange symbols. Boys with secrets. Clandestine meetings at Halfway House ... I wrinkled up my nose and peered at Gran. She was very straight faced, calm even. Except for her hands, they weren't spinning thread any more, they were twisting her rings, playing with her frilly pink scarf, fidgeting, wringing, clutching, until her knuckles were going all white.

'Go on,' I said more gently.

'What he didn't tell her was that if she did these things, she would never see him again.'

'WHAT!' I said.

'His secret was part of an ancient tragedy played out generation after generation on Snowdon, a curse that would end in him vanishing under the mountain.'

OK, this was all getting a bit too mystical and tales of King Arthur-ish for me. 'What did the girl do?' I asked.

'She did what he asked.'

'And he vanished?'

'Yes.'

'Are you sure he didn't just dump her and go off with someone else, while she was stuck indoors?'

Granny looked shocked. 'Absolutely.'

'How?'

'He told her that he could have loved her, but she was not the one he was waiting for. That didn't make any difference to her love for him, though. And his disappearance broke her heart. He told her that despite not being the one, she was more important to him than all the girls in the world.'

I snorted. Like who'd believe that!

'He dumped her,' I said.

Granny tutted very loudly in disapproval.

'And you think history is about to repeat itself, don't you? You think I'm the girl, and Henry is the boy.'

'If the cap fits.' Her mouth was drawn in a tight line. 'I'm just warning you, so you don't get hurt.' She left the spinning wheel and put Rod Stewart on. Soon the cottage was humming with *First Cut is the Deepest*.

'Ah, but I'm not the girl in your story,' I said. 'I'd make

sure the boy trusted me.' And I wanted to add, 'is that why you're so pinched up and weird? (Are you *really* the dumpee?)' But of course I didn't.

She fixed me with her steely look. '*Boed hynny fel y bo*. So be it then,' she said, 'But you must promise to do one thing for me.'

'What?' I said, ready to be completely stubborn.

'Don't go out after dark until it's New Year.'

I nearly burst out laughing. 'You want me to stay indoors for a week!'

'Don't scoff, Ellie. It's important. There's evil all around us.'

'Do you know what time it gets dark, Gran?' I said.

'Yes,' she said, 'be indoors and stay there.'

'Why?' I countered. 'Tell me exactly what the threat is — if it's so evil.'

She sighed. 'Let's say it's just one of my weird old fancies.' She flexed her knee and picked up speed on the treadle.

'You're going to have to do better than that,' I said, 'if you want me to stay in from 3.30 p.m. every day of my holidays.'

'You'll bring ill luck on yourself and your house, if you stray out after dark between Christmas and New Year.'

'Then Mum's going to bring it on us, anyway,' I said. 'There's no way she's going to miss seeing Jeff just about every evening.'

'Tis different for her. She does not share your destiny.'
Granny slammed the treadle up to full speed.

'Who was this girl?' I said, suddenly weirdly jealous.
'Was it you?'

Granny shook her head. But her voice softened. 'No pet,
it wasn't me. She was your grandmother. It's her story.'

'*My grandmother?*' I said surprised. 'Mum's mam?'

'She was like a big sister to me. I loved her, and 'tis for her
sake I'm telling you now.'

'But,' I said. 'My grandmother, surely she and granddad
… ' This was nuts.

'She made it her life's work to understand what happened
to that boy.'

Granny Jones is so Over The Top: *Her life's work!* My nose!

'Well at some point she must've forgotten about him,'
I said, 'because she married my grandfather, didn't she?'

'Yes, she married Dylan. He lived down the valley and
had always loved her. He stood beside her and faithfully
waited for her. But I've lived through this story once and
I don't want to again. Her heart was broken and yours
shan't be.'

I looked up then into her eyes. All the little crinkles
around them told me she meant it. She was trying to save
me pain.

'He told her about you, you see.'

That shook me. '*He told her about you.*' What the heck did she mean?

'The boy told Eleanor, your grandmother, that she would have a granddaughter, and she, the granddaughter, was the one he was waiting for.'

'*What?*'

'That's enough.'

It was definitely *not* enough.

'Before Eleanor died she told me everything. She made me promise to protect you.'

'Please Gran,' I said, 'start from the beginning and go slowly. What did he tell her?'

'That's enough, I've said my piece. I'm bound by my promise to protect you. And she made me promise as well, not to reveal the boy's story.'

'So she found it out?'

'You're to stay away from that boy. Keep in your house. Now come here. I've something for you.' Granny beckoned me forward.

She was *impossible*. I could've dropped a brick on my own head (or hers). What did she mean: *he told her about you?* Promises or not, I was going to get to the bottom of this.

Swallowing my frustration, I dragged my chair closer.

Granny Jones held up a thin chain with a small silver charm dangling from the end of it. The sun shafting in through the window sparkled off the silver. I held out my hand. She lowered the charm into my palm.

I examined it. The clasp was a bouquet of wild flowers and the fastener was a shining silver sun. The chain was exquisitely fragile, yet when I tested it, it seemed pretty strong. The charm was quite unique: a new moon held in the arms of the old one, like you sometimes see when the moon had waned right down. Between the circled moon and the crescent one was a constellation of tiny stars all set in diamonds.

'Wear it for me,' she said. 'Call it a Christmas present.'

It was very beautiful, and it was very old too. Maybe it had been Granny Jones' when she'd been a girl. Maybe it'd been my grandmother's. Anyway Granny Jones must have polished it up, for the chain was still flecked with tarnish and black oxide.

'Put it on.'

I slipped the chain over my head and let the circle with the crescent moon fall over my jumper.

'Tuck it in, next to your skin,' ordered Granny. She was being weirdly fussy. 'Not by sunlight or by moonshine,' she mumbled.

I slipped it inside my scarf, *his scarf*. The touch of the silver against my throat was soothing, cool. It made my skin tingle. 'Thank you,' I said, suddenly overcome. 'I don't mean to be difficult, Gran.'

'There, I know,' she said kindly, 'I was just hoping, it wasn't what I thought.'

'Meaning?' I said.

'Hoping that you hadn't already set your heart on him.'

'But what if I ... '

'You'll come to no harm if you follow what I've told you.'

'I'll try,' I said.

'You can't sometimes escape the old ways,' she said sadly. OK, she was going to start again. Time to go.

'Thanks so much for the necklace,' I said.

She waved her hand. I made a few more polite remarks. She ignored them and leant over to make sure the chain was well and truly tucked in. I hesitated, wondering what to do next. Granny started humming along to Rod Stewart.

I said, 'I'll go and see what George is up to,' (like I didn't know).

She sat there nodding away, humming her song and spinning her wheel faster than ever.

Outside I went over to George 'Oh God, how do you cope with it?' I said.

'Lots of boiled potatoes,' he responded. 'And being able to look out of my bedroom window and see the roof of your house.'

'Oh shut up,' I said.

'And knowing you are lying under it … in bed … in silk pyjamas … '

'You are such a perv,' I said.

George just rolled his eyes and chopped a few more logs. I watched him swing the axe. I saw the muscles ripple in his arms even through two layers of jumper.

'She's got something against Henry,' I said. 'She called me up here to warn me off.'

'Hope she succeeded,' said George. He swung the axe up high and brought it down with a sudden violent *thwack*.

'It is a well-known fact that if you warn a girl off a guy it makes her all the more determined to have him!' I replied archly.

'Pity,' said George.

'Why?' I said.

'You know, if I seriously thought this Henry was a threat to you, I'd crush him like this.' George placed two logs, one on top of the other, raised his axe over his head, slipped his hand down the handle and, in true professional axe-man style, brought the gleaming blade down at speed. Both logs split clean through.

'Wh-o-ah,' I said, 'I'll be sure to tell him to stay away from George and his mad axe!'

'Good idea,' said George. 'Tell him to stay away from the mountain all together.'

'I really have no idea why you two are so against him,' I sighed. It hurt actually. George was my best friend. Even though he teased me all the time – about fancying me and all that – I wanted him to like Henry.

George looked up. Maybe he heard the sadness in my voice. 'Hey Ellie,' he said, 'don't take it seriously, it's just Nan and her folk tales.'

'What folk tales?' I asked. 'She tried to palm me off with some Going Out After Dark Is So Scary Bad Luckish Crap.' But even as I said it I remember Henry had warned me against it too.

'It's all in the Mabinogion,' said George, tapping his nose knowingly. 'Apparently in the last quarter of the last full moon before a leap year, every seventy-two years or something, maidens shouldn't stray outside in the moonlight.'

'Why?' I said.

'On account of the Red Dragon of Wales,' said George.

'So?' I said. 'Is he going to jump down off his flag and toast me or something?'

'He's partial to a naughty nibble of little virgins for his Christmas din-dins,' said George, licking his lips. 'Can't blame him either.' George gave me his best ever pervy look.

'You're kidding me,' I said.

George laughed and made dragon claws and went to rake them down my face. I looked at him. He wasn't making it up, however much he thought it was bonkers. The silver moon inside my jumper suddenly felt icy against my skin.

George picked up his axe again. 'Yep it's true. The story goes that the Dragon of Wales must eat a sacrificial maiden once every hundred years. In days gone by they actually left a chosen girl up here to die on the mountain. So you know what to do, if you want to escape that fate … ' George leaned in closer, 'Just in case – you know – the virgin thing – if you wanted to rule yourself out – I'd be happy to oblige … ' he said, waggling his eyes again.

'George!' I said.

'And she had to be fatherless.' He paused as if he was sorry to point that out. 'Anyway Nan believes in all that sort of stuff, that's why she told you not to go out after dark.'

'She thinks I'm the next girl-burger, eh?' I tried to make light of it. Though I have to admit after seeing that creature fly down off the mountain I was no longer so sure.

'Yep,' said George swinging his axe.

I sighed. I always knew there were very good reasons why I needed to stop living halfway up Snowdon. Apart from the intermittent technology and no proper mains sewage, apparently now I had to plan my social calendar around the legendary behaviour of dragons. Brilliant.

'But don't worry,' said George, 'I'll be your knight in a shining anorak! Any dragon I find sniffing around your front door will have to deal with me and my axe!'

'Great,' I said, 'I'll sleep a lot easier.' I stuck my hands in my pockets and turned to go.

'You off, already?' called George.

'Got to get home, before I change into roast beef,' I said

'Cool,' shouted George. 'Next time you go out put the horseradish sauce in your pocket. You wouldn't want to be a disappointment would you?'

I didn't even bother telling him it'd take a whole super-market full of sauces to make him even the tiniest bit appetising. I stomped off instead.

'Hey cheer up, Ellie, I have to put up with it *every* day.' He called.

'But I don't understand what it's got to do with *Henry*.' I shouted back.

'Oh!' said George, 'Didn't she tell you? About the Annu-naki, the Royal Reptiles, maiden blood and Welsh gold?

'Wot?' I yelled.

'The *Annunaki* … ' he shouted back.

'Wot's that got to do with Henry?'

George stopped chopping. He stood silhouetted against the snow, leaning on his axe, laughing. His voice carried down the mountainside.

'Henry *is* the dragon.'

Fifteen

Recent updates between Ellie and Rhiannon:

Rhiannon

Thanks babes. I knew you'd leave George 4 me

Ellie

The pleasure's all mine.

Rhiannon

PLEASURE?

Ellie

?

Rhiannon

U so slow.

Recent updates between Ellie and Sheila:

Sheila

Word travels quickly. Henry Pendragon de Clare – eh?

Ellie

Is taken

Sheila

By me

Ellie

Not

Sheila

Then it's OPEN WAR.

It was a joke, had to be. If anyone was a dragon it was Granny Jones. She was one hell of an old dragon! George was just mucking around. But his words still rankled. I tried to wipe them out of my mind as I raced down the mountain.

My Henry = The Revolting White Creature I'd seen? Not.

George needed a good knock on the head. I hoped he got one. I hoped he slipped up on the ice and bashed some sense into himself.

It was only when I'd stopped seeing red that I got it, George was just being clever. Henry Pen-dragon equals Welsh for Henry, Head Dragon. Ha ha not very ha.

I slowed my pace a bit as I crossed over the upper pastures. And Granny's tale of my grandmother? How strange. Should I believe her? How far could you trust Granny Jones? At the best of times she was fanciful, embellished stories, exaggerated perils, concocted conspiracies where none existed. I'd ask Mum. After all my grandmother had been *her* mother. If there was any truth in it, she'd be bound to know.

George was just trying to be clever, *wasn't he*? Nothing to worry about? Just silly George comments?

The thing was, his silly comments had gone bullseye right on to the questions I'd been puzzling over. Where *had* Henry come from? Why was he up on the mountain? And it made me remember:

- How had Henry survived all day on the mountain?
- How had he got to the summit so quickly?
- How had he managed to appear and disappear and leave no tracks?
- How could he make you feel his eyes – make you feel his eyes could see you at ten times the distance of normal vision?
- How had he pushed open that door?
- And what about the fire?

Plus I realised I was still very shaky about yesterday, about Henry *being* a Pendragon, about his uncle … (And – don't worry – I hadn't forgotten how narked I was about Sheila.)

What right did she have to try and bag Henry? ~~The cow.~~

What the hell was I going to do about her? It was all very well to think: just rise above it, Ellie, don't ~~strangle her~~ let her get to you. But I *knew* Sheila! And I knew she wasn't going to give up. She was going to dig away at whatever she could – and once she knew everything, she'd haunt Snowdon herself looking for him.

By the time I got home, I was really flaky. I had two cups of tea, but it didn't help. Stuff kept jumping into my head. I made a whole pot of tea, but that unwelcome stuff stayed right where it was, right in the middle of my brain like a lump of cold porridge.

So I decided to spring clean the farmhouse to keep it all at bay. As you do.

I started by defrosting the fridge. I scrubbed it clean. I got a bowl full of hot soapy water and scrubbed up the puddles left by the defrost. Then the old flagstones (by the fridge) looked so clean, I decided to scrub the whole floor. There is something about the repetitive nature of scrubbing that makes you think everything is going to be all right. With enough scrubbing the whole world could be sorted out. Probably.

Mum was impressed when she got home, anyway. I helped her trudge everything in from the car. I made her stick to a path of old newspapers over the floor, and then put on slippers. I helped her stack the shopping in the pantry. I made her a cup of coffee. I offered to vacuum. She gave me a kind of odd look and said, 'Far be it from me to stand in the way of a clean carpet.'

So I sailed off with the vacuum cleaner for the next hour. Doing the stairs was actually the best bit.

But soon I ran out of floor, and even though I thought about wiping down every wall and polishing every door handle, I realised that might make Mum suspicious. She was already murmuring things about sending me off to see Granny Jones a bit more often. So I turned on the telly in my room. I told Mum I was going to stream Christmas films. She was fine about it. Jeff had called. She was curled up on one of the sofas in another world.

But no matter how I tried to get into the films, I failed. Without floors to clean, all those thoughts got out of control again. I couldn't help it. I flung myself down on my bed and surrendered.

Henry. Legends. Maidens. Mountains. Curses. Royal Princes. Dragons. Altogether they made a kind of horrible fairytale all of their own. What had George meant? Stupid George. Henry was obviously *not* a dragon.

He was a boy. A very attractive boy. His chestnut hair, his pale skin (and rosy glowing cheeks when he was climbing the mountain), his dark eyes – nothing like a dragon. And a very fit boy, all those muscles, those broad shoulders … OK, Godammit, a very Gorgeous Boy. (I am not going any further.) And he was a boy I'd promised to trust.

George was not just stupid, but jealous. That was it.

But try as I might, I couldn't get the idea to go away. Instead it got worse.

I remembered the girl on the mountain – her words: ' … *a boy… had to get warm … something inside the mountain …*'

And that Flight Lieutenant, Cecil Howard: '*I heard the story before … a girl too … years ago … lost at night … burn marks … bites … half crazed with terror … a handsome boy …*'

And then there was the speed with which Henry had got up to the summit during that first rescue; his glittering eyes that seemed to follow me everywhere; the lack of footprints; the sound of something beating the air; the enormous strength needed to push open the door of Halfway House (Dragons are powerful, aren't they?)

And the fire so easily made …

Oh My God! THE FIRE!

Dragons breathe fire, don't they?

Dragons can fly, can't they?

Dragons demand sacrificial maidens, don't they?

But how could he be a dragon *and* a boy?

Was there such a thing as a shape-shifting dragon?

And then more questions slid in: What about his uncle? That horrible whitish colour. Those hawk-like eyes, how they'd singled me out …

And the shrieking – what about the nightmarish shrieking?

I dragged out my laptop and started it up. The Windows sign took ages to appear. I actually started to panic. Just when I wanted to find out, the Whole Damn Internet would go down! I saw the box to type in my password. Quickly I entered it. And then I typed into the search engine:

Wales, dragon, maiden, sacrifice, royal prince.

First up came Human *Sacrifice* in Legends and Myths with a long story of how Merlin once came to Snowdon and warned somebody or other, Vortigern (?) actually, (where *had* I heard that name before?), that underneath the mountain at Dinas Emrys (? I *had* heard of Dinas Emrys, which is on the other side of the peak to us) were TWO dragons (?!) a white one and a red one and when they gave battle, terrible shrieking could be heard. (?!! – This. Could. Not. Be. A. Coincidence.) The only way to appease them was to sacrifice a virgin somebody and in this case, apparently, it was Merlin (phew).

Then there was a link to Dinas Emrys. I followed it and read the folk tale about the Beast of Dinas Emrys, but nobody had ever said it was a dragon … The word 'shrieking' was too much though. Hurriedly I typed in:

Dinas Emrys, shrieking.

And up came: The Dragons of Dinas Emrys !!!

I blinked. I bit my lip. This is what happens when you go snooping. You're looking for the bad news and As Sure As Hell You Find It! I took a big gulp. So the beast of Dinas Emrys *was* a dragon. (Two in fact!) I followed links. They led to the Mabinogion. So George had been right there too …

I read:

> '*A shriek that came on that sacred Yuletide eve, over every hearth and went through people's hearts, and so scared them, that the men lost their hue and their strength, and fell crippled to the earth, and the women their children, and the young men and the maidens lost their senses, and all the animals and trees and the earth and the waters were*

> *left barren. This plague,' said Llefelys 'is caused by dragons. Another dragon is fighting with your Red Dragon, and therefore do these dragons make a fearful outcry ... '* [1]

Dragons shriek.

Loudly.

Sound familiar?

Mystery solved then. At least the shrieking part of it. As for the rest – if only Granny had told me *everything* I might know what to do next.

I shook out my hair and rolled over on the bed.

Like should I believe Henry was a dragon?

And what should I do about tonight?

Well I HAD to see Henry again. So I had to decide some things, and I had to do them very quickly.

Firstly, what was I going to believe? The old stories clearly pointed towards dragons. Plus I'd seen one.

But if they did exist and if I believed in them, what then?

A sane little voice said: You could just stay at home. Do as Gran says, don't leave the house after dark until the New Year is here. If Henry really cares about you, he'll find a way to see you.

---

1. The Mabinogion, from the story of Lludd and Llefelys which survives intact in the Red Book of Hergest and in fragmentary form in the White Book of Rhydderch.

I often give myself excellent advice, although I seldom take it. And I knew straight away, without even debating it for two seconds, I wasn't going to take it on this occasion. I could no more sit at home knowing that Henry was waiting for me in Halfway House than jump off a cliff.

And I realised something then. *I did believe it.* Henry very possibly could be a dragon. He could be anything, but I loved him, so I was going to trust him.

And with that, my mind was made up.

I'd get to Halfway House before dark. When I got there, I'd ask him about everything: dragons, royalty, legends, Dinas Emrys, shrieking, my grandmother. Even about Granny Jones. I trusted him. He'd be there. If there were any secrets, he was going to tell me them.

Suddenly I couldn't wait.

Sixteen

The next few hours dragged by. Time went so slowly. It practically stopped. When would it be best to set out? How long would it take? How could I be sure to get there before dark? The earlier the better. Before dusk then?

Mum came up with a very late lunch. ARGH! Eating it took forever. And then there was the afternoon to get through. All those normal things that should have been fun, like using that nail polish, trying on those tops, playing those tunes, pinging all your mates, putting away your Christmas presents – none of them mattered any more. All of them lay like dead weights anchoring time to its slowest possible pace.

Except that the Christmas presents mattered to Mum.

'You've got thank-you calls to make,' she reminded me.

Distant aunties for crystallized lemon slices and £20

gift vouchers.

Sigh.

It was torture. And it took sooo long. In my family you can't get away with just saying, 'Hi there lovely Aunty Betty thanks ever so much for the … (slight pause whilst you scan through your memory to figure out what she got you) … um thing – and it was just what I wanted.'

No. You have to do the full year's catch up: How are you doing in school? What do you want to be in future? What did you eat for Christmas dinner? Have you grown at all? How's your mum coping? Bad time of year for her, isn't it? Is she still working as a mountain guide?

It goes on and on like that for-ev-er, and just when you get off the phone to Aunty Betty, you have to start all over to Aunty Marion, until you kind of get to hate presents and wish you could say, 'Thanks very much, but next year don't bother, because I can get Herbal Bath Soak in Tesco if I truly want it, which I don't.'

And then you feel all ungrateful, because it's the thought that counts – except that it isn't really, is it? They just send stuff, because if they didn't, Aunty Betty might say something bitchy about Aunty Marion, and how she never sends to the nieces any more, and that could start The Big Family Row Which Will Last For Centuries And You Will

Never Hear The End Of It. So you're doomed to receive fluffy hot water bottles and mugs with *Having A Bad Hair Day?* on them for all eternity. Amen.

And to make it worse, Mum hovered at the doorway. She had a wooden spoon in one hand, as if she was going to beat the crap out of me if I said anything about Jeff. But, of course, she was pretending she was going to mix Christmas pudding (?) with it, which she wasn't. But I wasn't allowed to point that out. Plus she was in a bit of a mood. She calls it The Three Day Blues. Mum reckons you can't sustain anything longer than three days before you get them. Especially Christmas rejoicings.

And all the time I was worrying and worrying. I couldn't tell her I'd planned to go out. I had to prepare in secret, in between the phone calls, and stash away the flares and the compass and the head torch and charge my phone.

Every time she stepped into my room, I'd start and go all guilty and she'd say, 'What on earth is the matter, Ellie? You're acting so OFF. Have I done something? I'd much rather you spit it out.' And I'd try to distract her, to stop her asking any more questions. And then she'd look sad and go away quietly, and do the I Am Creeping Around So As Not To Be An Annoying Mother thing, which is really annoying.

I wished I could tell her. Ask her: Is this how you feel

when you want to see Jeff? Do you have to hide your excitement and tiptoe around, so I don't feel cross or left out? Plus I wanted to know if I really *should* go. Everyone was so against it. What did *she* think? Was she on my side? Was I being really stupid? And did she believe in dragons? And if she did, would she trust a boy who might be one? And if not, what if he were Jeff? But of course, I couldn't ask her anything, because that would give everything away.

And how was I actually going to tell her I was going out?

I cringed as I imagined it:

ME: Oh! Hi lovely mummy. Sorry I'm a bit
   distracted. I think what I need is a nice walk
   in the fresh air to clear my head. So I think I'll
   just step out now before it gets too late.
MUMMY: But it is getting late!
ME: *GNASHES TEETH*
   Aside: *I soooo know that!*
   Oh is it? (practise sounding like a moron.)
   Oh, well never mind, I won't be long.
MUMMY: Don't be silly, darling. (Was being a teenager in
   her day so difficult?)
ME: Oh Mum I really must. I think I left my ~~iPod,~~

210

~~gloves, handkerchief (??)~~ um, new compass up on the top pasture. (Wasn't Going To Swallow It, Was She?)

My train of thought was broken when Mum came into my room. She stood in the doorway her hands planted on her hips. 'I just don't know what to do, or say to please you today, Arabella (ouch). I thought we'd have a cosy night in, but you're so distracted I might as well not be here, so I'm going to see Jeff. If you want to come, that's fine. I could drop you at Bethan's (Yuck, I hate Bethan. Didn't Mum remember that I've hated Bethan ever since primary?), or at the cinema. You could see the latest Horror-Type-Vampire-Movie (very reassuring), or you can come and watch telly at Jeff's, or you can stay here and do whatever you want.' And what she meant was that she had HAD ENOUGH.

And I felt rotten. I felt annoyed with myself, because I'd wanted to ask her about Grandmother and if she'd ever heard of a story that happened to her before she met Granddad. But I hadn't known how to start it and did I really want to ask her? Or should I ask Henry directly and not go snooping around in the past, as if I didn't trust him? I was acting so strangely, and I'd been worrying so much about how I was going to get out of the house, and now she was pissed off with me.

And now I didn't have to come up with any excuse, after all.

Mum went off downstairs. I felt guilty. Had I really been *that* awful? Or did she really just want to go out *herself* and didn't know how to tell *me*?

I distracted myself by thinking about what I was going to wear. What was I going to wear? I decided I was going to look stunning. I was going to wear something dark and silvery and clinging that showed off my shoulders.

I know you'll think that's amazingly ridiculous, given that I was going to walk up a mountain, over snow fields, dodging gullies to get up to Halfway House, but I didn't care. I could wear all my snow gear on the outside, and if he lit another fire, it'd be quite warm enough to take off my snow suit, wouldn't it? Well anyway I was going to choose the prettiest dress I had.

The prettiest dress I had was midnight blue. It was off the shoulder and had lace and shimmered. It frilled open a little across the front. And was, of course, completely unsuitable. I got it off the hanger anyway. I put it on. It looked great. I looked all dark and midnightish and mysterious.

Of course Mum came back in *yet again* and saw me.

She was about to tell me that she was going RIGHT

NOW AND WAS I COMING? Then she caught sight of me twirling in the mirror.

'Ellie,' she said, her voice quite hoarse with surprise, 'You look beautiful. That dress it's so … ' She stared at me. 'No, it's not the dress. It's you, darling. You look quite radiant.'

I flashed her a supersonic I-Am-A-Radiant-Being smile. Then just as suddenly she knitted up her eyebrows. 'But why're you wearing a summer dress in the middle of winter?'

'It's not really a summer dress,' I said, knowing full well it was.

'Well you're not going out in it, are you?'

'I'm staying in.'

Mum shook her head and shrugged. 'Well you're going to have to put on something warmer. The heating's up as high as it'll go.'

I nodded and slipped the dress off. I mentally crossed out the next line of my exit strategy. I didn't need it anyway.

ME: ~~Oh silly me, I'm just off to the top pasture to find my lost new compass, in my best summery blue dress, after dark, with lipstick on.~~

'I'll, stay in Mum. I'm going to sort out my stuff and put it away.'

I was lying to her. *Again.* I wasn't even sure why. I kidded myself it was because she was so engrossed with Jeff, and she wouldn't be in the slightest bit interested in the truth anyway. Which wasn't true and wasn't fair. Mum was always interested in everything I did and she was supportive. Maybe it was because I was afraid she'd be disapproving like Granny Jones and George. Also there was something about not telling things from the beginning. I'd never told her about staying out all night with Henry. If I started telling her now, she'd be bound to ask where I met him. And then I'd have to tell her. And then she'd asked me why I hadn't told her before? And it would all get lumpy. She'd find out George and Gran knew already. She'd feel left out. Someone was sure to get cross. Probably me.

It was just a lot easier to say nothing. Or lie. Although for how long I could do that, I didn't know. It depended on so many things. Which all began and ended with Henry.

'Ellie?' said Mum, 'Have you even heard what I've been saying?'

I looked up at her.

'I said, I'm going into Llanberis. RIGHT NOW. It's your last chance to join me?'

'Oh no,' I said, 'You go.'

'You sure?'

214

'Course,' I said, 'Although Granny Jones seems to think nobody should be going out after dark until the full moon is over.'

Mum tossed her head. 'Werewolves?' she asked.

'No. Dragons.'

'Oh, that old tale,' said Mum.

'What old tale?' I said. There you are: I should have asked her.

'Something about something that happened to her friend when she was your age,' said Mum, 'And you've been distracted all day so don't start getting chatty just when I'm leaving.'

Granny Jones' friend? My Grandmother? Mum's mum? Were we all talking about the same person? And now was just the right moment to ask – but she was leaving and we were both so stressy and I couldn't.

'I do love you, Mum.'

'I know Hon. Blame the Three Day Blues. And don't forget to turn the heating off when you go to bed.'

With Mum gone the house seemed suddenly empty, as if all the furniture had shrunk or was hiding up against the walls, as if everything was trying to get out of the way of something. I tried singing a Christmas carol, but the notes fell lifeless. I put on music, louder than I dared when Mum was in. It wasn't as if we had neighbours or anything. But the music echoed into the cold rooms and got swallowed up into the vast silence. So I turned it off. I didn't want to underline all that hollowness. But that seemed like surrendering. So I plugged the world out and stuck in my head phones. I marched around the house getting myself ready, daring all that quiet energy to come a step nearer. And I kind of succeeded too. By the time the shadow of the mountain started to fall across the back windows of the house and I was ready to go, I felt pretty safe. Safe inside my own little ear-plugged world.

What happened next I have no explanation for. The back of the house was in shadow and the sun was setting over Snowdon (I really should get going). It wasn't dark, but you know how sometimes the moon rises even when it's still light. You get this funny thing. From one window you can see the setting sun, all fiery and red, and when you turn around you can see the moon rising in the other, all white and ghostly.

So there I was in the middle of the front room. Out of one window was the sun, out of the other the moon. It was very beautiful, but it was very wrong. And that was when

I saw them. I'm sure I saw them. At first I blinked. I wiped my face, thinking a blob of mascara had got into my eye. But it wasn't mascara. It wasn't an eagle either. It wasn't an RAF helicopter, because that is huge and very yellow and could not be mistaken for a dragon – unless you really have had too many swigs from the sherry bottle.

You know those people who say they've seen aliens? You know the ones. They show you some dodgy bit of mobile phone footage, and point to a blob of dark squares that shimmer over the Californian desert in a plate shape. After what I saw over Snowdon that evening, I believe them. Because rising up from the direction of Dinas Emrys were two huge flying things. They were bigger than any birds I've ever seen. They had long tails that whipped the sky in snaky sideways motions. And they shrieked as they clashed together over the summit.

I ran upstairs to get Mum's binoculars. I couldn't find them. I grabbed her opera glasses instead. I ran back downstairs. I kneeled up on a chair by the window and steadied my hold. I trained the opera glasses on them and watched. I even had time to get out my mobile phone and put it on camera. That didn't really work so well. All I got was the same old blobby squares.

The two creatures seemed to be fighting. One of them

wanted to come down towards our side of the mountain –
the bigger, whitish one. The other was dark, reddish even
when it caught the light from the setting sun. And it seemed
to be trying to stop the white one. The darker one was
much smaller though and by the time the mist had rolled
in, I could hardly make anything out at all, except for their
shadows chasing each other round and round the summit.

I think I was beginning to understand. Two dragons.
Fighting. And Henry.

And if he was a dragon, then he was one of them. And he
wasn't that repulsive whitish one either.

I rang George.

'Did you see those creatures over the mountain?'

'Umm,' he hesitated. 'Not exactly.'

'Did you see *anything*?'

'Manchester United thrashing Spurs.'

'You're hopeless,' I said.

'What was it anyway?'

'Two things flying over the summit.'

'Buzzards probably. There's been a nesting pair up there
for years.'

'Bigger than buzzards,' I said.

'There're no albatross in Snowdonia, Ellie.'

'Bigger than albatross.'

'Um, let me think,' he said.

'Honest George, I'm serious.'

'Probably dragons then.'

'I think so,' I said faintly. 'Aren't you pleased?'

'Why?'

'That I believe you?'

'Does it mean I get to come and use my axe?'

'George, I mean it.'

'Shall I come?'

'No, I'm going out.'

'Where?'

'Up to Halfway House. Mum forgot to leave the key out.' I lied.

'You be careful then.'

I think I'd been half hoping he'd offer to come up to Halfway House with me, that I wouldn't have to go alone. Because I really had left it a bit too late. And it was starting to get dark. But that was ridiculous. And anyway he didn't.

'One was red, one was white,' I said.

'Just like Man U vs Spurs.'

He was still turning everything into a joke.

'Goodbye,' I said, and put the phone down.

Seventeen

I made it to the top pasture all right. I kept looking over my shoulder. I tried convincing myself: You Do Not Need To Be Afraid. But as soon as the farmhouse disappeared into the distance, I was. Maybe there were more than just dragons out on the mountain? *Anything* could exist. Snowdon is a tricky place. And I should have left home a lot earlier.

And it was colder than ever. It felt like the White Witch of Narnia had flown in from the North Pole intent on shrouding the place in her icy breath. As I walked, I flapped my arms and hugged my shoulders, trying to squeeze out the chill and I imagined what else could be out there. Werewolves? The Abominable Snowman? A shiver crept up my spine. All the little hairs on the nape of my neck bristled. I pulled my lovely Henry scarf tighter. Get A Grip Ellie, I told myself. None of that stuff exists.

But it was no good saying None Of That Stuff Exists. Dragons did, or something very like them. So why not other things too? *I'd seen them*. Not nice little friendly How-to-Tame-ones. Huge, mythical, hunting beasts. Great Beowulf monsters. Things to make your blood run cold.

Opera glasses don't lie.

They were out here and so was I.

The thought sobered me (which was a good thing, because knowing your enemy gives you a head start). I was going to have to be very careful. And practical too. There was no way I would survive if they saw me. All I had to do was get to Halfway House. ALL! I must be mad. Suddenly the whole mountain was one huge prehistoric landscape where demons worse than dinosaurs stalked.

Why on Earth hadn't I LEFT EARLIER? Or worn the white snow-suit? In this dark blue jacket I'd be spotted from outer space. How could I stay hidden? I was going to have to think like one of them, wasn't I? What had it said on that fireplace? *Fight Fire With Fire*.

It was a clue. Dragons are not afraid of dragons, are they? So I told myself: become a dragon; think like one then Ellie. So as I left the top pasture I tried to imagine how dragons thought. I tried to invoke their savage fiery souls and become one. How *did* a dragon think?

Hell, if only I knew!

If I'd played *Dragon Age* or read Tolkien, or done something dragonish … anything … it might have helped. I should have. I could have kicked myself. Why hadn't I forced Granny to tell me everything? Why hadn't I cross-examined Mum? But I didn't turn back, and I didn't give up. Nothing was going to keep me from seeing Henry. Not Mum. Not Gran. Not dragons.

I made it to the railway line. Dusk was falling fast, and a light blurring of snow had started. In the distance I heard the lonely drone of an aircraft. The air, stingingly sharp, bit into my skin. Already my nose was frozen, a film of flakes settled across my face, and a dreadful silence started oozing into everything; even my footfalls were nothing more than soft punches in the creaking snow.

It was majorly creepy. The snowfields had a strange luminous quality, as if they were reflecting back light from some invisible source. Everywhere glowed with a dull brilliance. And it all looked oddly arranged as well, as if it the whole of Snowdon were a stage, set for some ominous drama.

In school we did a drama once where the pagan God of Snow came onstage and threw cut up bits of tinsel at the mums. When the tinsel fell, it twirled and sparkled in the stage lights like falling snowflakes. Beautiful. Captivating.

Out here the Pagan God was real. There were no bits of tinsel. No mums. Only his arctic breath and this unearthly silence.

I went over in my mind what I knew about dragons: they were huge, strong, greedy, treasure-hoarding, fire-breathing, able to fly, demanding of sacrifices, reptilian. But shapeshifting? Did dragons shapeshift?

What did I know about shape-shifting? Werewolves, full moon, witches, owls, things of the night … yes, definitely the full moon.

The evil eyes of Sir Oswald suddenly flashed into my mind. Briefly, I squeezed my own eyes tight – willing the vision away. But through skin and flesh, his eyes bored, like a dentist's drill searching for decay.

'No,' I whispered.

'Yess,' he seemed to hiss.

If dragons could shapeshift, and Henry really was one – then who was the other?

'Yess,' the voice hissed on.

But that was nuts. How could Sir Oswald be the other? He was Henry's uncle not his enemy.

What had Granny Jones said? '*Do not underestimate Sir Oswald. He intends to harm you.*' And that warning muttered into the hearth? '*The Red one must always battle the White.*'

The Red must always battle the White.

Now I understood.

That was it. Henry was the red dragon and Sir Oswald the white.

And for some reason they were locked into some ancient deadly battle. That's why Henry hadn't wanted to get involved with me – because of Sir Oswald. That was why Sir Oswald had singled me out – because of Henry.

Granny was right. I'd got myself into something very scary. And if Sir Oswald was out here now, and he knew I was trying to reach Henry, he'd be stalking me, wouldn't he? Somewhere out there in the shadows …

I took a deep breath. But I'm strong too. I'm Ellie, the Mountain Girl. I wasn't going to be caught out easily. No, Sir Oswald wasn't going to beat me. I started scanning around for shelter, for high rocks to hide behind if the moon broke. (I was pretty sure there must be a connection between the moon and the dragons.) If moonlight streamed through, I was probably in more danger, if only from being seen more easily. And that was something else – the eyesight of dragons. Suddenly I realised that was how Henry had seen me, how he'd watched the rescue, how he knew where I was, even through storm and snow. Dragons must have exceptional eyesight. I shuddered. How on earth was I going to evade those hawk eyes of Sir Oswald?

But I *was* going to evade them.

I figured out how far up Snowdon I'd come. If I could make it up to Clogwyn Du'r Arddu, Arthur's Black Cliff, then I could stay hidden in its shadow. After that I could double back to Halfway House. I didn't think any living thing, dragon or not, could see through the gloom of the Black Cliff. Plus there was thicker cloud cover higher up the mountain. No moonshine would peep through there.

That was the route I'd take. I'd pass Halfway House, fool Oswald, who was bound to be watching the lower slopes for movement, and double back from above.

I felt Sir Oswald's hold over my mind weaken. I could beat him. I would beat him. Even if he was out there right now searching for me.

I switched on my torch and scanned for shelter. Then quickly I switched it off again. Darkness can work both ways you know. It can camouflage the predator, it can hide the prey.

And then I set myself to work. I climbed steadily, sleeper by sleeper, up the rail track. The air was so cold. My lips felt tight, like they were going to crack. I tried not to lick them. That makes them chap even quicker. Plus you lick off all your lip gloss. My boots creaked in the snow. There was no breeze. Everything hung sharp, icy. I felt like I was the only moving thing in the universe. Except I wasn't, was I? Up above me, just behind the clouds, were dragons. And they were no longer circling over the summit, were they? No, they were out hunting.

Two dragons or one?

No, only one.

Henry was waiting for me at Halfway House.

Henry wasn't out there hunting me.

Was he?

I watched the clouds like I was training to be a meteorologist. At the slightest suggestion they'd break, I got ready to hurl myself behind a railway sleeper and drag snow over me. That's the great thing about snow: it's like a blanket; it can cover you. It's like water; it can hide your scent. But I practised stealth. I tried to walk as quietly as I could. Burying myself in snow was The Last Resort. I might be trying to avoid a dragon, but I didn't want to look a mess in the process. So I moved noiselessly up the track. If I could hear them, they could hear me.

I pushed down my jacket hood, tucked back the ear flaps on my woolly hat, and trained my ears. Not just my ears, I sharpened all my senses, until I was listening with my eyes, my nose, my mind, even with all the tiny hairs that still prickled on the back of my neck. I promised myself: *I will win this game*. I will hear you first. Even the slightest sound will give me a head start. And in that great silence I did start hearing things.

At first it was just a faint rustling, a stirring in the darkness. My pulse beat faster. Maybe I was wrong. Maybe that was only the snow cracking, the ice cliffs settling. The mountain shuffling, as the Snow God bedded down for another polar night. I froze, every sense alert, waiting for that micro sound. Behind the cracking – there it came again. What was it? Thick muffled beats pounding against dry air? It wasn't my imagination. It was the distant thrash of giant leathery wings.

I looked up. The cloud hung dense. There was nothing to see, only bleak slopes, snow-covered grassland, a few gnarled and twisted thorn trees. But he *was* up there. Quickly I dived behind a railway sleeper, pulling snow frantically over me. The beating sounded louder for a minute, closer … and then it passed, faded away into the silence. Slowly I rose, shaking the snow off, mentally chalking up Round One to me.

Then I crept forward. I stayed in the shadow of the mountain, listening. Only the white glow of snow lit my way. A wind started. It moaned down the valleys, an unwelcome, eerie howling. It swelled and wailed, until I was sure that any muffled beat of sinew or skin would be swallowed up by the lament of icy air. But it offered me a small advantage; it would hide any sound I made too.

The wind was bad news though. Soon it was a gale. My scarf flew wide. Tufts of old yellowing grass shed their frozen load. Snow and ice twisted in little whirlwinds around me. The wind tore at my hair and face. (So much for hours battling with the straighteners. ☹) And I abandoned any hope of looking amazing when I got there.

Just let me get there.

I scanned around, looking for cover, anything that I could hide behind. The railway sleepers were becoming treacherous. (Already I'd slipped, banged my knee, hopped around, tried not to whimper.) Moreover the rail track was heading out on to open hillside. *I had to find cover.* So I clambered over the fence, and set out across country.

I was going to put my plan into action.

I was going to take the roundabout route, and head for the Black Cliff.

The going would be slower. And it was a much longer way round of course. But I figured Sir Oswald wouldn't expect me to climb nearly all the way up the mountain and then double back to Halfway House. And that consoled me it was a much safer route too. Because – in my thinking – if he was out here hunting me, then he knew I was out here too. And that meant he knew why and where I was going. So of course he'd expect me to take the Llanberis Path.

And that's where he'd be watching.

And that's where I wouldn't be.

Ha ha. Round Two to me (hopefully).

So I was going to take no path at all. I was going to head across the upper pastures towards the Ranger Path and then go cross-country up the mountain.

It wasn't easy. No tracks guided me between boulders, and it was all thick snow and undergrowth. But I made it to the shadow of Moel Cynghorion without hearing any more wing beats. Gratefully I melted into its darkness, and then struck out for the Black Cliff.

All the time I was thinking about Henry (of course). How he'd told me to be sure to get to him before nightfall. How he'd tried to warn me about his uncle. It was my fault I was late. And right now he was probably worrying and worrying. Granny Jones had him all wrong, didn't she?

And I was thinking too about Granny's story, trying to piece it together – and remembering the words of Cecil Howard, the Sea King lieutenant – and all the old stories

– those girls lost on the mountain for a start. They'd been rescued, though, hadn't they? But somewhere in the back of my mind, I remembered other stories about girls who hadn't. Loved ones who had gone missing – a long time ago, before I was born. They were never found, and that was odd. Even if someone died on the mountain, they'd find them in the end – when the snow melted – at the bottom of a cliff, under the ice of the llyn. Nobody had ever mentioned anything about dragons. The girls had run off to London or Cardiff (at least Cardiff) with somebody or other, long ago …

The wind dropped. The clouds thinned. I reached the Black Cliff. You know I never, ever thought I'd be grateful to enter the shadow of them, but as I slipped into their darkness I breathed a sigh of relief, and said a silent thanks to the great Snow God. Through their gloom I skirted the llyn on the north-west side and got ready to cut across dale, back to Halfway House.

How I longed to be there, to be safe within its walls, to be sitting beside the fire with Henry.

I left the shadows and the gloom of Clogwyn Du'r Arddu. I struck out for Halfway House, and I got a fair distance before my luck ran out. Suddenly the clouds parted. The moon bleached a circle in the mist, and from up above me came the rush of skeletal wings.

Holy Crap! The dragon!

'*ELLIE!*' someone yelled, '*RUN!*'

Without warning, a terrible shriek ripped into the sky. A rush of air belched through the cloud. It exploded down on to the mountainside. The force of it blacked out even the moon, and hurled me to the ground.

'*ELLIE!*' Henry's voice.

Dazed I looked up. Halfway House?

I staggered to my feet, brushing the snow off. Another shriek. Heart pounding, I ran. The mountain ahead was blasted smooth. I skidded in my tracks. The place had turned into an ice rink! I bent down and plucked at a shred of something. A thin white stalk which crumbled at my touch.

'*ELLIE!*'

Above me the gristly flapping started again. The wind picked up. It rushed down the mountainside. The clouds rolled back. The moon glinted through. I hesitated. I had to cross an ice rink!

Gingerly I stepped forward. I felt the silver charm burn against my skin. Underfoot the ground crackled, treacherous, slippery. Then I skidded, sliding out of control.

The door to Halfway House flew open. Henry rushed out.

He took one look up at the sky and bellowed, '*No!*' With supernatural speed he seemed to skim the earth towards me. And suddenly he was at my side.

I'm not sure what happened next. A dark shape seemed to burst through the clouds, except that it wasn't dark, it was white – like a huge ghostly phantom.

Except it wasn't a phantom.

It was fast and leathery and lethal and cold. It had huge thrashing wings, claw-like feet and talons that flashed like daggers.

And I remember thinking. This is it then.

And smacking into the mountain.

 Eighteen

ELLIE'S PHONE 27th December 22.30

Status: ... *no signal ... no signal ... no signal ... no signal ...*

PENDING ... Recent updates between Ellie and George:

George

Ellie you weren't serious about going up to HH were you?

George

Ellie?

My nose hit the ground. I bit my own lip and tasted blood. I imagined those razor talons ripping down. But before they could lay into me, Henry swept me up.

I felt his arms around me. He held me close, his grip like iron. And it hurt. Really hurt! But I didn't care. He wasn't a dragon. And he'd rescued me.

And then somehow we were at the door of Halfway House. I don't know how we got there. The dark bulk of Ugain Garnedd spun before me. The snowfields of the western ridges turned upside down. My arm felt dislocated, and all the while there was that terrible shrieking.

Henry kicked open the door. A wail of wind swept past. The shrieking rose to a crescendo until it was so loud, I thought my eardrums would burst. And then we were inside. And Henry was crushing me to him, and I was struggling to breathe.

As I spluttered in his arms, he uncoiled one hand and held my face and bent his head and stared at me.

And then (predictably) I couldn't breathe at all.

His eyes searched my face. 'You ok?' he said.

I nodded (just about).

'I'm so sorry … ' he said, as he let me catch my breath. 'I shouldn't have asked you to come … '

'*What was THAT?*' I cried, heart thudding, legs as soft as boiled spaghetti.

But Henry shook his head, and didn't answer.

I tried to stop trembling. Which Was Not Easy. Because outside there was something truly HORRIBLE, and it wasn't the wind or the weather. It was something that flung itself repeatedly against the walls of the cottage. It bashed at the roof, scraping it with a screeching that pushed my ragged nerves nearly over the edge. It screamed as if it were mortally wounded. But most disturbing of all, between the screaming, it seemed to chuckle, as if it was enjoying every minute too.

'*It's going to break in and kill us,*' I shouted. Desperately I looked around the room to see where we could hide.

'He can't,' said Henry.

'*Oh my God!*' I cried. '*Of course it will.*'

Henry dragged me to the hearth.

There was a fire already lit. The walls danced with golden shadows. Henry pointed at the plaque above the mantel. '*Halfway House … a safe house … where travellers can take refuge … magical world of Snowdonia.*'

'You're safe,' he said, holding me tight. 'He can't enter here. This is the Halfway House. It stands on the site where Merlin met Vortigern. It's stronger than him. He can't get in here, however hard he tries.'

I looked at Henry then. Full In The Eyes. (Trying not to see the soft curve of his lips.) 'What. The. Hell. Is. Going. On?' I said. '*For God's sake tell me!*'

Henry crossed the room and tried the door, made sure it was firmly shut. Then he returned, held me close and looked at me gently, almost sadly.

'*Henry?*' I screamed.

From outside came another GHASTLY shriek, a gnashing of bone and skin and a howl that echoed down the mountain. Henry held up his hand.

'Don't move. Don't say anything.' Henry warned.

The thing outside let out another scream this time of real fury.

'What. Is. It?' I said, determined now to understand everything.

'Sshhh.'

I was about to open my mouth and demand an explanation, but something in his tone stopped me. He seemed to be gritting his teeth, concentrating.

There was a new battering on the door. And a voice calling, '*Let me in. Let me in.*'

Holy Shit! What was going on now?

'*What is it?*' I clutched at Henry. The calling came again. Henry bent his head, listening intently.

'*Let me in.*' The voice was weirdly distorted like the wind itself was wailing through it. '*Let me in.*'

I let go of Henry and cowered down on the bench, trembling. Was this pleading voice some new kind of trick? A shiver of horror ran over me. I imagined that THING, shifting shapes, changing voices … only one stone wall between us and it …

Henry raised his finger to his lips, threw a glance at me. Then he tiptoed back to the threshold.

The assault on the door grew louder. The tone of the battering changed. It sounded as if iron was striking the wooden panels. In horror I saw one plank completely splinter and the sparkle of metal shine into the room.

I flipping FREAKED. If you think dragons are sweet little creatures on kids TV, FORGET IT. There Was Nothing Sweet Or Little About Those Steel Talons Tearing Through The Ancient Boards Of That Door.

'I thought you said we were safe – ' I started.

In the firelight his beautiful face was as cold as stone. 'Just stay quiet,' he said.

How could I? The thing outside was screeching and screaming. Its shrieks echoed into the cottage. I could barely hear myself think! The floor shuddered as each crash of dragon-tonnage shook the whole side of the mountain.

'It's going to break through!' I screamed.

'It's impossible … the magic here is too deep … ' said Henry, but I could see he was no longer sure.

I wanted to believe him, but I saw the pounding the door was taking. Nothing could withstand such a battering. In front of that fire I grew cold.

Henry stood very still.

Both of us stared at the door.

It bulged inward and squealed.

Wood and hinges shattered.

Henry sucked in air.

I watched. My eyes stretched. The door burst open.

And with a sound like railway engines screeching to a halt, something fell headlong into the room.

Nineteen

I don't know what I was expecting, maybe a monstrous claw, maybe a fire-breathing snout, maybe the whole scaly shoulder of a dragon – but definitely not a person.

And definitely not George.

It took a few seconds to register – I can tell you.

But it was George. All six foot two of him, with his pale gold hair, done in a Viking plait and his usually mischievous eyes looking deeply shocked.

Henry crouched down, as if at any moment he was ready to do something terrible. I just froze.

'Sorry to bust in like that,' George said, 'on a private meeting an' all,' he grinned his famous George grin. It stretched painfully across his face, and his eyes were not twinkling, 'Looks like you've got a little problem out there.'

At last I breathed. (I hadn't even realised I was holding

my breath.) Henry breathed too. And I swear the air around us crackled with sparks.

And then George stood up. And that's when I noticed he was bleeding.

Badly.

The whole side of his jacket was ripped wide and soaked red.

I raced across the room to help him. My throat dried up. *What if he was MAJORLY hurt?* (What on earth was he doing here?) With a gulp, I realised, it was my fault ... if I hadn't told him I was going to Halfway House ... if I hadn't been so pathetic ... more or less begged him to come ...

A blast of freezing air whirled into the room. Henry ran to fix the door shut.

With my hands all trembling, I helped George to the fireside. 'Ouch,' he said as he tried to sit down on the bench. 'Your bloomin' pet got me.'

Nervously, I removed George's jacket. It was soaked with blood and fell away in sodden red ribbons. I couldn't stop my hands shaking. I peeled the cloth away. George flinched. Fresh bright red outpourings followed every movement.

'I'm so sorry,' I whispered. 'I didn't know.' (Which wasn't strictly true, because I had sort of known.) But I really was sorry. *And* I felt supernaturally guilty. *What if he bled to death?*

Life Without George?

He couldn't die.

'Aw, give over,' said George faking a smile, 'I'll bleed for you any time, Elles.'

Only I didn't want him to bleed for me. Apart from it being just too *horrible*, he was Bang Out Of Order.

All I'd wanted was a bit of company up the hill. *What on Earth did he think he was doing, taking it upon himself to check up on me?* I was going to have to spell it out to him: U-N-A-V-A-I-L-A-B-L-E (in caps and underlined).

That's if he ever made it through the night.

But obviously I couldn't really say that with him sitting there bleeding.

George moaned and doubled up in pain. 'You're going to be ok,' I started, 'Just try not to move … '

Get the bleeding under control.

George couldn't die.

Press something against the wounds.

He was my best friend.

'George,' I said, 'Don't you dare die. You hear me? You Do Not Have Permission. Here, press this against your side as hard as you can.' I passed him the makeshift pad I'd been folding up. (My Henry scarf. That's how much I love you, George.)

All the while Henry stood in the shadows, looking at me, a curious expression on his face. What he was thinking? Was he angry? Did he think I'd asked George to come? Did he imagine I didn't trust him? His dark eyes gleamed. And at that moment he looked every inch the Royal Prince.

George groaned again, and I turned to him. There was no time to explain, George needed instant attention.

I removed the last bits of bloody cloth, and set about examining George's wounds. All down the left side of his body, his clothes had been ripped away. A great raking claw line had shredded everything – shearing right through his sheepskin coat, slicing his leather jacket, straight through his fleecy sweatshirt, right down to the skin, but luckily not much further. Gently I peeled off the last fragments of fabric. Under everything, I was surprised to find the skin over his chest, although bloodstained, unbroken. That was one good thing. But where the talons had got through, on his side, over his ribs, it was a different story; one gash hung open like a gaping mouth and two others looked serious.

'Christ,' I said. 'You need stitches, one inch deeper and you'd have been sliced like a tomato.'

George grinned up at me, his face pallid, sweaty, 'Wanna

kiss me better?' he whispered.

'Don't be silly,' I snapped, giving myself permission to feel narked now George Was Not About To Die. (Thankfully.) 'We need to clean up this wound and cover it.'

But I didn't need to clean it much. The tears were sharp and even, as if they'd been made by a kitchen knife. Henry nodded at me as if to say: You fix up George and I'll sort out this door.

By the half light I tended to George. I found some duct tape from my bag and improvised butterfly stitches. 'What happened?' I demanded as I pressed the lips of the gashes tight and taped them shut. 'And don't move.'

George bit his lip and shivered. The flames danced. The thing outside pounded on the walls again. I tried to be as gentle as I could, but I knew it hurt. George didn't flinch or complain, and when my fingers trembled so much I couldn't hold the wounds tight, he said, 'That's it, Elles, that feels so much better. You're a real natural at this,' until I felt tears filling up my eyes, and had to angrily brush them away, so I could see where to put the next bit of tape.

At last I managed to close the worst gash. It wasn't as bad as it'd first looked. The bleeding slowed to a sluggish oozing. And I pressed little wads of rolled up T-shirt against his side to stop even that.

'You should have seen the other guy,' said George.

Henry laughed at that. 'Hope you really gave it to him!'

'We need to get you to a hospital soon,' I said.

'Teach him to mess with the best,' said George.

Henry gave him a mock salute, clicked his heels and bowed.

I frowned. That wound needed proper stitching. The duct tape might peel off; the bleeding might start again. I tore the rest of the blood-soaked T-shirt into a bandage. 'Stop it both of you,' I said. 'George needs urgent medical care and how is he going to get it, with *that THING* outside?'

Neither of them had a reply.

'And I want to know What's Going On Right Now, or I'll … ' (I couldn't actually think of anything to bully them with, so I tied the bits of T-shirt together, tugging the knots tight.)

'Love it when you get bossy,' murmured George.

'Hold still,' I muttered and wound the bandage around him.

George flinched. Henry let out a chuckle, then he got the table from the kitchen and up-ended it, and wedged it against the broken bits of door.

'Sorry, bro,' said George, 'the door-bell wasn't working.'

Henry finished patching up the doorway. The noise from outside became muffled.

'George,' I said, when Henry returned to the fireside. 'What were you doing out there?'

'Fighting a dragon,' he said

I gulped. That wasn't quite what I meant. 'You're stupid,' I said anyway. 'It could've killed you.'

'Nearly did,' he said. 'If only you guys had opened the door a bit faster.'

Outside the shrieking lessened and seemed to rumble away. Henry took off his jacket, stripped off his own sweat-shirt, and handed it to George. 'Cover up your six pack, George, before I have to kill you myself,' he said.

But George couldn't raise his left shoulder to put it on. So I had to uncross my arms and help him. When I'd successfully guided the sweatshirt over his head and stretched it out, so he could get his arm into it, George flashed a warm smile at Henry. 'Thanks,' he said, 'you're all right for a toff, you know,' and tugged the remnants of his coat back around him, still shivering, but looking a lot more comfortable.

I stood there glaring at them both.

'Did you wound him?' asked Henry, a hopeful gleam in his eye.

'You bet,' said George, 'right now he's got my second-best axe imbedded in his sirloin.'

'Wow!' Henry looked surprised.

George grinned, 'I'm no lightweight with an axe, you know.'

'Stop it, George,' I said. Then I turned to Henry. 'Why Is There A Dragon Outside?'

'There is so much you don't know,' Henry sighed.

'Better tell me then,' I said. There was no way he was going to fob me off with any 'Not Now Maybe Later' excuses.

He shuffled his feet. 'Will you promise me something first, Ellie?' he said.

'No deal,' I said, nearly giving in to those huge dark eyes. 'Start talking.'

'Better tell her, old boy,' said George. 'She has a way of getting what she wants.'

'And *Why* Are *You* Here?' I snapped at George. He wasn't going to escape from Question Time either.

'Just checking you arrived safely,' said George, with a butter-wouldn't-melt expression plastered all over his cute face.

'I just don't know where to start,' said Henry, leaning his chin on his hand.

'Try the beginning,' I said tartly.

'Ok,' said Henry, his eyes suddenly sad, as if the whole world was about to end. He took in a deep breath and bit his lip – opened his beautiful mouth – and said nothing.

'Right,' I said, because I wasn't going to have any of That.

'Do you know *why* there's a dragon outside?'

Henry nodded.

George struggled to pat his shoulder encouragingly.

'Well?' I demanded.

'It's a long story ... '

'We've got all night.' I said, narrowing up my eyes and plonking myself down on a log.

'If only you would promise ... ' he started.

'Go on,' said George. 'Can't be that bad.'

'You. Be. Quiet,' I snapped to George. 'You *shouldn't* be here, *and* you went up against a dragon with your second-best axe, which in my books makes you Totally Psychiatrically Certifiable.'

'You mean, I should have risked my best axe and left Granny without firewood for the rest of the winter?' said George, all eyebrows raised in mock innocence.

'Stop it,' I said 'Going up against a dragon with any kind of axe is INSANE.'

'I wasn't trying to fight it,' said George defensively. 'I was trying to check you were ok. It started fighting me! I'd have been quite happy to have just given it a nod and a how'd'ya do,' said George. 'And actually it didn't really start fighting me. It just looked at me and scooped me up and flung me away. And it was so cold. Is it made of ice or something?

Anyway I played dead, then crawled round the corner and used my axe on the door. I only chucked my axe at it when the door gave way!'

'You wounded him, though,' said Henry, full of admiration.

'Right,' I said turning back to Henry. 'Start talking.' I tried very hard not to look into his eyes in case I got lost in them and went all weak-kneed and wobbly.

George rested by the fire. Henry shuffled his feet on the flag-stoned floor (AGAIN).

'You see,' he said. 'Like I said, it's complicated.'

'Then you better get on with it,' I said. Henry looked at me and I nearly melted. He was so impossibly beautiful. But I steeled myself and clamped my teeth tight. He *was* going to tell me *everything*. At that moment I was quite ready to DIE for him, but I needed to know why.

'A long time ago there were two dragons,' sighed Henry, 'a white one and a red one and they were fighting.'

'Long? As in?' I asked.

'Prehistoric,' answered George. 'Time of King Arthur and Fred Flintstone ... '

'Oh! So you're telling the story now, are you?' I challenged George.

'Ow!' said George ducking his head down and pretending

he hadn't heard me. 'Ow! Ow! My ribs! My ribs!'

'Try not laughing,' I said unsympathetically.

'When the dragons fought they shrieked. Their shrieking made the cattle die and the grass wither … ' said Henry.

'Yeah, yeah, I know that legend,' I said. 'The people couldn't stand it so they found the dragons' lair and poured alcohol into the pool, and the dragons got drunk and the people entombed them in the mountain. End of story. Bye bye dragons.'

Henry looked at me in a strange way.

'Try telling me the truth,' I said.

'But it is the truth, and it wasn't the end, Ellie,' he said. 'It was only the beginning. Imagine it: entombed under the mountain day after day, every minute cramped up in darkness, the air stiflingly heavy, the earth thick around you … ' he looked at me with an expression of horror.

For a second my mind flicked to my dad, pressed up against that cliff in the Himalaya, waiting, dying, and a wave of ice seemed to engulf me.

'Imagine the dragons confined in that small space, breathing each other's stinking exhalations, compressed against scales, against bony claws, no room to stretch, wings stiff and aching, no food, no water other than a tainted pool. And always the need to fight.'

'Jolly,' said George.

'Dragons don't die, and they don't sleep, you know, they go on and on living, when life is torture, until men forget them. Imagine it: trapped, squashed against your worst enemy, pressed close to the one element you can't stand for one is made of ice and the other of fire. Imagine it hour after hour, day after day, year after year ... '

I blinked. I hadn't thought of it like that.

'And I wish you'd just promise me ... '

'Jesus,' said George, 'Now I'm starting to feel sorry for dragons!'

'Please finish the story then,' I said, 'because as sure as hell that dragon is not under the mountain any more.'

'Well,' sighed Henry, 'A man called Vortigern decided to build his castle over their lair, and their dragon hearts filled with hope. They made a desperate plan to shake the earth so much that the castle walls would fall. They pledged to work together, for once, to fight and fight but not to maim, but to shake the ground forever until someone came and released them.'

'Hang on a minute,' I said 'It sounds like they teamed up. I thought you said they were fighting; why exactly were they fighting?'

Henry ignored me. 'They shook the mountain, and the

castle fell down. Day after day Vortigern tried to rebuild it, and night after night the dragons destroyed it, until the people claimed the place was cursed.'

George nodded, 'I know this part of the story too,' he said, 'Look it's written up there.'

I looked up again at the plaque over the fire place.

HALFWAY HOUSE

HALFWAY HOUSE, A PRIVATELY OWNED MOUNTAIN SHELTER, STANDS ON THE SITE OF THE LEGENDARY MEETING OF KING VORTIGERN WITH THE GREAT MAGICIAN MYRDDIN EMRYS (OR MERLIN, AS HE IS CALLED IN ENGLISH). IT WAS TO HALFWAY HOUSE THAT MERLIN WAS BROUGHT, FROM MOEL CYNGHORION (THE HILL OF THE COUNCILLORS), BY VORTIGERN'S ADVISORS TO RESOLVE THE CURSE HANGING OVER DINAS AFFARAON. MERLIN UNFOLDED THE MYSTERY OF THE WORMS OF DINAS AFFARAON TO VORTIGERN. THE MOUNTAIN ON WHICH HE PROVED HIS MIGHTY POWER WAS CALLED IN AFTERTIME DINAS EMRYS INSTEAD OF DINAS AFFARAON, IN HONOUR OF MERLIN. HALFWAY HOUSE HAS LONG BEEN KNOWN AS A SAFE HOUSE, A PLACE WHERE TRAVELLERS CAN TAKE REFUGE FROM THE REAL AS WELL AS THE MAGICAL WORLD OF SNOWDONIA.

'Yes, the "*worms*" of Dinas Affaraon,' said Henry sorrowfully. 'Was it their fault they were born dragons?'

'Vortigern's councillors advised him to sacrifice a fatherless virgin to the dragons. And they brought Merlin before him, claiming he fitted the job description,' quoted George. 'We actually did a PowerPoint on it in junior school, and I was the presenter.'

I rolled my eyes at George. I didn't know whether he was helping or not. 'I want to know WHY there is a dragon outside,' I said, 'and neither of you has explained that, so far.'

'I'm getting there, Ellie,' said Henry. 'I did say it was a … '

'I'll help you out, bro,' said George, turning his blue eyes on me. 'Elles,' he said, 'you're pretty – probably the prettiest girl in Snowdonia – but you gotta realise us guys are weaklings in the sight of such great beauty, so you gotta treat us gently. We probably forget why we're telling the story at all – every time we look at you, you know: Instant Juvenile Male Amnesia. So, my lil' London rude-girl (George is sooo funny when he does a London accent) you gotta be patient and listen to the man's story, innit?'

I suppressed a smile and squinted at him. Right now George wasn't going to charm his way into or out of anything. Henry's mouth twitched. He looked like he was trying to stifle a giggle. George looked round all wide eyed.

'Merlin's an old man with a pointy hat,' I said. 'How did he fit the description? And what's he doing in this story anyway?'

'No, he was a boy then,' broke in Henry, 'He was young and quite ... ' he suddenly shut his mouth as if he'd given something away. 'Merlin told Vortigern that sacrifice wouldn't save his castle and he'd be better to dig up the dragons and allow them to fight.' Henry stopped. The flickering light of the fire lit up the lines of his face. He was so impossibly handsome my heart missed a beat.

'Yeah,' said George, 'time for the proper battle scene: WHAM! BAM! POW! WOW!'

Yes, George is right. He IS juvenile. I crossed my arms. 'I'm being very patient,' I said, 'all I want to know is why there's a dragon out there trying to kill us.'

'Kill you,' said George. 'It wasn't very interested in killing me.'

'The dragons, you see, always want to fight when the sun goes down. It's in their blood and under the mountain there was no sun ... ' Henry frowned.

'Though if he had been trying to kill me, I'd have given him WHAT FOR and KERCHUNK – but I didn't because my first mission was to rescue you ... ' George pulled something that was supposed to be a mean, badass face, but looked more like he was trying not to pee himself.

'So Vortigern dug up the dragons, and … ' said Henry.

'And you haven't explained what they were fighting about, either.' I said.

'The Red Dragon won didn't he?' said George. 'Isn't that why he's on the Welsh flag? Although, now you mention it – I never heard about the WHAM! BAM! POW! WOW! bit.'

'Well that's strange,' I said 'Not only have you *not* explained why there's a dragon out there, but you also don't seem to know much about the legend either.'

'That's it!' said George, as if he'd suddenly realised something. 'They didn't fight did they? That's why there's a White Dragon out there. The Red Dragon never killed him.'

'They fought all right,' muttered Henry.

'Let me get this right,' I said. 'The dragon out there is one of a pair that was buried under the mountain zillions of years ago?'

'And they're still fighting,' Henry said grimly, 'whenever it grows dark.'

'So where's the other one?' I said. I fixed Henry with my best steely eye. I wanted to hear him say it.

Henry stared into the fire, his handsome head sunk in his hands.

'I *really* DON'T get it,' I said. 'Something as big as two dragons cannot stay hidden – even on Snowdon.'

'Yeah, what did happen to the dragons once they got dug up?' added George.

'Well killing dragons isn't simple,' said Henry. 'They don't actually die. So Merlin had to be very clever if the whole of Snowdonia wasn't going to be plagued by shrieking again and Vortigern was going to get to build his castle. So he offered them a choice. Either they go back down under the mountain to that dark torture again, or choose to live out their lives as humans.'

'Cool,' said George, 'Dragon men!'

'And to make sure they'd never be a nuisance, he forbade them to fight in human form. And he forbade them to fight during daylight hours – even in the reflected light of the sun – should they choose to stay as dragons. He wove part of the spell thus:

> ' ... *Not by moonshine, nor by sunlight,*
> *shall the Worms of yr Wyddfa fight.*
> *And if under cave or cliff ye stay*
> *All Dragon strength shall fade away ...* '

'And his magic was greater than theirs, for his powers were young and strong. And to bind them forever, he removed their dragon hearts, and sealed those hearts in enchanted crystal under the mountain.'

'That doesn't sound quite so cool,' said George.

I thought that was kind of nice of Merlin, giving them the chance to become human. He must've had his reasons for not trusting them though (obviously).

'So give. C'mon, what was the rest of the spell?' said George.

'There you can read it for yourself,' said Henry. He removed a golden band from his wrist and passed it to George, who read:

> *'Give your heart to a woman and live as a man,*
> *Or to the lair under Snowdon as fast as you can.'*

'What does it mean?' I asked.

'There's always a catch to spells,' sighed Henry.

'You mean, you had to literally give your heart to a girl to live as a man?' asked George.

'The hearts were encased in crystal,' said Henry, 'so, yes.'

'So the Red Dragon gave his heart to a girl and became a man and lived and died and RIP?' I said.

'No.' replied Henry.

'And the White Dragon didn't give his heart to a girl and somehow got out from under the mountain?'

'No, again.'

'So WHAT happened?' I said puzzled.

'The White Dragon did not want to age and die, but he didn't want to live under the mountain either. He wanted the best of everything, so he appealed to the Stars, to the eternal constellation of Draco that winds itself around the Pole Star. He appealed *against* the magic of Merlin. And Draco, the constellation of the Dragons – so old and powerful – showed him a way to cheat Merlin's spell by twisting the words around.

> *'Give a woman to your heart and live as a man*
> *Or to the lair under Snowdon as fast as you can.'*

'Give a woman to your heart?' I repeated.

'Sneaky,' said George.

'Evil,' said Henry.

'What exactly does giving a woman to your heart mean?' I said.

'It means sacrificing a girl to his Heart's Crystal,' said Henry.

I jumped up from the log, like it was burning.

There was a terrible silence. 'The girl on the mountain, on Christmas Day ... ?'

'One of the ones that got away.'

'The girl that disappeared way back in Granny's childhood?'

257

'One that didn't,' said Henry.

'But the girl on Christmas morning?' I said, 'She said a boy lured her, asked her to go somewhere warm with him … ?'

'It was me and I wasn't luring her. I was trying to save her, to keep her warm, to get her help, to rob him of his prey … I'm always trying to save them. I heat the very boulders under them, to keep them alive, if I have to. And he is always trying to capture them and chain them in the lair, ready for the Hour of Draco.'

I could feel the blood draining away from my face. All those years I'd wandered over the mountain feeling so safe, feeling so free, all those years there'd been danger under every rock, death behind every peak …

'And I fight for them even up until that eleventh hour.'

'But if,' I said, 'that's the White Dragon out there. Where's the red one?' I wanted now to hear it PROPERLY from his lips.

Henry turned his face to me, his eyes beaten, pleading. Telling me he could no more speak the name of the Red Dragon than fly.

Except he could fly, couldn't he?

'Ok,' I said weakening. (Those Eyes Should Come With A Health Warning!) I took a deep breath: 'I'll help you.

Just nod. That's all.'

George moaned a bit, as he lifted his arm to pat Henry's shoulder again. 'Go for it, boyo,' he said. 'Like I said, she has a way of getting to the truth.'

I took a deep breath. 'Did the Red Dragon use the same cheat as the white one?'

'No,' said Henry.

I breathed a sigh of relief. I wasn't about to be sacrificed.

'Did the Red Dragon give his heart out and die?'

'No.'

I breathed another sigh of relief. So the Red Dragon never found his true love.

'Is the Red Dragon very near us now?' My throat was dry and my voice barely squeaked out.

Henry nodded.

'In this room?'

Henry nodded again.

All around the room the shadows danced crimson red in the firelight.

'Are you:'

Henry looked at me his eyes dark as coals.

'a) human

'b) dragon

'c) none of the above?'

Henry twisted his mouth, but he did not shake or nod.

'Oh!' I said,

'Are you:

'a) human

'b) dragon

'c) *both* of the above?'

A slight nod.

'Which?'

'*Both*,' he whispered.

I nodded. It was enough. Henry's face looked more impossibly beautiful than ever. George wisely kept his mouth shut.

'I couldn't find anyone to love me,' he said, 'Not enough to keep me from turning back into a monster.'

'I don't understand,' I whispered. 'What about the spell?'

'I couldn't find the one to give my heart to. The one I could love forever.'

'But?'

'So I had to protect the world from myself.'

'What did you do?'

'For hundreds of years I've lain under the mountain, waiting.'

'Waiting?'

'Waiting for the right girl.'

Twenty

I gulped. I pressed my lips together. My pulse felt weak. My hand flew to my chest. 'Henry?' I managed.

He came to my side, put his hand on my shoulder. 'I'm sorry Ellie,' he whispered, 'I tried to stay away from you. I ... '

'I know,' I whispered back.

'I should never have ... ' he said.

'Don't ... ' I mouthed shaking my head.

'But, Draco help me, how *could* I stay away?'

'I ... ' I began again.

He paced the room and punched the stone wall.

'No! Listen,' I said. 'I don't care what you are. I don't care.'

'You don't care that I'm a monster?' he said, his eyes wider and darker than they ever should be. 'That I'm driven to fight and shriek and terrify?'

George coughed. I spun round and looked at him. My eyes saying: 'No George! NOT! NOW!' He looked back at me, his eyes saying: 'I can't stay away from you either, Ellie.' There was something so desperate, so pleading in them, but he saw my face and dropped his gaze. He groaned and adjusted his position on the low bench.

I swung my head quickly between the two of them: George and Henry.

'Ellie,' Henry whispered, 'You've got to promise me something?'

I looked back at him. I'd promise him anything. Everything he needed.

'Promise you'll stay here, in Halfway House, for three days.'

'Three days?' I squeaked in surprise. Quickly, I dropped my voice. 'What on earth for?'

'Just promise.'

'Not until you tell me why.'

'Trust me?' his voice pleaded.

'I do,' I said, 'I trust you to tell me WHY.'

The time for secrets was over. I knew he was the Red Dragon, Y Ddraig Goch; I knew he was Sir Henry Pendragon de Clare, Lord of Chandos and Viscount of Carnarvon; I'd faced the worst, there couldn't be anything else, could there?

George straightened up and groaned again. 'Yep – you better tell me why too. You don't want me to have to go an' fetch my best axe, do ya?'

Jokes apart, there was something in his voice that told me he wasn't feeing so friendly towards Henry all of a sudden.

Henry crossed back to the bench, sat down and stretched his hands out to the fire. 'You've got to stay here,' he said. He took a deep breath. 'The whole point of everything was to get you here and keep you here.'

'Get me here? Keep me here?' I sat back down on my log puzzled. 'Look at the place, Henry, I *can't* stay here.'

'You think I'd have jeopardised your life, asked you to come here, for anything less? Do you think I'd ever have forgiven myself – for risking you – even for one second, unless I had to? You were supposed to come here safely in daylight and then stay here.'

'Hang on a minute,' said George 'You knew the dragon was out there, and you still asked her to come?'

Henry turned his flawless face, now as white as ice, to George. A blue flame of defiance rippled in his eyes. 'Once he'd seen her, I had no other choice.'

'Once who'd seen me?' I looked questioningly at Henry. But already I knew. I remembered those piercing eyes, that hooked nose, those thin hands; I saw again those silver eyebrows, felt their menace.

'Sir Oswald,' I whispered.

Henry brought his head up sharply, the muscles on the side of his jaw tightened as he looked at me.

'Your uncle? Isn't it?' I said. Those sinister eyes, that predatory stare ...

'Yes,' whispered Henry. 'Sir Oswald Pendragon de Clare is the one outside.' Henry hung his head. 'He is the White Dragon of Wessex.'

'And he means to kill me.' I could hear the tiredness in my voice.

Henry raised his eyes and looked squarely at me. 'He means to sacrifice you to his Heart Crystal.'

'What!' cried George clutching his side, voice shrill.

Henry swung round and addressed George. 'It's my fault. He saw how I felt about Ellie. He saw that for the first time ever, since the people of Wales put us under the mountain, he was in grave peril.'

I tried to figure out what he meant.

'Why?' said George.

'That is not a subject fit to discuss in front of a lady,' said Henry, suddenly his full regal self. 'But man to man I will tell you.' He bent down and whispered something to George. George clenched his fists as he listened.

I tapped my foot, trying to think up some smart comment about 'fit' behaviour.

Henry straightened up and turned to me. 'I am sorry to whisper in your presence. Please be assured my words were nothing but full of respect for you.'

'What did you say?'

But Henry changed the subject and I could see pursuing it further was useless. I looked at George and raised an eyebrow. He scowled back and changed the subject too. 'So your name's Pendragon?' he said.

'My royal name,' said Henry.

'In Welsh, 'pen' means head,' said George. 'Pendragon means The Head Dragon.'

There was an awkward silence.

'Henry means Home Ruler.' said Henry. 'In Welsh it's Harri.'

The Home Ruler: Head Dragon of Wales. He really was Y Ddraig Goch.

All of us went quiet. Even the noise outside stopped, as if Sir Oswald Pendragon de Clare was listening too.

'So he means to kill me?' I said.

'You are the one he's chosen,' said Henry, his voice as hard as diamonds.

I did not mind the hardness, but he said it with such

inevitability. A lump started, it grew in my stomach until I felt a bit ill. I wasn't scared of any dragon, but that look of finality on Henry's face terrified me. I fell silent and looked into the heart of the fire where the coals burned red.

'Well at least tell me why I need to stay here?' I said.

'This place is protected. He cannot get to you here. Look, see the plaque, look at the fireplace, look at the herbs.' Henry waved his hand at the room.

I looked again at the plaque:

HALFWAY HOUSE HAS LONG BEEN KNOWN AS A SAFE HOUSE, A PLACE WHERE TRAVELLERS CAN TAKE REFUGE FROM THE REAL AS WELL AS THE MAGICAL WORLD OF SNOWDONIA.

I looked at the stone dragons carved into the hearth. I looked at the four corners of the room, carved into the stone work of the cornices were wild flowers. They looked familiar, like the small bouquet Granny had given me.

'And here too, I can keep my human form – even after dark – and not feel driven to change back into a monster to go out on to the mountain and fight him.'

'And why me?'

'Because … '

The silence lay heavy between us now.

'Just tell her,' said George wearily from the bench.

'Because of me,' said Henry.

'You?' I wanted to get this very clear.

'Yes me.'

'For a toff you didn't get much of a education in speaking in full sentences, did you?' said George.

I felt the tension then. I felt Henry stiffen. I half stood up, worried.

Henry clenched his jaw tighter, glanced angrily into the fire, 'I've been fighting the White Dragon of Wessex since the Dark Ages. He seeks to control all of Wales. He wants to eradicate me. He wants a White Dragon to fly from the Welsh flag. And only when all of Wales mounts his emblem above their roofs and he can have unhindered access to the mountains, to the valleys and the coastlines; only when all the free men of Wales no longer think of themselves as Welsh, will he cease.'

I frowned. Something jogged my memory. 'There *are* flags with White Dragons,' I said. 'There're sort of like the normal flags, but like someone screened in the red only as a background. Sheila has a T-shirt with one on.'

'Yes, he's already been at work,' muttered Henry. 'And yes, the White Dragon of Wessex has always had his own standard. In days of yore it flew from the ramparts of every castle in England.'

George sighed. 'So all this, all my wounds,' he made a painful gesture at his side, 'are tiresome episodes in the Great Chronicles of Henry Versus The White Dragon.'

'It's more than that,' Henry said coldly. 'I have been charged to defend my country. This is no "tiresome" endeavour.'

'Well,' said George, 'If you can manage to speak in a few paragraphs perhaps you'd deign to let us lesser mortals know how you've managed to *not* quite do that and we've ended up here.'

'It's complicated.' Henry stared moodily into the fire. 'Dragons do not die easily, and Oswald was always prepared to be more ruthless. And there are rules that govern magic, too,' he said. 'Once Merlin released us, everything changed. For a start Merlin offered us only *one* chance at living as a man; one life span.'

'And that was a mistake?' asked George.

Henry looked squarely at George. There was flint in eyes. 'Oswald wanted to be a man AND to have immortality – AS WELL AS freedom. Even the great sky serpent, Draco, couldn't change Merlin's offer. Although he did his best by twisting the words of the spell.'

'Yeah, so you said.' George shifted uncomfortably.

So, once in every lifetime a new victim must be sacrificed to the White Dragon's Heart Crystal, so that he can live again as Sir Oswald.'

'For a further lifespan?' I whispered.

'Yes, the White Dragon was given eighteen days at the end of every seventy-two years to find a sacrifice to fulfil the magic. And during that time he can shapeshift at will.'

'Fabulous,' said George.

'And once in a lifetime I get the same chance too.'

'Not to find a sacrifice?' I asked, my voice rising.

'No, no, no,' laughed Henry 'Long, long ago I foreswore that. No, once in every seventy-two years, I get the same eighteen days to find someone to give my heart to. Draco is quite fair in his deeds.'

I took in a deep breath, hardly daring to think about it.

'How long have you got left?' I whispered.

'Until midnight on New Year's Eve,' he sighed.

'But,' I exploded, *that's only three days …* '

'Yes, three days … ' said Henry.

'And you want me to stay here for all twenty-four hours of each one of them!'

'I want you to be safe,' he said. 'I want you to stay out of the claws of Sir Oswald, and now the time is pressing, he will try to snatch you, to get you to the lair at every opportunity.'

'But,' I mused, 'say I did stay here and he didn't get me … '

George snorted something like 'Get you? Over my dead body!'

'Say he didn't. What would he do?'

'He'd take another, he'd hold out for you until the eleventh hour,' said Henry dully. 'But he'd take someone, though he'd have me to reckon with, for I have dedicated myself to stopping him.'

George laughed, 'Bad luck ol' Sport,' he said. 'He gets eighteen days to snatch any woman he can – unless he takes a particular fancy to yours – and you get eighteen days to stop him! That way you never get time to give your heart and he always wins!'

I think he muttered 'loser' under his breath too.

'George!' Oh why had I ever told him I was coming here?

'Tell me,' continued George, 'why seventy-two years? Why not eighty-two, or ninety-two for that matter? We live longer these days, you know.'

'Every seventy-two years is when the procession of the equinoxes moves one degree in the constellation of Draco,' explained Henry. 'The Magic of Draco must be renewed then.'

'Is there a time when Draco's magic fails?' I asked hopefully.

'No,' said Henry 'There are no days when Draco is not above us. He coils himself around the Pole Star. The Magic of Dragons is immortal and unchanging.'

I sighed.

'But there are eighteen days at the end of each procession and that is the time when we can slip between shapes; that is the time in which Oswald must find his sacrifice and I can walk as a man ...'

'Why eighteen days? I don't get it,' said George.

'It is the accumulation of the leap years in the procession of the equinoxes, one day for every fourth year in seventy-two years.'

'Is it a leap year this year?' I asked.

Henry nodded.

George laughed. 'Yeah, I was kind of hoping you might get up steam to ask me ... ' he said, 'Don't you remember I invited you to the rugby club to watch me play on the 29th Feb?' He raised his eyebrows in quick succession and gave me a feeble smile.

I rolled my eyes at George and gave him a Please-Shut-The-Frick-Up look. Then I turned to Henry. 'So if you don't give your heart, you're going to go back under the mountain for another seventy-two years?'

He looked at me and nodded. And my heart started

breaking. *Seventy-two years!* I'd be old. I'd be different. I might be dead.

Henry shot a look into the hearth that would have shattered stone.

'I had from the Feast of St Lucy on the 13th December,' he said. He seemed to be examining the flagstone floor. At length he raised his eyes. 'On midnight of the old year I must go to my Heart's Crystal in the lair and either give it to my true love or prepare to be entombed.'

'So little time,' I said, horrified.

He smiled. 'I would wait in the darkness of the mountain for an eternity and beyond,' he whispered. 'Just to have seen you.'

I caught my breath. My throat tightened. A pain shot into my chest.

'I knew about you,' Henry murmured, as if he was fondly remembering some past time when some secret knowledge had sweetened his darkest hours. 'Centuries ago. I knew you were coming. Dragons have much more than long eyesight. Every day since the hour fell and I was released from the lair, I have been near you.'

'So it *was* you on the Devil's Bridge?'

'I saw you long before that.' He smiled as if the memory pleased him.

'When?'

His eyes lit up. 'On my first day of freedom, I found you on your way home from college. The late afternoon sun sparkled on the gold in your hair.' Spots of colour highlighted his cheek and his face suddenly looked radiant.

'But I didn't see you.'

'No,' he said.

'You were watching me?'

'From that moment I have not ceased watching you.'

'What-*ever*,' said George, acidly. 'This is getting boring. I watch you too you know Elles. I watch you all the time, and what's more I watch OUT for you.'

'And I saw you even before *that*,' said Henry a faraway look coming over his beautiful face.

'How?' I said puzzled.

'In my dreams, he said, 'In my dragonish dreams under the mountain.'

'You saw me in your dreams?'

He smiled, 'It gave me the strength to bear it all.'

And then I remembered what Granny Jones had said: '*The boy told your grandmother that she would have a granddaughter who was the one he was waiting for.*'

'You were different from all the others.'

'Different?' I said.

'I knew you were coming. We dragons have the seer's gift. We can foretell the future, if it comes to us in dreams.' His dark eyes filled with shadows. 'It is strange to dream when you don't sleep … ' The spot of colour on his cheeks dimmed and disappeared. 'And I was right. You saw me. You saw me through the mist. You saw me on the summit. *You came out to rescue me.*'

'Yes,' I said, faintly. 'I did, didn't I?'

'You proved something.'

'Yes?' I said eagerly.

'You proved that I had not waited in vain.'

'Can you be rescued?' I said, my heart flaring with an impossible hope.

'You did rescue me when I was struggling on the mountain, that Christmas night, waiting for you to find me, determined not to give in to the change and become the Dragon, determined not to answer the call of the fight, though it robbed me of all strength, for there was no moon and the darkness and his shrieking nearly drove me mad.'

'But is there any way to rescue you from going back under the mountain?'

Henry's smile faded and a look of determined hopelessness settled over his features. 'Once I hoped so,' he said, 'A long time ago, but I've known for many centuries that the magic

Merlin offered me can never be used. I can never become human. I can never give my heart.'

'Bring out the violins,' said George, 'Oh and a box of tissues, while you're at it.'

'George,' I said, 'Please.' I turned to Henry, 'Why?' I think my bottom lip was trembling.

'Because until I destroy Oswald forever, he will not rest until he destroys me. Anyone who has the keeping of my heart would not survive his malice. It would be unthinkable to drag any other to that fate.'

'So there is no hope?' I said faintly.

'There is always hope,' said Henry, 'but not of me becoming human.'

'You better tell me, how much danger I'm in,' I said, 'if I leave Halfway House.' A sudden determination fired through me. I wasn't going to skulk here like a frightened rabbit. If I didn't do something I'd lose Henry forever.

'You must not,' said Henry, his voice as hard as forged steel.

'Well she can't stay here,' said George, 'and neither can I, so you better think of something to distract your pal the White Dragon until I can get her safely down the mountain and myself to A&E. Surely another minor skirmish in the Annals of The Red and The White won't be too hard to arrange?'

Henry took his arm from around my shoulders. He put his face in his hands. 'You speak the truth, George,' he said, 'I have brought this upon us. I must do something … ' His voice trailed away. Then suddenly, he brought his head up, as if something had occurred to him, and he'd made a decision.

In the light of the dancing flames, I looked into his eyes. No light danced back. 'Henry!' I said, suddenly irrationally alarmed.

'Ellie,' he said. 'Now, you *will* do as I say.' It was not a question.

'I will?' I said.

'Yes,' His voice stern. 'There is only one other way.'

'Soon, when Oswald knows there will be no fight tonight, he will go back to Caernarfon and take his human form. He does not like the shape of a dragon, especially when it is daylight and he must hide in the lair with only bare rocks around him. Tomorrow when he is in human form he will try to besiege this place with those bodyguards he keeps in his pay – in an attempt to pry you out. All will be a ploy to get you away from the safety of Halfway House. At first I had decided I would guard you in monster form, if need be, but now I see he will force me to keep my human shape by employing the use of others. So instead when the time is right you will go home. You will pack a bag. You will do all this as quickly as possible. You will call your mother and tell her it was high time you met Jeff properly, formally. You will go into Llanberis. George will go with you. You will persuade your mother that you should be allowed to go and celebrate New Year at the Pen-y-mynydd-gwryd Hotel and have a New Year's Eve supper there with her and Jeff. You will find a way to make her let you stay the next three nights at the hotel – that this should be your Christmas treat – if possible you will go with her, George?'

I smiled then. I'd thought of Rhiannon. I knew exactly how I was going to manage it.

'He cannot hunt at that hotel.' Henry's eyes lit up with hope. 'Yes! Perhaps after all this is a much better idea. It is a rule of Draco that he cannot hunt anywhere in his monster form when the stone dragons of our common ancestry guard the place.'

I nodded, as I remembered the stone dragons, and Granny passing her hand over them.

'But you must be careful; the place is not as secure as this, and should he enter there in his human form, you will have no protection from him.'

I nodded.

'She'll have me,' said George.

'And you?' I said.

'Do not worry about me,' he said. 'I am not the one at risk.'

'Can't you come there too?' I asked.

'Ellie,' he said looking at me with that darkness in his eyes. 'I will come, if I can. But when Oswald realises I've tricked him, and he cannot get you, he will find another sacrifice. I must stop him, for at midnight on the 31st of December, the two of us must visit our Hearts' Crystals in the lair under Snowdon, to either give our hearts or return to darkness. If he hunts for another, I must save her – if I can.'

'And on New Year's Day?' I said. 'What happens then?'

'You will be out of danger.'

'And you?' I said, tears blurring my eyes. 'Will I see you?'

Henry laughed at that, a small sad laugh. 'It will be a New Year, a new chance for you. You will forget about me.'

I know my jaw dropped then, but I let it. I was too busy trying not to tremble. The tears in my eyes brimmed over.

'George, will you help me?' said Henry.

George nodded.

'Promise me, you will get Ellie to the hotel somehow. I can confuse him during the daylight hours, when he prefers to keep the shape of a man, but by nightfall he will return to the mountain as a monster and try to find her.'

'No problem,' George winked at me. 'Pack your silk PJs Elles,' he said. 'That penthouse suite needs checking out.' Then he yawned and said. 'But if neither of you mind, and the plan's agreed on, I'll get some sleep. Maybe you've both forgotten, but I'm injured, and tomorrow could be a long day.'

He lay down on the bench and yawned again. I moved across and folded his tattered sheepskin and put it under his head. I shook out the foil blanket and covered him. Henry put more logs on the fire.

And Henry and I sat on in silence, there in the firelight. My heart was trembling, and I was fighting back the tears. The flames flickered. Warm shadows danced on the walls. Outside everything was quiet. Henry's beautiful face was as cold as stone, his eyes impenetrable.

'You better tell me if … ' I said at last.

'Come closer. Stay quiet,' he whispered.

'Please?' I said. 'Seventy-two years is a long time to wait … '

'Can we forget the future for just a little while?' Henry said. He held out his arms to me. I moved into their embrace, and we sat there close in silence. Through everything I could feel his heart pounding.

'Why can't we … ' I asked eventually, torn between the

need to know if there was any hope at all, and the stillness of not knowing.

His arm stayed around me. 'It was worth it,' he said gently.

I felt the warmth of the fire, the impossible pleasure of his arms.

'Worth what?' I murmured.

'Worth eternity to be here now.'

I put my head on his shoulder.

'If anything had happened to you … '

'It didn't.'

'Thank God,' he said.

'Why didn't you tell me you were a prince?'

'I'm not a prince.'

'Ok, a viscount.'

'Does it make a difference?

'Yes and no.'

'How?' he asked.

'It makes it harder. It makes me feel like I don't matter,' I said truthfully.

He laughed as if that was absurd. 'And no?'

'Because I don't care what you are. I don't care if you're a dragon or a prince or a king, I'd still want to … '

'A viscount,' he corrected.

'Or anything.'

'Well it should.'

'Well it doesn't.'

We sat, staring into the flames.

He looked at me, turned my face round, and gazed into it.

'Ellie,' he said, 'You give me hope.'

I smiled, 'Is there any hope?'

'No,' he said. 'Right from the beginning there was none, but no one knows the future and hope is the only thing we have.'

'Yes,' I said. 'And tonight.'

'Ellie?' he said again.

'Yes,' I murmured again.

'You're right. We have tonight, and there's something you need to understand.'

'Yes?' I said.

His eyes swiftly became alive. He stood up and tiptoed to the doorway. He pressed his ear against the upturned table. 'Shush,' he said.

I held my breath. Only the murmur of George breathing rhythmically, only the sighing of the wind.

'He's gone,' said Henry.

'You sure?'

'Dragons have pretty good hearing,' he said. 'Come on! We're going outside.' He lifted back the table as if it were a feather. He raced back to my side, caught my hand. 'Expect the unexpected,' he said mysteriously.

And together we stepped out on to the mountainside.

Twenty-One

Outside the air was crystal sharp, the sky above us a deep indigo blue. There were no snow clouds, only a mist hovering above the summit of the mountain and the perfect darkness of the night. The moon sailed high, and beyond that, a myriad of tiny pinpricks of light sparkled like diamonds. To the north, the constellation of Draco curled around the Pole Star, looking down on us, as if he were entertained by the events unfolding in the winter hills of North Wales.

'Close your eyes, Ellie,' laughed Henry.

'Why?' I said.

'Just trust me,' he replied.

So I closed my eyes.

'You don't have to do this,' I said, suddenly understanding exactly how to 'expect the unexpected'.

'But I want to,' he said, 'I want you to see me as I really am.' There was a tremor in his voice as if he was unsure.

I was unsure too.

'Don't look,' he said, 'it's vitally important,' and as he said it, I could hear the tenor of his voice changing.

'Henry?' I cried out – a bit alarmed.

'There's nothing to fear,' he laughed. 'Oswald knows he's defeated for tonight. He's gone back to Caernarfon to eat and sleep as a man.'

'That's not what I meant!' I said.

'Well, don't look anyway, because I'm taking my clothes off.'

Immediately I felt the blood rush to my face. *Taking His Clothes Off!*

'We're safe. Don't worry. I told you Oswald doesn't like being a dragon. He uses our shape unwillingly. Besides, George has cut him. He'll want to deal with it.' His voice was oddly deepening as he spoke.

Slight crackles filled the silence. The snow rustled. I nervously twisted the sleeve of my coat.

'Unlike me,' said Henry and now his voice was cavernous and huge. 'I like my natural form. I love to be the Dragon.'

There was a movement very near me, a swish, a troubling of the air. The ground under my feet trembled.

'Hen-ry?' I said.

'Are you ready?' he asked.

'Ready for *what?*' I said.

'To see the world as I do.'

OMG. A Dragon?

My heart beat fast. I felt an urge to open my eyes.

'Keep your eyes closed tight, and prepare to be amazed.'

The air shook. A mysterious energy sent an eddy of snow up into my face.

'Stretch out your hand.'

I stretched out my hand.

'A little further.'

I leant forward, struggling to keep my eyes shut.

'There!' he said.

My fingers touched something. It was hard to describe the texture: rough but soft, scaly but smooth, cool yet filled with warmth.

'If you promise not to faint you can open your eyes,' said Henry, his voice odd, echoey, as if he was standing in a cave or had the chest capacity the size of a whale.

'Ok,' I said, shaking, half-terrified at what I'd see.

'You can look now.'

I opened my eyes just a little and peeked. There through the white glow of the icy peaks, through the darkness of the winter night, was something reddish. I opened my eyes a little more at what looked like a vast scaly flank covered with a film of crimson. A little more and I saw sliced rubies, scarlet foil and rosy discs of light. The discs glittered like jewels, and the light from them bounced around, reflecting off the sparkling snow, until I became aware that the entire area around me was dancing in shades of gold and red and cherry pink. It was as if the most glorious sunset had been trapped in the air all around me and spilled itself on to the ground and was pooling around my feet.

'*Henry?*' I said.

The flank of the thing in front of me was so huge it filled my vision. I took a step back, and realised what I was looking at.

Y Ddraig Goch.

A huge horned gleaming head swung round at me. I gasped. My legs trembled. My jaw opened. My eyes went wide.

There looming in front of me was the Red Dragon of Wales.

'Ellie?' said that huge creature, 'You Ok?'

'Just a bit – like – WOW,' I said.

OMG. I am in love with a dragon!

'Don't you like me?'

But before I could answer, the dragon snorted out, '*I got it wrong. You weren't ready for the truth* ...'

'SHUT UP!' I said, trying to contain my surprise. *The colour! I'd never seen anything like it!*

'I'm too close.' With one earthquake motion, it jumped back. His voice boomed. '*You must like who I really am.*'

'Bit small for a dragon, aren't you?' I joked. *My God, he was unbelievable!* Bigger than a dinosaur. GARGANTUAN!

'You like me, then?'

And he burned like the setting sun.

'I can be fierce too,' he boasted and opened his wings, raised his massive head and roared. A jet of hot air shot up through the clouds and the snow around him steamed. Then he curled his long neck round towards me and, looking at me out of his golden eyes, he pushed his head into my chest. 'SCARED?' he said.

It was Henry's voice, but not his voice. It had an echoing hollow ring to it, and it was so deep it seemed to be coming from inside the bottom of the mountain.

'HENRY!' I shrieked.

'It's still me,' he said, laughing a little. And he very gently nuzzled his head against me.

Oh. My. Double. God! I thought. I. Am. Being. Nuzzled. By. A. Dragon.

And I stood there frozen to the spot.

'Ellie?' he said 'You *are* scared?'

'NO,' I shrieked. 'Absolutely Not!' I reached out to touch him 'You're astonishing. You're awesome. You're – I don't know. I'm NOT scared.'

'Sure?' he said. *'Awesome*, eh?'

I stroked his face, felt silky smooth skin: softer than velvet, harder than diamonds. 'How d'you glow like that?' I asked.

'Like what?' he said.

'Like, well, you're covered in sparkles?'

'Ah!' he said. 'Does it look ok?'

'OK?' I said, 'Incredible. Unbelievable. Dazzling.'

'It's because I'm a fire dragon,' he said. 'I glitter like light. I smoulder like flame.'

'What's it like?' I said suddenly aware of how ignorant I was about dragons, their anatomy, their feelings, every-thing.

'Well,' he said. 'I can feel you. I can see you. I can hear every-thing about you. I can hear your heart beating. I can hear every chamber of your heart pumping. Dragons have height-ened senses – maybe some you can't even guess at,' and he chuckled a deep booming noise, like a furnace roaring.

'Can you breathe fire?' I asked.

'Easily,' he said, I can breathe flames that could melt ice caps.'

A part of me suddenly realised how dangerous he was!

'But I won't,' he said.

I breathed a rush of relief.

'Would you like to see Snowdon as I see it?' he asked.

I hesitated, not sure what he was asking. 'Ye-ah,' I said at last. A dragon's eye view of Snowdon. I mean why not?

He sank to the ground, stretched out in front of me and rested his head at my feet. 'Then climb on.'

'*Climb On!*' I shrieked.

'Yes, climb on my back and settle yourself between my wings.'

'Oh My God!'

'I promise I will take care of you. You will not fall,' he said.

I took a deep breath. I touched his flank. I looked up to where his wings lay folded. How the heck was I going to climb up there?

'Step on my foot,' he said.

Heart pounding, I stepped on to his outstretched leg. As soon as I was balanced there, he curled a huge wing down towards me and scooped me up. Before I knew it, I was rushed through the air and set down in the hollow of his back.

'Now, hold on,' he said.

'Hold on to *what?*' I squeaked.

He laughed that deep roaring laugh.

Instinctively I clutched at the spines that stuck out on his neck.

'Yes,' he said, 'hold them tight.'

It was a good job I did. He beat the air with those two humongous wings. There was a rushing, and I felt myself rising. I screamed, (at least I think I screamed), but the icy air tore my voice from me, suddenly and dramatically, as I hurtled upwards.

And up we went.

And, just like that moment on Lovers' Leap when we stood sailing over the world, I felt the dizzying rush of vertigo. My knees trembled with the effort of hanging on, my stomach somersaulted, my arms went totally numb. And there we were chasing our own moon-shadows on the mountain below, and diving amongst the stars.

And the speed!

The land below blurred, the skies above spun.

His huge wings beat the air. We rose, and rose, and rose again. We pushed higher and higher, right up to the top of the world. And then we soared. Below me the entire panorama of Snowdonia spread out. All of Wales.

'Hold. On!' roared Henry, 'We are going to touch the stars.'

He swooped. I held on. He swirled around for one last dizzying turn. He rocketed straight up at such speed, it left my breath behind. We rushed to meet the clouds, way over the peak of the mountain. And everything exploded around me as we burst through the highest cloud belt, right over the summit, right into the starlight beyond.

And I was left breathless and dizzy,

And hanging on for dear life,

As we rushed into the heavens.

Act Three

'Deffro Mae'n Ddydd Y Ddraig Goch Ddyry Gychwyn'
('Awake it is the day! The Red Dragon will lead the way!')

Welsh Tradition ~ Deio ab Ieuan Du (*fl.* 1450–1480)

Twenty-Two

If Henry thought George and I were going to hide out in the hotel and then go quietly back to our little mountain lives while he went off and fought with his uncle – and got them both entombed under the rocks of Dinas Emrys for another three quarters of a century – he was wrong.

For a start that was not my idea of true love. In my book, true love meant like it said in Corinthians:

Love never fails.

It always trusts.

It always hopes.

It always perseveres.

So if there was a fight to prove it, I was in. And if I was in, that meant George was in, because George is George and will do anything for me, including trying to save the boy I love (even when it isn't him), because George is totally like that.

So we were both in.

And if you're in – you've got to play your part, innit?

So as we walked, we made a plan. We'd go to the hotel all right, and George would get himself to the hospital, but before we did that, we were going to find out if there was anything else we could do. We were going to ask the one person who might be able to help us: Granny Jones.

George was pretty sure she knew a lot more than she let on, and I was *convinced* of it. She'd known all along about Henry, about him being a dragon, about Merlin and Oswald, hadn't she? And despite the promises she'd hidden behind (and after all it was MY grandmother), I kind of wondered why she hadn't just told me straight up, right at the beginning. I mean how hard would that have actually been?

GRANNY: Listen up, Ellie; Henry is a shape-shifting dragon. He's a lot older than you and has a serial killer for an uncle. He probably has an insatiable lust to devour young maidens as well. He has set his sights on you. If you hang out with him, don't blame me if you get ravaged.

ME: Oh I see. Fair enough then. I'll dump him.

Lol.

Actually, Granny *had* been trying to tell me, but she probably knew that warning me off, as sure as hell, was going to egg me on. She'd tried to protect me too. She'd laid charms around the farmhouse; she'd got the herbs for me; she'd been there at the hotel, invoking the help of those stone dragons, stepping forward to thwart Oswald, tracking me to the frozen lake. She'd called me up to her cottage and tried to let me know the danger. And I realised, as I strode along beside George, there wouldn't have been anything else she could have done to make me change my mind, and she probably knew that too.

A sudden surge of love for her caught me unawares and my throat dried up and I gulped.

Granny Jones is all right, you know, probably one of the most all-rightest people eva.

Along with George.

I glanced up at him as he walked beside me, tall, golden haired, strong: trying not to show me how much pain he was in. I was so lucky to have a friend like him. I promised myself to value him more, to be kinder to him. Because if he felt as passionately about me, as I did about Henry, his heart must be breaking.

Poor George. I fought back an urge to hug him and

slipped my arm through his instead. I was definitely going to be massively nicer to him.

He squeezed my arm and together we passed into the shadow of Moel Cynghorion towards our side of the mountain. I was a bit scared, so I said, 'Do you think asking Gran is *really* a good idea?'

He stopped and turned to face me. 'Elles,' he said, 'You want to help Henry. Right?'

I nodded.

'So,' said George, 'let's do it.'

'Right,' I said.

'And let's do it now while Oswald is being De Man in Caernarfon.' He faked his Elli-South-London voice.

'Right,' I said again.

'And getting Gran on our side is best.'

I nodded.

'She's a funny old thing,' he said, 'but she won't bite your head off. She's too wise. She knows just about everything, including when being all bossy won't help.'

I took a deep breath. I looked out across the peaks. I realised I'd changed. Last night had made me grow up. And in the process, I'd lost confidence. I didn't know everything any more (don't smile). Maybe it was because I'd touched a dragon. (And that meant there were things I knew now, that I didn't yesterday … So therefore there would be more things tomorrow, obviously.)

The future wasn't so certain any more.

But no matter the uncertainty, I must act and NOW.

We hurried. The snow crunched underfoot; everywhere shone with a sinister brilliance. George waved his hand towards Caernarfon. The view was scarily fantastic – low clouds circling distant peaks, a terrifyingly blue sky blazing icily above us. The sun rose steadily, clearing the distant ranges. Red streaks from the dawn drained across the sky like fresh wounds. A low wind howled.

'Hey Ellie, it'll be all right,' said George. He raised his good hand in a kind of thumbs-up gesture. 'We'll save your prince. Try not to worry.'

'Viscount,' I said.

'Aw,' said George,' don't demote him for my sake.'

But he didn't roll his eyes, and I know George. He never gets serious unless something really is serious and then he goes like this, all trying to be positive, when you can tell he thinks the chances are worse than a zillion to one.

Perhaps George had changed too. Perhaps both of us had grown up.

Suddenly I sighed. I turned and stopped. George stopped too. I buried my head in his shoulder. 'Oh George,' I said

'You don't have to, I won't mind. This isn't your fight.' My voice went wobbly.

'I know,' said George, putting his good arm round me. 'But hey Elles, I'll stay and fight the Evil Dragon if you promise to give me a snog.'

I had to smile.

Typical George!

'You can snog me now, if you can't wait, or you can snog me later … ' He was joking again.

I took my head off his shoulder and braced myself.

'I'll see,' I said playing along. 'I'll only snog you, if we defeat Sir Oswald and only if – ' I was going to say if Henry doesn't mind: but of course he'd mind. *I'd* mind if Henry kissed anybody – even if they'd saved my life.

'Oh Elles,' said George giving me a squeeze. 'I know you probably think I'd rather Henry was out of the way again, but it's not as simple as that. If he was out the way, you'd be gutted. If you were gutted then I'd be gutted. So that would mean two of us majorly gutted – well three of us actually – if you counted Henry.'

George's voice took on a determined tone. 'So we'll save Henry if we can, and if we can't, we won't give up. We'll try and figure out a way to get him out of the lair – we'll go to Great Draco himself and ask him to come up with any plan that doesn't involve killing off all the pretty girls in Llanberis. Although come to think of it … ' he rolled his eyes, 'Howsabout we send Rhiannon a ping – that way we could fix everything!' George looked at me, his eyebrows dancing.

'Oh stop it!' I said. 'Poor old Rhiannon, all she ever did wrong was fancy you.'

'Oh well,' said George, 'it was just an idea … ' and he shot me such a hangdog expression that it made me want to burst out laughing. And actually I did snigger, and George started twitching his lips, and you know, even when everything looks completely hopeless, and you are probably about to die, and your heart is totally broken, it's amazing how you can still manage a laugh.

And pretty soon we were both giggling and then snorting manically at the thought of Sir Oswald chomping up Rhiannon. And by the time we broke out of the shadow of Moel Cynghorion and stepped into the bright sunlight, the snow-scape looked less sinister, the sky less terrifying and the morning more hopeful.

Maybe there was a way. Fingers crossed Gran knew something that would change everything.

I don't know exactly what I was hoping for – a talisman, a spell, a cure for being a dragon, some detail of some long forgotten legend. *Something*, anyway. So as we hurried down the hill, I crossed my fingers (both hands), and my heart beat faster. Under my breath I prayed, Please Let There Be A Way. Oh Great Spirit of Snowdon Please.

When we saw the smoke from Granny's cottage, I turned to George. 'She is going to believe us, isn't she?'

George pointed to his side: 'Unless she thinks you did this in a moment of passion,' he said, raising his eyebrows.

'Oh God,' I said, 'I really hope she can help.'

But all George muttered was: 'I wish she did love potions,' in a sad, crestfallen sort of way.

I took his arm. 'I *do* love you George,' I said, 'just not like that.'

He smiled sadly.

'But you're my best friend.'

George tried to sling his arm over my shoulder, shuddered in pain and let it fall limply back, 'I know Elles,' he said.

Sometimes I think it's a shame I *don't* love George. He's so nice – and he's cute too – and tall and muscly and fit and everything. It would be so much easier if I fancied him. But I hanker for stranger, wilder things: the big wide world with all its adventures.

Although we seem made for each other, that's not enough. And I can't fool myself that it is. He's just George. He'll always be the-boy-next-door, and I don't think I'm the kind of girl who can settle for the-boy-next-door and live out the rest of my life in a little neighbourly bubble. Well, maybe I could, but then there's The Spark, isn't there? There has to be The Spark.

I'd just make him unhappy.

And think how awful it would have been, if I'd promised George, I'd be his – and then I'd met Henry.

Henry. My mind went over everything he'd told me.

He *was* the unknown.

He *was* the adventure.

I couldn't step back from him, not for all the Georges in the world. It felt like I'd been waiting for Henry ever since I was born.

And now I'd found him.

And I was going to lose him.

And there was nothing I could do about it.

I squeezed George's arm. I realised that it wasn't just Henry who needed saving.

It was me too.

We curved out of the top pastures and saw Granny's cottage settled amongst the snow drifts. With a pang, I remembered all the other mornings I'd arrived there: mornings with George bringing in fresh logs, yelling and grinning and waving at me; mornings full of the smell of bacon and honey-roast ham and toast and mushrooms; mornings all charged with spicy sweetness, with blue wisps of wood-smoke curling up from the chimney; mornings that belonged to a past I could never get back to.

It was all gone. I was not the girl who'd left her home yesterday to brave the mountain.

I'd looked into the eyes of a dragon.

I was changed. I was different, and it made me terribly sad.

I glanced sideways at George. He still belonged to the land of bringing in the logs and putting the kettle on. I bit my lip. Part of me wanted to get back there as well, to be again the carefree Ellie, that Mountain Girl Who Knew Every Rock and Stone. But that part of me was already fading. I had to become this new self; this sad-eyed girl who had rushed beyond the summit of Snowdon and touched the heavens.

Henry had changed everything. And I was so deeply and hopelessly in love with him that it hurt.

But worst of all I knew none of it could come to any good.

I think I was very near to tears when I got inside the cottage. It would only have taken one more tender word from George and one kindly hug from Gran and I'd have sobbed my heart out.

Luckily there was no time for that. Granny rushed us in and sat us down by the fire, as if she already knew something was badly wrong.

We told her everything. We told her how Henry had lain under the mountain, how Oswald hadn't. We told her about the magic of Merlin, how he had offered the dragons humanity in exchange for immortality, about Oswald's cheating heart, the magic of Draco and about the cold-blooded sacrifices. We told her how dangerous Oswald was, and how he'd set his sights on me. I even told her how much in love I was with Henry. Well I tried to. She just nodded and shushed me, but I could tell she knew everything anyway.

George added in bits, all modest, all praising Henry, all pretending he wasn't badly hurt, all designed to make me feel good and reassure us all. And Granny said 'It is as I feared.' Then she handed me a hot mug of tea, and George a steaming bowl of herbal broth. 'Drink it, quickly, Siôr' she said, a note of worry in her voice. 'It has healing powers.'

I sipped my tea while George took his broth.

'The time is short,' she continued, 'and there is much to do.' At those words my heart leapt. Perhaps she did know a way.

Granny turned to me. 'How much of all this does your mother know?'

'Nothing,' I replied

'Good,' said Granny. 'She must not know, or she will blunt your confidence. Your love for her will hold you back, for you have set yourself on a terrible mission and goodness knows where it will take you.'

'So what've we got to do, Gran?' asked George

Granny turned to him. 'If Ellie doesn't help Henry, he will not be able to defeat his uncle or save any girl in this round of history. He has not been able to in the past and there is no reason to believe he can now. In fact if he is in love with Ellie, he will be less able than ever to defend any girl Oswald chooses to sacrifice.

'I sighed. I knew she spoke the truth.

'And there is no magic that I have that can protect her or anyone from Oswald in his dragon form.'

'Then she better get to the hotel?' asked George. 'I'll take her, I'll stay there … '

'You will not!' said Granny, 'You'll get to hospital and stay there until you can be of any use to us.'

'I'll do what I want,' said George, looking squarely at Gran. 'Once I've been stitched up, I won't leave Ellie's side.'

It was the first time I'd ever seen George stand up to Granny so openly.

'You would risk everything to help her?' asked Granny Jones, looking at him with her piercing blue eyes, holding him in a steady gaze.

'Yes,' said George firmly. 'I'll go with Ellie anywhere. I'll do what I can to protect her and use what I know to help her. I only have my axe, but … ' he turned to me, 'I pledge my best axe to you.'

I was overcome. I didn't know what to say. I had just told him I was in love with another. It made my heart rise up in my throat, and I threw my arms around him and gulped.

'Ouch,' he said nearly spilling his broth.

But even as I was hugging him and feeling so much better, I also knew that I could not let George sacrifice himself for me. Deep inside me the new Ellie was taking over. Nobody must suffer for me. This was *my* destiny and if I was to die or lose Henry, it must be my curse alone. So I turned to Gran. 'If you know anything that can help, please tell me,' I said.

'I know nothing new,' said Gran, 'but, the solution of the ancients is wise enough for us. The legends say they found a pool in the lair and filled it with mead and the dragons drunk deeply from the pool and fell asleep and were thus entombed under the mountain.

'The same solution will serve us. I will brew you a potion,' said Granny Jones, 'I have that art with herbs and flowers. I will steep it so well that it will dull even the wits of a dragon. Any that drink of it will fall into such a deep trance that for three days and three nights none shall wake them. You must take this potion and be prepared to use it.'

'I'm ready,' said George.

'Me too,' I said.

'If Sir Oswald in his human shape stalks you at the hotel, you must find a way to pour it into his drink or drip just a few drops on to his food. That is the only defence I can help you with there – but more importantly before New Year, you must go deep into the cavern below Dinas Emrys. You must find the pool that the dragons drink from when the times comes for them to change into their dragon forms and confront their Heart Crystals. You must pour the sleeping potion into the water.'

'I'll do that,' said George.

'I'll come too,' I said.

George stuffed toast into his mouth and shook his head at me.

'When they change into their final shapes, at the year's end, they'll drink it. They'll fall asleep before the hour set for them and fail the spell of Merlin. Even Draco's arts will not wake them, and thus we will be rid of them for another procession of the equinoxes.'

My heart contracted. 'Then Henry will be lost too!' I said.

'That is the only sure way I can help you to save yourself or any other girl.'

George swallowed his mouthful, shushed me with a look and said, 'I'll take the potion to the lair, as soon as Ellie is safe at the hotel and armed with some of it – just in case – and as soon as I'm through at the hospital.' There was a glint in his eye that alarmed me.

'Is there no way we can tell Henry?' I said, 'So that he doesn't drink the potion? A way that I can meet him there and save him?' Already an idea was forming in my mind. I would go there myself, I would tell Henry, we would fool Oswald …

'Do not try,' said Granny in a voice so stern and yet so soft, it sent shivers into my stomach. 'Once he is in his dragon form Oswald cannot be fooled. Not by you. Not by Henry. He has already fixed you with his dragon eyes, and now he can read your intentions. When you are in his presence, you will not be able to make any pretence before him. But Siôr may stand a chance. So far he has overlooked Siôr.

He has not bothered to understand him and he knows his talons have already poisoned his flesh.

'Poisoned?' I shrieked.

'Yes, poisoned,' said Granny Jones. 'If Siôr had not come straight to me, by tomorrow night when the moon rises, a fever so powerful would have snatched him from us. But someone passed here in the early morning and left me dragons' bane and self heal and warned me with a note.'

Gran produced a slip of paper on which was written:

'Mae eich plentyn wedi cael ei anafu gan y Ddraig Wen. Paratowch y tonig iddo yr ydych yn gwybod amdano.'[1]

Henry, I thought. He left the note.

'So I prepared Siôr a broth with it – and added dried white snapdragon and tamed it with ground dragon's teeth from the rocks on Snowdon. It will drive his poison away.'

Hastily George slurped down the rest of his brew.

'Now,' said Granny, 'weary as you are, you must get to the hotel and Siôr must have his wound properly stitched and dressed.'

'Thanks Nan,' said George handing her back his bowl.

---

1. 'Your child is wounded by the White One. Prepare for him the tonic which you know of.'

'Go quickly,' said Granny, 'I too must start my work and brew the potion.'

~

We left Granny's cottage. We walked to the end of their valley and down the snowy slopes.

My shoulders drooped. I knew Granny was right to think of saving the life of another girl before everything else, but my hopes of helping Henry were dashed. If only Oswald could be defeated and kept under the mountain; Henry would give me his heart, I knew it as surely as I knew the sun shone. But I also knew that if there were any risk of Oswald alive and abroad as a man, Henry would rather spend eternity entombed underground that risk my safety. My safety was the thing holding him back. So I resolved to make his life as easy as I could, (until I had another plan). I'd go straight to the hotel.

George walked beside me. I saw he had his best axe, (hand forged in Sweden with a polished handle of hickory wood – Which He Is Always Boasting About), slung across his back. He, too, was worried about my safety. (Right when he needed to get to the hospital.) It seemed both George and Henry would stop at nothing to protect me. It was very humbling.

I pulled my mobile out of my pocket. I held it up to see if I could get coverage. George's part of the mountain sometimes goes down completely. There were a couple of bars on the coverage scale. A couple of bars was enough. I sent a ping to Rhiannon:

> **Ellie**
>
> Coming to yours to help get the party started. Find me a bed.
> XXX

She pinged me back.

> **Rhiannon**
>
> Hehehe I know just which bed to find you.

I didn't bother replying except: '*Thanks will be there soon,*' and then I rang Mum. She was on her way back from Jeff's.

'I'm going down to the hotel to chill out with Rhi and Darren,' I said.

'Ok Hon,' she said. I could tell by her tone she was happy.

'I won't be back til after New Year's.'

'Oh,' she sounded a bit surprised at that. 'I could come there, with Jeff, for a drink on New Year's Eve,' she offered.

'Ok,' I said, 'Rhi is having a party then, so come early.'

'I could stay. I mean, we could stay and see the New Year in together ... '

'Ok,' I said. 'It'll be quite a loud party. But if you want. With Jeff too?'

'Well ... ' began Mum.

'Because its gonna be a teenage kind of party,' I said.

'Well if you'd rather not ... ' her voice trailed away.

'Come early,' I said, thinking of empty lairs and dragons' spells and hearts' crystals. 'And see if you want to stay.'

'Jeff's invited me to see in the New Year with his family,' said Mum, 'but I'd rather...'

'So go,' I said. (What teenager wants their mum at a party?)

'But ... '

I could tell I was being harsh, but I pushed home my point. 'Honest Mum, Jeff wants you at his and I don't want you at mine ... '

'Well, we could come over to the hotel on New Year's Day. We could do brunch or – '

'Good,' I said. 'Perfect. Love you. Gotta go. George is waiting on me ... '

'Or supper earlier on New Year's Eve?' she said.

Great. That was just what Henry had suggested, but I didn't have to do everything exactly as he said, did I? If I was stuck having supper with Mum and Jeff all New

Year's Eve – there'd be no hope that Henry could ever be mine. So I pretended I hadn't heard and hung up.

I caught up with George. The sun shone bright through the clouds, glancing off the snow. We said little as we trudged past the stony outcrops, past the dark rise of low foothills. George looked pale and moved slowly. From time to time he glanced behind us, or stopped and made me wait while he explored the path ahead. At last we saw the trail of smoke from the chimneys of Llanberis.

As I stepped over the thin brook that gurgles its way through bracken and under bridges as it winds from its source at Marchlyn Mawr, the reservoir of Llanberis – where they say Arthur's treasure lies, my phone pinged. I stopped dead in my tracks.

I pushed my hair out of my face and tried to stand still. My heart was racing and my eyes were smarting, as I read the message.

Recent updates between Ellie and UNKNOWN:

UNKNOWN

Go straight to the hotel. I won't let anything happen to you. Know that I love you. There may not be any chance of a further meeting. Please understand this. I cannot come to the hotel.

> So fare thee well Heart's Crystal. I will love you for as long as
> Draco embraces the Pole Star.

I stood there. A chill ran through me. Was that from Henry? How did he get my number? Or was it from some far more sinister source? Someone who was trying to get me to believe it was. Someone who was trying to groom me into trusting an UNKNOWN text message.

Even little kids know better than to trust UNKNOWN texters.

So I sent a message back.

> **Ellie**
>
> If this is Henry, know that I love you and I will love you forever
> and I will never stop loving you, even though it takes a lifetime
> to see you again. I hope I will see you again, though.
> If it is not, BE AWARE I WON'T BE FOLLOWING ANY
> INSTRUCTIONS YOU GIVE ME.
> NB Soz if it was you H XXXXX E.

And then I sent it.

But even though it went, the message on it read: '*Pending.*'

Twenty-Three

George and I couldn't have got a warmer welcome anywhere in Wales than we did at the Pen-y-mynydd-gwryd Hotel. Darren raced around like a puppy let off the leash, and Rhiannon nearly swooned when she saw George. And that was nothing to when she saw George Was Hurt.

She led him to the downstairs reception suite. She made him strip off. She made him lie on one of the upholstered chaises longues and then she gently peeled back his T-shirt bandage. When she saw the wound she shrieked so loudly a couple of the long-term guests came hurrying out of the Bwlch y Saethau (The Pass of the Arrows) saloon and cried out, 'Oh! Oh! What is it? What can we do?'

Rhiannon ignored them superbly, and fell weeping over George (who tried not to flinch or say 'ouch' too often).

'My GOD! OH MY GOD! How did it happen? OH MY

GOD you could have died!' shrieked Rhiannon.

'I tripped up in the wood shed. It was dark. I fell on the blades of the combine harvester.' said George, being supernaturally inventive.

'OH MY DAYS!' shrieked Rhiannon. 'YOU COULD HAVE BLED TO DEATH!'

'True,' muttered George, suddenly grinning as if he'd just discovered a new computer game. 'I had to drag myself bleeding and in agony, all the way to the door, and pound and hammer on it before Granny even realised what had happened.'

I cast a sneaky look at George. He winked. Like who the heck ever heard of a combine harvester halfway up a Welsh mountain? Luckily Rhiannon came from the valleys and didn't notice and Darren was too busy rushing around with Cokes and crisps to pay attention to anything George said.

But Sheila eyed the two of us thoughtfully.

'Anyway I can't stay,' said George. 'I've got to get to hospital.'

That was it. Suddenly Rhiannon was organising the hotel courtesy shuttle coach, getting the driver to bring it round to the front door, folding back the seats, pushing George into it, making him lie down, fetching bandages and more Cokes and a huge chicken salad wrap and declaring she was going with him 'RIGHT NOW', 'RIGHT AWAY', into Caernarfon Outpatients, and probably to John o'Groats if need be.

George just grinned his famous George grin and let her fuss. But as I bent down to say goodbye, he caught my hand and pulled me close. 'Keep inside. Lock the door of your room. Don't go anywhere alone. Keep Darren with you. I don't like the way he's drooling over you, but I'm glad he's here. Don't forget what Henry said – Oswald can get in here as a man – and he looks like the kind of man that won't let a pair of stone dragons stop him.'

'You just get better,' I said, 'I need you. Come back as quick as you can.'

I went to straighten up, but George kept hold of my wrist. He half raised himself up. 'I love you, Elles,' he whispered. 'Don't forget it, and don't let Darren snog you.' Then he sank back on the coach seats and started groaning in such a fake way that Rhiannon nearly went mental.

For the rest of the day, Darren stuck to me like glue, which annoyed Sheila, so she stuck to him like superglue, so we all rolled through the afternoon and evening in a glued-up little knot.

Mum passed by, gave me some money, said what a 'nice boy' Darren seemed, that she'd come over for a meal on New Year's Eve, 'not too late' so I could party with my friends, that she'd bring Jeff, and it'd be so nice if I got to 'know him' a bit more (like he hadn't lived in the village forever) and that I wasn't to 'bankrupt' Rhiannon's parents, and I was to pay for my drinks, even if they let me eat from the buffet. And she handed me another twenty-pound note.

Then she found Rhiannon's dad in his office and thanked him, apparently (Rhi said later). He was surprised, but said that frankly 'the more pretty girls' he had 'floating around the hotel' the better it was for 'business' and that absolutely outweighed any bits of 'salad' they 'nibbled' on, and the New Year's Party was a 'promotional event' anyway.

The afternoon passed. When 4 p.m. came and George still hadn't come back. I started worrying. He wasn't picking up his phone either. I tried not to stress. I told myself that in hospitals you can't take calls, but that worried me even more, because he shouldn't be IN HOSPITAL.

He should have been seen long ago. And discharged. And if he wasn't, that meant it was all Very Serious and he was undergoing emergency surgery.

At last I got a ping from Rhiannon.

Thank God! I sank on to a handy, crimson, Jacquard
loom, upholstered chair.

By the time Rhiannon did get back and gave us the
full story: twenty-eight stitches, tetanus jab, antibiotics,
dressing to be changed in three days' time, stitches out
in ten, George was taken home, by Order Of Gran Who
Turned Up At Hospital Much To Everyone's Annoyance
(and for dessert, a complete breakdown on how George
had taken it: Brave, Kind, Humorous, Gallant, Handsome,
Gorgeous, Divine, Amazing, Sexy and Oh My Days) – we'd
all settled down to watch telly (with Sheila, because she
couldn't miss the next episode of Corrie) and pigged out
on huge plates of food straight from the evening buffet.

By evening, I'd seen no sign of Oswald, but when I went up
to my room, I made Rhiannon come with me – just in case.

I made out I was dying to know more about George. She then spent half an hour, sitting on my bed, wowing over his Viking looks and muscly torso and fantasising about A Life With George.

When she left, I turned the key on my hotel door. The lock was a flimsy thing. I remembered how Henry had pushed open the door at Halfway House. One shove. So that stupid lock was really going to keep me safe, wasn't it? LOL.

I shivered beneath the flimsy bedding (Question: why do even posh hotels always have flimsy bedding?). I huddled down, drawing the starched cotton sheet up to my chin. I glanced nervously between the door and the window, until I couldn't stand it and got out of bed, drew back the thick folds of curtains and looked out at the mountain.

The moon was nearly full, and sailing high over the summit. From here Snowdon looked even more remote and mysterious than ever. It looked capable of hiding all kinds of secrets (amongst which, dragons seemed commonplace). I stood mesmerised by its beauty, looking out over the rooftops, over the foothills to that white mountain top. Another world was out there, a world of wizards, magic, myths and curses, a world where dragons gave their hearts or lay entombed in ancient dark caverns or walked abroad with nothing but death in their thoughts

... I shuddered and when I returned to the flimsy safety of the bed sheets, I huddled beneath them again hardly daring to breathe.

Twenty-Four

And so it came that the last day of the old year dawned. I shivered. One way or another, today would seal my fate. I reached under the bedding for my phone, expecting a message from Henry or an update from George. There was nothing.

I stared unhappily at my mobile. George must have done *something* since we talked to Gran?

Had she given him the potion? Had he put it in the lair? I'd done my bit, not put a toe out of the hotel, and I can tell you, That Wasn't Easy. I am Arabella Morgan, Child of the Mountain. I am used to roaming free, and right now I wanted to be back up the slopes of Snowdon DOING SOMETHING. Instead of locked up in a hotel, like a pet poodle.

In fact I'd had enough. This was not how it should be at all: me hiding in a hotel room, doing nothing to save the boy I loved. I was going to go back up on to the mountain. And I'd brew the potion myself and put it in the lair too, if I had to.

Filled with a new Can Do attitude, I sprang up in bed and knocked my head on an ill-placed shelf. Ouch! That hurt! I rubbed the spot. Then I called George.

His phone rang and rang, and he didn't pick up.

So I sent a ping:

Recent updates between Ellie and George:

Ellie

George, please let me know what's going on. I have had enough. I am going MENTAL. So I am coming up to your place to KICK ASS.

And then I sent one to UNKNOWN, just in case it *was* Henry.

Recent updates between Ellie and The Most Gorgeous Boy in History, UNKNOWN:

Ellie

How are you fy ngwir gariad melys? I'm flipping fed up with being here. I've really tried hard, but I need to help you too. TBH I'd rather be dead than live on knowing I could've tried

to save you, but didn't. I know you'll understand. Sending
prayers to Great Draco, and the spirit of Yr Wyddfa for tonight.
Love you xxxxxxxxxxxxxxxxxxxxxxxxxxxxxxxxxxxxxxxxxxxxxxx
xxxxxx

Enigmatic enough? I hoped so.

Please note, I'm not very good at soppy stuff, but I did
try with the 'ngwir gariad' darling dear bit. Then hoping
my Welsh was ok, I sent it.

So with my new daring plan in mind, I pulled on some
clothes and started trying to figure out how to get into
Llanberis.

That's when there was a knock on the door.

I jumped. Scooping up a heavy glass paperweight (just
in case) I flew across the room. *'Who's there?'* I hissed.

'Me.'

'George?'

I placed the glass weight back on the table and unlocked
the door. George stepped into the room, breakfast tray
in one hand, freebee newspaper in the other (Great!
I suddenly realised I was starving!). I looked from his
anxious face to the steaming coffee pot and demanded,
'What's the story?'

He put the tray down and poured coffee.

'Eat first,' he said (infuriatingly). 'And I don't need my ass kicking.'

'So tell.'

'I was your Guardian Angel for a whole twenty-four hours,' he said with a radiant smile. 'Yesterday Was The Happiest Day Of My Life.'

'Oh shut up!' I said. 'And get on with it.'

'Ok,' he whispered. 'Now listen – we may not have another chance. They're gonna be here soon.'

'Who?' I sat bolt upright on the bed, eyes wide.

'Last night on the mountain I heard them,' he said. 'They must have had a pretty serious fight. All over our side – there was lightning, rock falls and that shrieking noise. They carried on right till dawn – it's all over the news this morning: *Caernarfon Castle involved in freak accident. Castle wing occupied by Pendragon royals struck by lightning.*' George slung the newspaper across the bed at me.

'Henry?' I said.

'Don't worry. He's ok,' said George. 'They're claiming the cuts and bruises and burns were due to the lightning strike, but … '

'Cuts and bruises?'

'He's … ' said George.

'*What?*' I stared at George searching his face.

'Ok' he said. 'Except … '

'*Except what?*' I was off the bed and about to shake him.

'They're both coming to the hotel.'

'*Coming to the hotel?*' I screamed. (They probably heard me in Cardiff.)

'Yep, they're cutting their stay in Caernarfon short, due to the damage to the royal apartments. They're going to relocate to *this* hotel for tonight – they still have New Year's engagements or something to do. That's the excuse.'

I don't know whether my heart was soaring or might need emergency CPR.

'Everyone's in a tizzy downstairs, upping security, buying food, hiring in extras – some of the royal staff have arrived already.'

'What about Rhiannon and the party?'

'Apparently Sir Oswald wants no other guests at the hotel during his stay.'

'He's trying to get us out … ' I said.

'Definitely,' said George.

That was it. Clever.

I got it – cause a fight, destroy the castle, get relocated, enter the hotel – no questions asked – *force Ellie out before she's had a chance to think*. My heart started beating faster. Oswald was trying to outwit us.

'Don't panic yet,' said George. 'Rhiannon kicked up such a stink, her dad was literally screaming. I mean he can't decline the royals and if Oswald says No Other Guests For Security Reasons, he's bound to put their comfort and safety first, and ... '

My mind raced. Where would we go? What should we do? What about the potion, could I stay and somehow get it into his drink?

'So the party's moved to the annexe. You know, the old stables converted last year, to the conference hall section and apartments. That's where Rhiannon's dad's put us – With No Further Discussion. We've all got to relocate there ... like *NOW* ... '

'What about the potion?'

'Right here,' said George.

George pulled out a tiny glass bottle, not unlike an old-fashioned perfume bottle. In fact, now I come to think of it, it *was* an old-fashioned perfume bottle. He held it up. It seemed to glow in a strange way. 'But we need to think about You First,' he said.

'The old stables are outside the hotel, beyond the safety of the stone dragons, right?' I said.

'Exactly,' said George.

'So if outside is outside, we might as well go straight to

the lair?' I reached across to take the potion from him.

George swatted my hand away and sat there looking grim. 'No. Way. Ellie.'

'Look,' I said. It Was Time To Give George The Talk. 'You know I'll accept Henry – if he offers me his crystal?'

George nodded miserably. 'I know,' he said. 'I'd get down on my knees and howl like a dog – beg you to accept *me* – if I thought you would – but I might as well howl at the moon, I s'pose.'

'But don't you see,' I said. 'It means that I've got to be up at the lair by midnight too.'

'No, I don't,' said George flatly.

I explained to George my new daring plan. 'I'll go and lure Oswald there, he'll drink the potion and sleep, then Henry will be able to offer me his crystal and be freed … '

'Forget it,' said George. 'We need to focus on just staying alive. There's no way you can get safely up to the lair, and I can't go and put the potion in the pool with Oswald loose in the hotel. That plan is dead.'

I folded my arms. I could see he wasn't going to give me the potion, but I wasn't going to give up that easily, either.

'Here's my idea,' said George, 'both of us should go down with a tummy thing and retire to your room straight away after breakfast,' George raised his eyes invitingly and waggled his eyebrows. 'We won't be able to be moved, and we won't have to go to the party.'

'But what if Rhi's dad just sends us home in the shuttle – in case the royals catch it?' (Plus that wouldn't save Henry either, would it?)

'Pity her stupid cousin isn't up to looking out for you,' said George. 'He's keen enough on sniffing round though, isn't he – useless creep.' George shot me a look like it was my fault, and I was encouraging Darren.

'You don't like him much, do you?' I said.

'Not much,' agreed George.

I was a bit surprised. George is Mr Nice Guy. He likes everyone.

'I've got to put up with Henry, I don't have to put up with him,' snorted George.

'Please George,' I said, 'You've *got* to put the potion in the pool. If I promise to find a way to stay in the hotel all day, will you? I'll do whatever you want?'

A wicked grin spread across his face. '*Whatever I want?*' he said.

I leaned over and squeezed his arm. 'Oh, George,' I said, 'You're the truest friend any girl could have.'

He smiled. 'Wanna shift up in that bed?' he said, 'you know, as a sort of down-payment, thank-you gesture?'

330

'Typical!' I snorted.

'Look, seriously, Elles,' George said. 'It'll take all day to get there and back.' He put the potion in his hoodie pocket and zipped it shut. 'So give that idea up. I was going to go straight there this morning, but when I heard they were coming here, I had to act quickly. Things change and that's that.'

If George wouldn't put the potion to the pool and wasn't going to let me, either, then there was no hope.

'Looks like we'll just have to slip this potion in his gin'n'tonic then,' joked George, making dragon claws. 'And I think I know of a really convincing way of getting Rhiannon to reserve us a bedroom – if we invite her along – you know – just the three of us … just a chat and a … '

But I wasn't listening. I was on a desolate mountainside where there was no comfort. Out there, I saw only the empty march of days – one after the other – each as meaningless as the one before – and me alone forever.

And that made me really sad.

And furthermore that Was Not In My Life Plan.

So, I thought, say what you like, George, but by fair means or foul, I'll get that potion off you and I'll go to the lair myself.

The royal entourage arrived at the hotel by noon. Expensive cars choked the yard, stewards in livery flooded the reception area, and chefs in tall hats filled the kitchens. The best rooms and the Great Hall were cordoned off and the whole of the front drive, lawn and conservatory became a no-go area. Only the buffet bar and the Cadair Idris restaurant stayed open for the public. There was no chance of me staying in my room, however many tummy bugs I complained of, as while I was down at breakfast my room was cleaned, locked and my stuff taken over to the annexe.

Just as well I'd decided not to.

Rhiannon, George, Darren and I sat and watched everything from an upstairs balcony. I kept my eyes glued on that zipped hoodie pocket, timing George's every move. Sheila arrived and joined us.

I saw how the chauffeurs rearranged the cars; how the police escorts tore up and down between Caernarfon and Llanberis. The council sent the gritter up and it gritted away, as if we were expecting another severe weather alert rather than a royal entourage. Overhead, RAF helicopters swept the sky as if aliens were going to attack Snowdon from Mars.

I wondered at it all, shaking my head: all the fuss, all the pomp, when Henry could wander the hills as he liked and

Oswald could take to his dragon form every night to hunt me down. All a pretence.

'Well we can't loiter around all day,' said Rhiannon, 'We need to set up in the annexe and sort out the food and get in the drinks and … ' She started to get shrill.

'I'll do the food,' I said. 'I'll go and grab a corner of the kitchen where the royals aren't jugging hares and start up some sandies, 'k?' That would keep me inside the hotel for the time being.

'Open baguettes like bruschetta style,' said Rhiannon.

'Tuna toppings, chopped tomatoes, basil?' I said. 'George will help me.'

'Ok, you do the food,' said Rhiannon. 'But as for George, I need strong arms.' She looked at my thin ones. 'There's a tonne of stuff in that conference room. Dad's been using it as a furniture store.' She smiled at George, as if nobody in the universe could be stronger than him.

George looked at me.

'You don't need Ellie's permission,' snapped Rhiannon.

'He does,' I said. 'Granny Jones put me in charge of him. And as his In Charge Person, I don't think he should lift tables and old wardrobes. His stitches might split.'

Rhiannon gasped. '*Oh My Days!*' she said. '*How awful! I forgot!* No! George mustn't lift anything! Darren can shift the stuff. I'll get a footman to help.'

Darren didn't look too pleased.

'I'll keep you company,' said Sheila and wrapped an arm around Darren's neck.

His scowl didn't shift an inch.

'I'll give Elles a hand in kitchen,' said George.

Rhiannon jumped up. 'Ok, troops let's to it! Let's get everything sorted by five; let's wangle a supper with the royals, and get this party started!'

'My mum's coming over to have supper,' I said, thinking, why, oh, why does Mum have to come? Right at this point?

Darren sidled up to me and whispered, 'Expect me in the kitchen, Sugarbabes, to give you a hand with opening the tuna tins – as soon as I'm done doing Man Stuff.' He snorted at George and turned again to me, 'I'll help you titillate your toppings too.' He winked in a leery, yuck, kind of way.

I shuddered and was about to say something, but before I could open my mouth, George sprung to his feet and glared at Darren.

'Boys, boys,' simpered Sheila, 'No need to fight over a little minger like Ellie.' She laughed and ruffled my hair, which annoyed me as much as being called a 'minger'.

Darren smiled. 'Calm down Georgy Porgy boy – go on – off to the kitchen with you'

George struggled to control himself. I could see his jaw working. At last he laughed. 'Ok,' he said. 'I'll go and put my pinny on,' and the ugly mood seemed to clear.

We spent a long time in that kitchen, and I discovered catering was not going to be one of my preferred life choices. You can get pretty tired of slicing tomatoes. You can get pretty tired of adding mayo to tuna, and buttering garlic bread too. And you can get pretty tired of buttering SOMEONE up, trying to get them to Remove Their Hoodie.

I tried: you need to put on a proper chef's outfit.

I tried: come and slice over here (by the huge ovens).

I even tried: do you need your stitches looking at and a back rub?

No joy. George knew what I was up to.

And so the buttering continued. And so did the work load. I thought Rhiannon was just having a nice cosy little New Year's gig for only the gang – but it turned out half of Birmingham were driving over to see Darren, and the whole of Caernarfon had been invited on Twitter.

I don't think her dad had any idea of the size of her party (if he had, I don't think he'd have been so keen on having pretty girls wafting around everywhere).

All afternoon, in between trying to find a way to get the potion off George and not slice my fingers to the bone, I kept my eyes on the window watching out for Henry. Had he arrived? Was he here already? Was Oswald by now sneaking through the lobby on some plan to get me? Would Henry swoop down, rescue me, carry me off to the mountain and give me his crystal? If I got the potion before evening, would I still be able to get to the lair? Would taxis be running? Would Henry take me? My dreams and fears spiralled in and out of each other – one minute showing me magical fantastical endings, the next plunging me into horror.

George was nervous too. He kept saying, 'I'm really sorry Elles. I do want to help.' And, 'How can I slip the potion in a gin and tonic if I'm here?' And I knew he meant *stuck* here: babysitting me.

So I said, 'George, I'll be fine. I've got a sharp kitchen knife and I'll use it. Please find a way to stop Oswald.'

But George just sighed and said. 'I'm not leaving you, Elles. I've thought this through, and the only reason I'd be leaving you is to help Henry, and for me that's no reason at all.'

My heart shut down at the thought that we wouldn't save Henry. By midnight tonight he would be entombed under the mountain for another seventy-two years. I stopped sprinkling basil over the bruschettas and let my hands fall slack.

George looked at me, his eyes full of something that made me catch my breath. 'When you get that expression on your face,' he said, 'I don't know what to do. It's like you're dying inside.'

I nodded, tears welling up. George put his arms out to me. I buried my face in his shoulder and sobbed, dry, shaking sobs. 'Please?' I whispered. 'Please George. If you love me even the tiniest bit, let me go to the lair.'

George held me and sighed. 'Ok,' he said at last. 'You win. We'll borrow Darren's Range Rover if we have to. I'll drive right round the south spur and over the foothills.'

'He'll never lend it you,' I said bitterly. George'd changed his mind too late.

'I won't bother asking him then,' said George and he dangled a set of car keys in front of me.

My heart jumped, my eyes popped. 'George!' I hissed, 'However did you … '

'She who asks no questions, will be told no lies,' he smirked.

'But how?' I marvelled.

'Didn't offer to help the valet to park the cars round the

back for nothing,' laughed George. 'You gotta have a lot more confidence in me, Elles. I've been thinking of nothing but your peace of mind, ever since I woke up.'

I brushed back my hair and wiped my eyes on a tea towel. Then I blew my nose on a piece of kitchen roll.

'Much better,' said George. 'Now that must be worth a snog or two?'

'It is,' I said and reached up and kissed him lightly on the cheek.

He snorted, 'You and I do not share the same definition of the word,' he said. But before he could grumble any more, a fanfare sounded and the hotel fell curiously silent.

'They're coming,' he hissed. Both of us dashed to the window. A cavalcade of shiny cars pulled into the front drive of the hotel. The late afternoon sun blazed coldly from their sleek rooftops. Six, maybe seven white cars drew up to the main door, each with the Welsh flag fluttering from their bonnets – Welsh flags in which the red had gone from the dragon – except on one dark maroon Jaguar.

'Henry,' I murmured.

The cars slowed to a stop. Footmen in olive-green livery danced to attendance.

'Come on, Elles,' said George. 'Let's finish the chicken wings and get going,' but nothing could drag me away.

Just one glimpse of Henry. Just one glimpse.

The car nearest stopped. The footmen opened the doors and out stepped Sir Oswald. He limped slowly round to the front of the car. ~~Well Done George You Really Mashed Him Up!!~~ Oh Dear Poor Oswald! He swung his gaze around, sweeping to and fro, searching the windows of the building, his hooded pink eyes more menacing than ever. I ducked back behind the curtain, my hands clutching the cloth. I let out a silent, 'Oh,' but not even the evil eyes of Sir Oswald could stop me peeping out again. I had to see Henry. Just had to.

The maroon Jaguar had already stopped. Its doors were already open. Its one passenger was already out. There in the glow of the setting sun was Henry, his thick auburn hair aflame with the rays of the setting sun, his face turned straight towards me, as if he already knew exactly where I was, and how I'd been longing to see him.

He smiled as he saw me, and I pressed my face against the window and smiled back.

But no sooner had I smiled, than I felt the cold creep of other eyes searching me out. Eyes that knew I was bound to be at a window, bound to be smiling out at Henry. And those eyes found me and the jolt of malice from them sent me spinning back into the kitchen counter behind.

One of the stewards pushing a trolley said, 'Steady on!' as I crashed past and nearly sent him flying.

⁓

From then on I felt the chill of Oswald's gaze fixed on me. Maybe if we'd left earlier, things might have worked out. Maybe if I'd stayed holed up in the kitchen with George, I could have kept out of trouble.

But that didn't happen, and anyway trouble was already out looking for me.

It arrived first in the unexpected form of my mother. Yes, no sooner had the Royals arrived than Mum was there too.

They (of course Jeff was with her) were both all done up in their best. They found me out and invited me down for supper. Immediately.

In snatches of excited chatter, Mum explained they must get back, and clear up, and pop down to the off licence, and get the wine in good time (so that it would be properly chilled), and pick up Jeff's suit from the dry cleaners – oh, and there were the nibbles to sort out – and a whole heap of other stuff that I wasn't really listening to.

And as if that were not enough, at exactly the same time Rhiannon came back from the annexe, and latched on to George. And trouble made its second appearance.

Rhiannon fussed over George in such a sickening way that he seemed to have no choice but to go and eat supper with her despite Mum inviting them both to stay with us, and George saying YES PLEASE (to Mum) and NO THANKS (to Rhiannon) very loudly, more than twice.

And so he was dragged off.

And that freaked me out.

And I was left sitting with Mum and Jeff in the Cadair Idris restaurant.

And that's when the best bit and the worst bit of the whole day happened:

Henry and Sir Oswald walked in.

A ripple of whispers went through the restaurant, which was actually embarrassing, because they could plainly be heard. (There weren't many people there – only those who'd made their reservations before the Pendragons had announced theirs.)

And I was metres away from Henry.

Blood rushed to my face. My heart went wild. I started fidgeting with my napkin. *Henry was here – in the same room – breathing the same air!*

A thin chuckle came from Sir Oswald. My heart checked

341

its crazy beating. I felt the blood in my cheeks draining away. My hands fell into my lap, trembling. The napkin dropped to the floor. Sir Oswald laughed again, a queer thin hissing laugh.

And Henry didn't look at me.

Not Once.

Mum raised her eyebrows as if to say: We Are So Lucky. And Jeff shuffled around in his seat like he was really unsure that he was wearing the correct tie. A waiter approached in spotless white with the royal fleur de lys embroidered on his waistcoat. He stepped up to the table and looked from Jeff to Mum and back again and then offered something on a silver platter to Jeff.

On the platter lay a thick creamy envelope with the royal crest embossed on one corner. Jeff took it, his mouth dropping slightly open. He turned it over in his hands, uncertain what to do with it.

'Open it, then,' hissed Mum.

All the time I was watching Henry, waiting to catch his eye. But he didn't raise his face or turn his chin in my direction. In fact he seemed to smile and bow to every other point of the compass – except mine. The same was not true of Sir Oswald. In rude contrast, he deliberately stared straight at me, his pale eyes malevolent and his mouth drawn into a thin cruel line.

'Well?' hissed Mum.

'Hang on,' said Jeff, as he fumbled with the envelope.

Christ, I thought, he can't even open an envelope.

At length he managed to draw from inside it a thick cream card, which also had the royal seal imposingly embossed into its papery depths.

'Well?' said Mum.

Jeff opened the card and read the message.

'Well?' said Mum for a third time, and I could see she was getting rattled.

'It says,' coughed Jeff. 'It says:

Sir Oswald Pendragon de Clare &
Sir Henry Pendragon de Clare, Lord Chandos
and Viscount of Carnarvon invite you to join them
for a preprandial drink.'

Twenty-Five

Mum flashed her eyes from Jeff to me to Sir Oswald to Henry. Immediately Sir Oswald sprang to attention and bowed politely. Mum blushed. Jeff stammered. Henry bowed too. Sir Oswald gestured with his hand toward the small VIP room attached to the restaurant, and said in a high thin voice, 'It would be my pleasure to make the acquaintance of your good selves and residents of Snowdonia while you wait for your meal.'

Jeff stood and nearly fell over his shoelaces. Mum pulled herself together, and did a made-up kind of curtsey. Henry flashed his eyes up at me once. The message: SAY NO, very clearly written in them.

'Mum,' I said straight away. 'I don't think we have time.'

Mum turned her face on me as if to say: Are You Mad?

And Jeff had already left his seat and was walking towards

Sir Oswald, with his hand outstretched. 'How very kind,' he said.

I looked up at Henry, my eyes saying: WHAT CAN I DO?

He did not look back, but politely showed Mum into the bar.

Immediately a waiter appeared. Sir Oswald ordered a bottle of champagne. Within seconds the bottle was brought in a silver ice-bucket with the best cut-glass champagne flutes. The waiter popped the cork very professionally, twisting the bottle with skill. He poured out a little for Sir Oswald to endorse, waited a nanosecond and then poured for us all.

Sir Oswald picked the first glass off the tray and straight away offered it to me saying, 'Perhaps this once we can put beauty before age?' His pale blue eyes fixed mine, and like a mouse staring into the eyes of a snake, I found myself frozen.

I'm not quite sure what happened next, but suddenly Henry tripped. It seemed as if the waiter accidentally bumped his shoulder, as he was walking past to offer the tray to Mum, but it was much too quick for me to be sure.

Henry went sprawling after the waiter, knocking the drinks, tray, ice bucket and champagne flying. The bottle catapulted up into the air and drenched me on its way.

Mum squealed, Jeff gasped, Sir Oswald cursed in a language I'd never heard before: '*Cha d'fhuaireadh facal Beurla mar sa Bhriathrachan Bheag.*'[1]

'I'm so sorry', stammered the waiter. 'I don't know what happened; let me fetch another bottle … '

Sir Oswald let out a strangled yell and turned rudely on his heel.

With Oswald gone, Henry stepped forward all gallantry, all bowing, all smiling and all good manners. 'Just an accident,' he said, 'don't worry, we are slightly ahead of schedule anyway.' He took Mum's arm and gently steered her back towards the restaurant. 'We'll send a fresh bottle to your table,' he told Jeff. Perhaps you'd like to assist your daughter in a change of clothes?' he said to Mum. 'I promise I'll make this up to you,' he said to us all. 'After you've changed and eaten, do allow me to treat you to coffee and liqueurs? I'll have them sent to your table.' As I turned away towards the toilet, he whispered quickly in my ear, 'I'm sorry to ruin your dress. I had to act quickly. *Never* accept food or drink from a dragon unless you truly trust him. Once you have eaten or drunk from his hand – it's too long to explain – but he will have powers over you'.

---

1. 'You DARE to foil me, serpent's spawn. You will pay!'

He brushed my elbow, pressed it slightly as if he was trying to tell me something else too and slipped a note into my hand.

At Henry's insistence Mum helped me towards the toilets to change. My heart was hammering. *Powers over me? That was so close! Thank God for Henry.*

But I couldn't change of course; all my clothes were packed away in a bedroom in the annexe, and I wasn't going over there to get them. No way. Not with Oswald on the loose.

Mum wasn't too keen on going either.

Inside the ladies' I moaned at her. 'But look at me Mum,' I insisted, 'I'm soaked, I can't go out in the cold like this – can't you get them for me?' Mum dabbed at me with pieces of loo roll and reluctantly left in search of my valise. I breathed a sigh of relief.

From my pocket, I dug out the dried flowers Gran had given me. They were soaked through like everything else. As I patted them dry in a wad of toilet tissue, I realised with a shudder that I knew virtually nothing about the powers of dragons. *What if Oswald tried again? What could I do to protect myself?* Hastily I checked to make sure Gran's silver charm was still around my neck. What had she said when she'd given it to me? *'Not by sunlight or by moonshine?'*

I suddenly felt so grateful to Gran, so glad she'd kept it all those years and given it to me. I was never going to take it off, never going to let go of my dried flowers. I needed all the protection I could get.

And with that decided, I waited impatiently for Mum and dry clothes, in the VIP visitors' toilets.

And I read the note.

'In the conservatory after supper. Come alone. H'

Throughout the meal, all I could think of was Henry. I pushed the little pieces of designer food around my plate and wondered what the hell was going to happen. Was there a different plan? Or was this goodbye? Was Henry still determined to go under the mountain at midnight? And when I thought of that, my face drooped, and I could feel tears pricking at my eyes. Even Jeff noticed, 'Cheer up Eleanor,' he said, 'It's only a dress. I'll pay the dry cleaning bill for you,' which was sweet of him, except that it wasn't the dress and my name isn't Eleanor. But I forced myself to look more cheerful, and whispered, 'Thanks Jefferson,' which paid him back.

After all, maybe Henry *had* found a way. Maybe we would defeat Sir Oswald, maybe *he'd* end up under the mountain …

Maybe Henry was going to offer me his heart.

Blood pounded against my temples. I could scarcely swallow. I dared not even think.

And whilst I was wishing the dessert already over and imagining accepting Henry's crystal, Mum chattered on about how she'd hardly seen me much this holiday, and did I feel neglected? And would I like to come over to Jeff's on New Year's Day, in the afternoon sometime, as she was going to invite a few of her friends to a late lunch party there? And Jeff's brother was coming up from Hereford tonight, and it would be nice for everyone to meet everyone before he went back, wouldn't it?

I could see exactly where her mind was drifting, and I thought to myself: on New Year's Day I will either be with Henry forever – and so happy I'll scarcely be able to think straight – or I'll be alone and so sad I'll be completely suicidal, if not already dead.

Jeff was saying how amazing it was to have been invited for drinks with royals and what a shame it was that the clumsy waiter had messed the invite up, but that nice Sir Oswald had been so apologetic and sent more champagne and that charming Henry had promised brandy, (quite forgetting Oswald had stomped off and it was *all* Henry) and what gentlemen the royals were, and could he get a photo – did we think he could? – something to show the grandchildren when they came along (Grandchildren?!).

I reminded myself to be on guard. Sir Oswald had shown himself quite capable of thinking on his feet and setting up a manoeuvre while drinking his cocktail.

'Well?' said Mum.

'Oh,' I said. 'I don't really know … ' my voice trailed away. What did Henry want to tell me? Would we be able to be alone … ?

'Ellie?' said Mum.

'Oh,' I said again, thinking on my feet too. 'Rhiannon has invited me to a New Year's Day lunch here,' I said, 'it's a post-party sort of thing, after all her hospitality, it wouldn't be very nice if I didn't show.' There I was lying to Mum again.

Mum didn't look too upset though. If anything she breathed a little easier. She probably was dreading me being there with all her friends, getting to know all Jeff's friends. I shuddered at the thought of them all mutually admiring each other and congratulating themselves on being just the 'right kind of people'. And then I suddenly saw it. She was starting the New Year as she meant to go on! She was moving into a much more solid relationship with Jeff! Perhaps I ought to be there. I ought to raise objections, before everyone got too cosy. I opened my mouth to say something, and then closed it again. My heart just wasn't in it.

'Maybe I'll come over in the evening,' I said.

'Oh yes,' breathed Mum, and I could see that would suit them both very well.

At last they served the coffee and the cheeses and a little platter of white grapes and the courtesy brandy with delightful petit fours along with another royal calling card. I said I was full, and how yummy it all was, and how lovely they'd been to invite me; and Jeff pulled out his wallet and made a big show of the fact that he was going to pay, which was making some kind of point that I didn't really get.

Anyway, I thanked him very prettily and even gave him a quick kiss on the cheek. I hugged Mum and said I was literally busting and how fab it was being with them – and how Rhiannon needed me now, because I was doing the catering for the party – and if I was away from the kitchen much longer the chicken wings might re-animate and flap their feathers and fly off all on their own – and Rhi would be pretty upset about that.

And after being very flattering and appreciative and

wishing everyone Happy New Year a zillion times I was
allowed to escape.

Henry was waiting for me in the conservatory.

He had arranged one of the carved wooden settles near
to the window, and sat there, looking out towards the
frozen lake. Heart pounding, I slipped in beside him.
He put his arm around me.

'Where are all your bodyguards and man-servant
thingies?' I whispered.

'You look amazing,' he said. 'Beautiful as the stars.'

'Won't they see?'

'I love your hands, your dress, your tiny feet in those
sparkling slippers.'

I forgot about his entourage, as his nearness enveloped
me.

'Oh how I've longed for this,' he murmured.

I felt his heart thudding against me, felt the pressure of
his arms, as he crushed me close.

'*Oh Ellie* … ' He held me, and I felt my head spin.

'How much time have we got?' I whispered.

'Not much,' he sighed. His eyes clouded over. 'Oswald
is up to something, and I dare not leave him alone long.

He'll use his influence to corrupt someone – one of your friends maybe – he's already tried with your family – or he'll give me the slip and snatch another girl.'

It seemed weird to me, how these two creatures – who so violently hated one another – somehow lived in each other's pockets. I said as much.

'Ha,' laughed Henry, 'Our relationship is as complex as the stars in Draco. Until one of us triumphs, we are locked together in deadly combat. In our human form we cannot fight – such was the will of Merlin. But he can no more leave me alone than I can him. He believes the minute he takes his eyes off me, I'll settle on someone to give my heart to – and he fears that more than anything, for he knows it is the ultimate way to destroy him.'

'Why?' I said (I had to stop myself asking anything else).

Henry shuffled and looked at the floor. 'You might as well tell me,' I said 'You told George. You whispered it to him and I'll get it out of him somehow,'

'I'm sure you will,' he said, 'with your beautiful eyes, you could coax the stars from their orbits … '

'Don't try to derail the subject,' I said brusquely.

Henry sighed a long deep exhalation 'It's kind of embarrassing,' he said.

I looked at him puzzled. How could the reason that your

arch enemy wants to kill you be embarrassing?

'And?' I said

'Well,' Henry took a deep breath.

'Yes.'

Henry started shoving something around on the floor with his toe.

'After all if you give your heart to someone, you will lose your dragon's immortality and eventually die,' I said. Suddenly I gulped at the thought of Henry dying. Because much as I wanted him – more than anything or anyone I'd ever wanted – I realised with a pang, that I didn't want him to age and die.

'There are other ways of living forever.'

I didn't know what he meant and I feared he'd change the subject altogether, so I brought him back to the topic. 'Why is he afraid you'll give your heart?'

'He cannot tolerate the thought of the bloodline.'

There it was. He'd said it.

I opened my mouth and stopped in mid action. The penny dropped. The bloodline. His bloodline. Henry's bloodline. His *children*. Children he would have with … I blushed. 'But … ' I stammered

'Yes,' he said 'Oswald fears my children and my children's children and he knows that those born of the dragon will oppose him and instead of one of me there will be a myriad of me, and whilst my sons may not be able to shapeshift they will have dragon souls, and they will be true Welshmen and will not rest until they have outwitted him and made Wales safe forever.'

'I see,' I said and chewed my lip. 'But who says your wife will want a myriad of kids?'

I looked at him, I loved him right enough, but the role of women has changed a bit since The Days Of Yore, and being in love didn't mean I was up for the whole mortgage and two kids deal (and anyway it certainly would be nice to be asked).

Henry looked at me with his strange dark eyes. 'Not masses all at one go,' he said, 'but over time there would be many, who would multiply and besiege him throughout all his life spans.'

'And what makes you both think they'll all be sons?' I said.

Henry turned to me. 'Ellie,' he said, 'if you would have my heart, I would give it to you a thousand times. I would not need children – no, I would need neither sons nor daughters – I would only need you close beside me. But I have been trying to explain why my heart can never be given. For Oswald would try to kill you as soon as my heart was yours. He would make it his sole purpose – to prevent any bloodline of mine outliving, outwitting and outranking him – please understand. This is why I have tried so hard to stay away from you.'

I bit my lip then. 'But can't Oswald have his own children?' I said, randomly, at last, as a way of deflecting the bitterness of his decision.

'He has chosen to sacrifice women to his heart. And that means he can never have a woman himself. He is impotent and no woman will give herself willingly to him. It is the choice he made. It is part of the magic. Even in my case, if the woman I give my heart to dies or deserts me, I can never take another – that too is part of the spell.'

'Oh?' I said again, and fell silent.

We sat for a while looking out over the frozen garden. I imagined little children born with dragon souls out there, leaving their footprints in the snow.

But there would be no children.

No future.

I'd lost and Henry had lost, and all we could try to do was make sure that Oswald lost too.

At last I looked at my watch. It was nearly 8.40 p.m. Less than four hours before the year closed. 'What are we going to do?' I whispered.

'You are going to go down with a headache and go to your room and stay there. George will stay with you. I have only to see him and ask him and he will stay with you forever – and I *will* ask him, for it will ease my mind – so that while I lie cramped under the mountain, day after day, night after night, I will rest easy, knowing that the truest of hearts guards yours. Oswald will have no interest in you once I'm gone. He will not blight your life again.'

'But … ' I wanted to tell him I couldn't actually 'go to my room' any more, because there was no room for me to go to – except in the annexe – and that George and I had a different plan, but I didn't. I shut up.

'I will go to the lair before midnight to make sure Oswald has not taken another girl and chained her there already, if I can.' Henry looked thoughtful.

Of course he must.

'And after that, he and I are constrained to meet on the summit of Snowdon, as is destined by the will of Merlin, and to arrive together at the lair and make our choices in front of the crystals.' He paused, 'So there will be no more talk about the future, now.' Henry bit his lip.

The footprints of little dragon-souled children faded in the snow.

'I would go there, straight away, if it were not for you.

But whilst the hope of capturing you still drives him, he will remain at the hotel. And therefore so will I.'

I knew I should say something, convince him to check up on the lair immediately – convince him I'd be ok. I was going to, but at that moment the door to the conservatory flew open, and in charged Sheila, Darren, George and Rhiannon.

'So *hell-ooo* mystery mountain man,' said Sheila, a wicked gleam in her eye. And she swooped directly down on us and squeezed herself – without warning – straight in between Henry and me.

In shock, I drew back – this was exactly what Sheila had been hoping for. She turned very briefly to me and licked one finger and drew a line in the air, in front of my face. 'One up to me,' she gloated. 'Plus I got bought a royal drink at the bar just now. Beat that!'

If Henry was startled, he didn't show it. He dipped his head slightly and said, 'Please excuse my manners, I should have relinquished my seat to you, as soon as I saw you,' and he promptly stood up to allow Sheila to sit properly.

A look of thunder scrolled across her face. She uncere-moniously grabbed his arm and tried to pull him back down beside her.

And failed.

I resisted the temptation to lick my finger and stroke the air. One Up To Me.

Henry moved across to a nearby table and picking up two chairs, quickly arranged them so that Rhiannon could sit too. He gestured Darren to the second. He turned to George and bowed slightly, 'I'm sure you'll stand with me,' he asserted.

George grinned, 'Course,' he said, good-natured as ever.

Sheila was not happy. She made as if to stand up too, but Darren pulled a face and said, 'Don't worry, Sheila, if you can't sit beside me, there's always my lap,' and he trotted his legs up and down as if he was dying for her to sit on them.

Sheila shot him a withering look and stood up anyway. She went and squeezed herself in between George and Henry saying, 'If you two think you're the only ones who can stand – that's so sexist.' She managed to say sexist like it was 'sexy' and tilt her chest up, and thrust her bosom out, so that from the angle occupied by George and Henry, they'd be able to see straight down her front.

George turned red and rolled his eyes, Rhiannon rolled hers too. Henry was absolutely perfectly behaved. He cast his eyes down, away from Sheila and said, 'Could I offer anyone a Coke or a coffee?'

'Mine's a double Scotch on the rocks,' Darren said. He got up off his chair, and plumped himself right down on the now empty seat beside me. 'If your bloke doesn't want to sit by you, and George is too much of a loser to grab the chance, that leaves the way open for your favourite boy from Birmingham,' he said. He stole his arm along the top of the settle and sneaked it down around my shoulder. 'You know what they say: if you're not the only pebble on the beach you've got to be a little bo(u)lder.' He raised his face at George and stuck his tongue out in a stupid childish way.

George's face darkened. He took one step forward. Henry moved away from Sheila and laid a hand on his arm.

But George wasn't having it.

'Back off,' he said in a menacing tone straight at Darren. I looked up at George amazed. I swear, never in my entire life, have I seen him so angry.

'Calmness, Georgy Porgy,' said Darren, and all of a sudden his arm (which had moved even further over my shoulder) snaked around me in a horribly intimate fashion. 'There, that's what you like isn't it?' he said, 'A nice cuddle.'

I tried to draw back. Blood rushed to my face. But before I could move, George had stepped forward and yanked Darren up from the seat and punched him on the nose.

Blood spurted down Darren's face. 'You just hit the wrong guy, buster,' he said.

George, beside himself with fury, raised his fist again. 'Take Your Hands Off Her,' he snarled.

'Why? She likes it, doesn't she?' sneered Darren. 'She was out here, getting all loved up with Mountain Man, wasn't she?'

Rhiannon burst into tears. 'Just stop it both of you,' she said, racing to get hold of George's arm, trying to drag him back.

'I'm sorry Rhiannon, but he had it coming to him, the *prat*,' said George.

'Oh,' sobbed Rhiannon.

All the while Henry was looking at me in a strange way.

Then one of the bodyguards (who'd been discreetly staying out on the corridor) rushed in and put George in an arm lock.

Rhiannon looked shocked. Sheila looked shocked. Even Darren looked shocked.

I suddenly realised they didn't know who Henry was. They'd assumed he'd been someone I'd just met in the restaurant, someone who maybe was going to the party.

Only George didn't look shocked, but as the guards wrestled him to the conservatory doors, he shuddered in pain, twisted towards me and whispered, '*Had to do it. Sorry. I'll get to the lair. Henry'll take care of you. Don't give up.*'

I looked into George's face, at the set of his chin; George defending my honour, George setting out alone across the ranges. My throat dried up.

'*Of course you're Sir Henry Pendragon de Clare?*' breathed Rhiannon. '*I thought you looked familiar …* '

'Oh My Dayz!' said Sheila, immediately pretending to stagger, (so that she could land herself right on him).

'Nice one, bruv,' said Darren. 'Wot a little loser our Georgy is!' He sniggered as the guards marched George to the glass doors and pushed them open.

Henry raised an arm to stop them. But the bodyguards had already thrown George outside, 'Clear off,' said the bigger guard. 'If we see your hide around here again, it'll be the worse for you.'

'No, let him stay,' said Henry.

But George, shooting us a grim smile, turned on his heel and strode off.

'Oh Sire,' said Sheila huskily, with all the coquetry she'd been practising, like forever, 'I'm so sorry I didn't recognise you before.'

'There is no reason why you should,' said Henry coldly.

'Oh, but Sire,' she said pressing herself even closer.

'I certainly have never seen *you* before.' Henry was stiff, his voice wooden. I saw that he hadn't either, and I

362

remembered how at the Boxing Day reception Sheila hadn't been there. She'd been skiving off with Darren doing the sales in Caernarfon – or so she'd said (mia-ow).

But it puzzled me. Why was Henry being so formal, so rude even? It wasn't like him. Don't get me wrong, I wasn't *sorry* about it. Sheila had it coming to her, and inside, a part of me was cheering. But it was still odd, and unlike the well-bred Henry I knew.

'We'll have to get to know each other much better then,' purred Sheila. 'So that next time you'll know me *intimately*.'

She lunged forward.

'There will be no next time,' said Henry, abruptly stepping back.

Sheila wasn't giving up that easily. She stepped after him and said, 'Then I'll have to let you get to know me better, right now. I can be very charming, you know.' She raised one eyebrow and her voice went silky sweet.

'You have no charm for me, and as to what other charms you have – BEWARE!' Henry's face flashed, a hard gold gleam sparkled across his eyes.

Sheila drew back affronted. (Ha ha. Two up to me!) But I was alarmed. I'd *never* seen Henry behave like that before. I moved forward to stand beside him, to show him whatever was going on, I was on his team.

Sheila gulped, as if she was suddenly aware what a fool she was making of herself. She stood up, looked wildly from Darren to Rhiannon, looked at me, saw all our blank faces and promptly rushed from the room.

Darren who had been staunching his nose with paper napkins from the bar, turned to go too. Rhiannon looked like she didn't know what to do. 'I better help him,' she said and fled after Darren.

All of them gone!

I looked at Henry. Our eyes met. 'What is it?' I mouthed.

Henry tilted his head in a quizzical way.

'I know she's a flirt, I know she goes too far – I know it's embarrassing. She was trying to prove a point … '

'Yes?' said Henry coldly.

'But she's my friend,' I finished, rather lamely.

'She is no friend to you,' he said.

'But …' I said, and stopped. Somebody had left their mobile on the settle and it was ringing.

I picked it up. Sheila's.

Darren calling …

'I better go and give it her,' I said, 'I'll be quick.'

Henry raised his hand, as if to forbid it. But her phone was ringing and she was my friend … (and I had just won that round), and your mobile is like part of your BEING and I ought to give it her, maybe Darren needed her … and I was pretty sure she'd just rushed to the bathroom.

'She'll be only down the corridor.' I said, biting my lip.

'Go then,' he said, seeing my distress. 'Take no more than a minute. But beware she is *not* your friend and I need you here with me.'

I nodded. I wanted to be there with him, too.

'Be quick, I do not often feel my dragon's heart calling, but right now I hear the fire in the crystal clearly, and it warns me. Follow her if you must, but do not stay with her, listen not to her words, and come back to me, my dearest heart.'

I rushed to the bathroom, but Sheila wasn't there. In a way I was glad. I turned to run back to Henry. *Why had I left him? Was I crazy? This was our last night. What had come over me? Why did I feel it was so urgent to give Sheila her phone? Who cared if it was ringing? I could give it her later.*

Why had she behaved in that stupid way, anyway?

Let her panic. She deserved to.

The corridor outside the rest room was empty. Suddenly I shivered. There was no George around any more to look out for me. I should have stayed with Henry.

A door slammed. I jumped. Sheila rushed down the corridor, her eyes red, her nose running. 'Your lousy boyfriend wants to see you on the terrace,' she said. 'Not satisfied with being rude to me, I now have to run his poxy errands for him, when all I wanted to do was get my phone and apologise!'

'Shell,' I said trying to think of something to say. 'I'm sorry … here's your phone … '

'On. The. Terrace,' she repeated, snatching the mobile without a thank you.

I was confused. Surely not on the terrace? That was outside – or was it?

Maybe the terrace didn't count as outside. Plus it was closer than going back to the conservatory.

'You sure?' I said.

'Don't go then,' she said. 'I don't care.'

'What exactly did he say?'

'Go and ask him your bleeding self,' she said. 'Maybe he wants to fly you to the moon or something.'

Fly me to the moon! *That was it! She was more right than she knew!* If he wanted me on the terrace – he wanted to fly me to the lair after all!

My heart soared. I raced down the hall, my feet already flying, down to the private terrace. I pushed open the double doors on to its wide patio.

There he stood at the far end, leaning over the balustrades with his back to me, a long cloak swirling around his dark form.

'*Henry*,' I called. '*Henry!*'

He didn't turn or answer, but leant further over the balcony, as if there were something out there in the snowy evening that he was intent on understanding.

'*Henry?*' I called again.

He was probably checking to make sure no one was looking.

I raced to his side. I touched his shoulder. 'I'm here!'

The long cloak swayed. The figure whirled round. The hood fell back.

It wasn't Henry.

'*Well hello,*' hissed a high thin voice.

There in front of me was Sir Oswald Pendragon.

Twenty-Six

'At last we meet alone, Miss Morgan,' he said, his voice thin and sharp as the north wind.

I made to step back, to turn and run to the safety of the hotel, but he was far too quick for me. His long arm snaked out and clasped mine. I found myself held in a grip of steel.

'Not so fast, my pretty,' he said, 'now you're here, I think you need to be a little more civil.' He sucked in his breath.

'Let me go,' I said, my voice rising in panic. *'Henry's looking for me. He's out here.'* I don't know why I said that. Maybe I wanted to scare Oswald, make him think twice. Maybe part of me still believed that Henry was out here somewhere.

Surely Sheila couldn't have made such a huge mistake?

Oswald laughed. 'Oh I don't think so,' he said.

I looked wildly around, but there was no Henry anywhere. I tried to wrench my hand free.

'You'll only hurt yourself, if you squirm,' he said, his voice softer now and hissing like the wind.

My heart hammered in my chest, my knees went weak. My wrist under his touch went icy cold. *Henry where are you? Surely you must come?*

Sir Oswald dragged me slowly towards the edge of the veranda.

'Come, come,' he said. 'Why fight me? You know you can't win – all this silly running and hiding – you knew all along I was going to get you.'

I didn't bother to answer, instead I opened my mouth and screamed '*HENRY! HENRY!*' but the wind whipped my words away, and I knew with a sudden terror that Henry was still sitting in the conservatory, still waiting for me and not even his sharp ears would hear me.

But my cry alarmed Oswald, for as I opened my mouth to yell a second time, he raised his free hand and struck me hard. My neck snapped back, my head reeled. I literally saw stars, and then I blacked out.

When I came to, Oswald was no longer human. Instead a huge white dragon loomed over me, a gigantic monster with its claws around my wrist.

Ice-blue eyes, as cold as glaciers, looked into mine, and its tongue snaked out, '*At lassst,*' it said.

Around us the night howled. The mists from Glyder Fawr swept down from the head of the pass. My head spun. My mind swam. I cast around trying to fasten on something – anything. *How could I save myself?* I struggled, but the monster's hold tightened with every twist I made. A disembodied voice seemed to whisper in my head, '*You cannot fight. You have been waiting for this. You know it's what you want. Give up. Give in …* '

But deep inside there was a spark that was still me. A spark that would not go out. It struggled and fluttered like a tiny flame. And I knew what I must do: Find A Way To Tell Henry.

But how?

The wind wailed across the empty terrace. Even if I could manage to scream again, would he hear me?

The white dragon leant closer. It stared into my eyes. Its hooded lids sliding down so low that its irises, pale polar blue, were almost completely hidden. My heart nearly stopped. My throat closed. I shrank in panic against its steely grip.

'You *cannot fight. You can never win. Give in* … '

It dragged me across the balcony. But I was thinking fast. You can't break free. You can't scream. Nobody will know you've gone until it is too late. You must leave some clue, like Hansel and Gretel, *like Cinderella*, and as I was hauled relentlessly to the very edge, I slipped one shoe off.

One of my little star-speckled slippers that Henry had so admired.

And there it stayed, sparking in the moonlight, tiny on the balcony. Yet I knew when Henry came to look for me, he would find it, and he would understand. He'd see how I'd gone outside the safety of the hotel, and know what had happened next.

At the balcony's edge where the parapet rose in stone balustrades, Sir Oswald pounced. My chest froze. I swear my breathing just shut down. I had the feeling that I was tearing in two. His grip on my wrist eased; my hand dropped free. But before I could move I was clasped round the waist by huge talons. I flapped my hands around, feeling for my side, feeling to see if I was still in one piece. And then I was wrenched into the air.

I felt the stonework of the parapet knock against my shins. I felt myself rising, being hoisted, lugged, like cargo.

My head spun, my arms flailed, my hair ripped and streamed in the wind.

A great rushing began. I looked down. I saw I was far above the hotel, above the stone balcony, above the gardens and the annexe and the car park. Icy cold. Mind numbed. I heard a dreadful cracking like the tumbling of a skyscraper and I saw the two stone dragons that stood guarding the hotel entrance shatter. They exploded into a thousand fragments as quickly and as easily as if they'd been made of glass.

And that was it. I was carried fast into the mists of Glyder Fawr.

But before the mist closed around me, the last thing I saw was my little slipper sparkling on the tiles of a very distant terrace.

Twenty – Seven

I don't want to remember that dreadful journey; how cold blasted against me, the clutch of those claws, how the whole of Snowdonia was swallowed up in mist and darkness, how the pounding of my heart burst my ears, and the dull thrash of bony wings beat the air above me.

I tried to search in my bag, tried to find my phone, only to have the whole thing ripped from me by Oswald and dropped on to the rocks below.

I struggled to breathe – Sheila? – she couldn't have known? My face froze. Sir Oswald had done what Henry feared – my lips cracked – found a way to me through my friends – did she know? – she'd warned me – she'd said 'It's War' – so dizzy – so cold.

Poor Mum.

She'd never know what happened to me.

Would Granny Jones – or George – tell her – and George …

George?

A sudden ray of hope. Breathe. Fight the pain. Stay alive. Hang on to life. George might have made it to the lair.

If he'd taken the Range Rover – Darren boasted it could climb a cliff – George might have put the potion in the pool. There was still a chance. Breathe the air so icy. Oswald might drink it …

One thin thread of hope.

I hung on to that, until the moment we landed outside the lair, and I was deposited, only half alive, on to the frozen hillside.

I looked up. There in front of me rose the ruins of Dinas Emrys. Mossy ramparts and the base of an ancient tower. Somewhere under there was the dragons' lair.

For a second I turned away and looked down at the slopes below. If only I could escape, get back to the hotel, get back to Henry.

Would he find my slipper?

Low clouds covered the valleys. An inky sky above. A full moon rising fast. Already in the east the blue-black of low clouds stained the horizon. I shivered and shivered. Everywhere frozen. And there in the shadow of Dinas Emrys my hopes started to freeze too.

Desperately, I searched for a glimpse of George. A trace in the snow. But there was no sign of footprints or the Range Rover. Beside me the hill fell away, covered in part by trees. Everywhere reeked, a horrible rotting smell.

I stood up, slipped on the ice and looked down the bank to see what stank so. Oswald must have seen me turning, for his sinister chuckle rang out and he hissed, 'Welcome to the lair of Dinas Emrys.'

He shot out one taloned foot and grasped me again. He lifted me up and dangled me. Behind the snow-covered branches, the ground was strewn with a gristly mess. Something had felled a sheep; ripped it open from its throat to its bowels. Half of its insides had been guzzled away. The other half lay spilled on the rocky hillside.

Unceremoniously Oswald dropped me back to earth. He pushed me with his claws, and I staggered to my feet. There on the side of Dinas Emrys, under a steep crag, was a low opening, and towards that hole I was half dragged, half shunted.

Before we reached the entrance to the lair, I saw four more sheep carcasses in varying stages of disembowelment. The air was stale with their decomposition. I wanted to vomit. Inside the entrance to the cave were the remnants of other kills. Tufts of blood-stained wool, chewed particles of limb and hoof, a torn off jawbone still half attached to a bony skull.

Feeling sick, I tried to pick my way over the mess, my one unshod foot – half numb with cold – recoiling from the touch of frozen entrails.

Further inside it was worse. The stench of animal hung so heavily in the air, it would have made even the strongest stomach turn. In addition, inside the cave, the winter's chill hadn't managed to keep everything frozen. Every surface was slippery with putrefaction. I hugged my arms around me, my teeth chattering, my ears aching. I searched the ground for traces of George, but there were none. I gave up. George hadn't been here – and if he arrived now it would be too late.

As Oswald dragged me on, I slipped and cracked and crunched over God Knows What. All around rocks hung precariously. They looked so fragile: one shout, one misjudged thump, and the whole lot might come tumbling down.

At length we reached a huge cavern, deep underground. Something in it shone, strange and brilliant. Although I could not make out the source of the light, I was glad of it. The floor was littered with sharp stones. My poor shoeless foot was cold and torn and bloody, and every step hurt, and being in the dark made it worse.

Once in the cavern we stopped and I saw the source of light was coming from a place high on one wall. Edging closer, I squinted up at it.

Two huge crystals shimmered from a niche in the rock face. In their eerie glow the chamber looked vast. Not wide, but tall; it seemed to stretch upwards under the mountain. From its jagged roof, long stalactites hung, like swords poised to fall. But it was the crystals themselves that were the most staggering. They seemed to be embedded in the rock, each one about the size of a tall plinth, square-ish, but tapering to a sharp point, like an obelisk. A light emanated from their brilliant centres and every facet glittered. And deep inside them something beat, as if it were alive.

Oswald let go of me. I fell back against a rock and knocked my shin on an old chain. With a great rush of stinking air, Oswald beat his gargantuan wings and flew up to the crystals.

'*I have brought her to you*,' he hissed. '*As the constellation of Draco turns once more around the pole, as the procession of the equinoxes meets its zenith, you shall drink her blood and renew your strength – you shall fulfil your magic.*'

At those words, he dropped like a stone to the ground, and before I knew anything, he snatched my arm, yanked my wrist out and snapped an old iron manacle around it.

'*Now,*' he hissed. '*While I meet Y Ddraig Goch, you can despair.*'

And with that, he left the way we'd come.

I pulled at the manacle, but it was heavy and made of solid metal. I twisted my wrist, but even though the thing didn't fit properly there was no way I could slip out of it. In panic I jerked and jerked at it, until my wrist was sore and bleeding. Then I slumped down and sunk my head into my arms. And as I dragged my hand up to wipe my eyes, the ancient chain clanked against the cavern wall.

I sat shivering on the floor, the manacle dragging around my wrist, my teeth chattering, my head drooping. But just when I was giving up all hope, I heard a voice.

'*Ellie!*' it hissed.

I looked up; I scanned the cavern. Shadows lurched at me from every angle.

'*Here!*' hissed the voice again. And there in the entrance to the cave, I saw something move. '*Ellie!*'

'*George?*'

'*Yes,*' hissed the whisper, '*it's me.*'

It *was* George. My heart leapt in my chest. *It was George!*

'*I'm here – chained up.*'

'*Can you free yourself?*' he asked. His voice ran in sighs round the edge of the cavern.

Hastily I lifted up my face and looked even more anxiously towards the entrance. '*Oswald will be back soon,*' I called. '*Once he's met Henry – he'll be back.*' I tested the manacle one last time, but despite the smallness of my hand and the ill fit, it stayed firmly where it was.

'Hang on,' said George and in an instant he was beside me. '*Oh Elles,*' he said. He examined the chain. 'OK. Try to be heroic,' he warned. 'This is going to hurt.'

I gritted my teeth, but they were chattering so fast they would not hold steady; I braced myself, but all around me was sharp rock and ice.

George took my manacled hand in his. He made me hold my fingers straight and bury my thumb in the hollow they created in my palm. Then he grasped them and *crushed*, his grip like a vice.

The pain was Un. Bear. A. Bull. But George yanked the manacle upwards, and it ground forward, until it massacred the knuckles of my hand.

'*Don't scream,*' whispered George and then he bent my hand downwards, grasped my wrist with his other hand, jamming my knuckles tight in his. Then he yanked.

I mean REALLY YANKED.

A silver bolt of pain shot up my arm. I opened my mouth to cry out, but found my lips stopped by George's.

With his lips pressed full on mine, he folded my freed hand into his chest. I didn't know what to say or do. But with no way to cry out, and the pressure of my hand clamped against him, I found enough strength to burst into tears.

Slowly George withdrew his lips. I gasped. I spluttered.

'Sorry,' he said, 'I'm not trying to take advantage of you. I just had to find a way to keep you quiet. I needed my hands to … '

'How did you do it?' I said in wonder, feeling my hand burning.

'Just a trick I learned in judo – how to make the hand thin and pointed to effect a proper thrust,' he whispered.

I didn't even know George did judo!

'It feels dislocated, but it's not. Although tomorrow it may be swollen.'

Tomorrow. If only!

'*Quick now, follow me,*' said George, '*this way.*' And off he sped.

Up ahead in the gloom, ripples of reflected light washed over the side of the cave. I heard dripping, and a strange hollow bubbling. I limped nearer, and I could just make out George, already bending over a pool. If you could call it a pool. It looked more like a puddle really, a big dark puddle. But as I looked into it, I realised that this must be the pool the dragons drank from.

George dug his hands into his pockets, pulled out the small potion bottle. He struggled to unplug its top.

'Quick! They'll be back soon,' I cried.

George tried to hurry, but in the darkness he fumbled. 'Blast!' he whispered.

'*Hur-ry!*' I urged. Already a low ray of moonshine had pierced the cave mouth and lay like a finger of silver across the rocky floor.

'My fingers are so numb,' George groaned. He tried to hurry, but instead of removing the cap, he dropped the whole thing. The bottle spun out of his grip and rolled away into the darkness. '*Oh hell!*' George cursed, and instantly crouched down and began searching the floor.

Anxiously I listened. I could almost hear the beat of leathery wings as they smote the air over the mountain. I straightened up.

I *did* hear them.

What were we going to do?

'George?' I pleaded.

Leaving his search for the potion, George grabbed hold of my hand, '*Quick Elles, hide,*' he hissed.

I took his hand and limped away from the pool, into the recesses of the lair. I tripped and stubbed my poor toes. I gritted my teeth and I ran. I knew how hopeless it was, but I ran anyway, looking for a place to hide. We'd failed to put the potion in the pool. We'd failed to get out of the cavern. Oswald was coming. Oswald was beating his way back to his crystal. George would be useless against him. Midnight would come. The finger of moonshine would strike the Heart Crystals. Oswald would find us. Oswald would catch us.

Henry must come.

Henry would come.

But in time to save us?

Twenty-Eight

They did not arrive as huge winged beasts. I wasn't expecting that. If I'd thought, if I'd had my brain half turned on, I might have guessed. Of course Henry would try to keep Oswald in his human form; try to give me a chance. But I didn't guess, I just heard the voices of two men and froze against the cavern wall. Two voices and the step of expensive leather shoes on stone. George shot me one warning look that said: *HIDE. NOW.*

Desperately I searched the gloom of the cave. At the back were four huge stalagmites with a low space behind them. I made straight for that. George read my mind, and together we raced into the darkness and scrabbled around to conceal ourselves.

Within seconds we were crouched down behind the biggest stalagmite. Its rocky pillar, thick at the base, hid us from the two approaching shapes. George's jacket was rough beside me, but I huddled into it all the same. George slipped his arms out of it and put it round me.

Heart pounding, I watched. *Did Henry know I was here? Had he found my slipper?* If he knew what had happened, how could he talk to Oswald so calmly?

Then I remembered his words: '*Our relationship is as complex as the stars in Draco. Until one of us is defeated, we are locked together in a deadly dance for all eternity.*'

Then there must be more stars in Draco than I guessed at.

George's hand found mine and squeezed it (ouch). 'Don't be scared,' he whispered, 'I won't let him get you.' His words cheered me, although against a dragon, both of us knew he stood No Chance.

Maybe up until then, I had been hoping that somehow, magically, it would all come right, that I'd be left with Henry, holding hands, looking into the sunset. But as I crouched in that cold lair, my heart sank.

I squeezed George's hand back (with my good hand), and braced myself. The finger of moonshine crept in behind the two men, soon it was a river of quicksilver flooding across the cavern floor. In only minutes. it would rise up the wall behind us and strike the crystals.

And the final moment would arrive.

And one way or another it would all be over.

George put his arm around me. I noticed his other hand was firmly clenched around the handle of his axe. From far away the sound of an aircraft droned into the evening. The last sound of a civilised world, far beyond our reach now.

'So nephew,' I heard Sir Oswald say. 'Have you brought your sweetheart here? Have you got your pretty little true love ready to accept your heart?' He laughed, cold, mocking.

I peered into the darkness trying to see if I could spot where the potion bottle had fallen.

'Prepare yourself, Uncle,' I heard Henry say. 'You shall not taste human flesh tonight. Prepare yourself for the long internment. Release whoever you have brought. Beg Draco to alter his course. Beg the stars above to once again reshape the magic. Maybe they will still listen. Maybe there is still a chance – even for you.'

'Never!' hissed Sir Oswald. 'I shall sacrifice a girl to my crystal tonight and it will be the very same one that you have set *your* heart upon. It is *you* Henry, Y Ddraig Goch, who will lie here in misery for another lifetime, not me.'

I heard Henry laugh then. 'I think not. She promised me to take refuge elsewhere and I trust her.'

At that Sir Oswald threw back his head and let loose the

most horrible sound. I saw him raise his chin and sniff the wind. His tongue flickered over his lips. He stood silhouetted in the cavern entrance, glowing pale in the white moonshine like some kind of huge maggot. He laughed again. 'You're wrong, nephew, your girlfriend is not to be trusted. *She is already here!*'

'WHAT?' cried Henry, in a terrible voice. Then he too lifted his face and tested the air. He let out a low moan. 'NO!' he cried with such ferocity the rocks themselves might have melted. I hung my head in the darkness.

Sir Oswald sniffed the air again. His thin tongue snaked across his lips. Then with a snarl in his throat, he strode forward into the interior of the cave. My mouth went dry. I couldn't breathe. *He knew I'd escaped.* I broke out in an icy sweat. *He was going to find me.* I clutched at George. My hand fastened on rock. I squeezed myself further into the darkness. I felt something beneath my grip, something round and smooth with eye sockets and a row of bony teeth.

A shudder ran through me. How many girls had run here, to the back of this cave? How many? Had Henry tried to save them? Had Oswald always won?

How many had died?

A scream of fury sprang from Sir Oswald's lips. He must have found the manacle and the chain, found the prey had slipped her tether.

'*Ellie?*' shouted Henry. A note of hope.

'*ELLIE!*' his voice broke, '*RUN! For God's sake! RUN NOW* – before we change.'

My knees trembled. I looked for a way past them. Something by the pool glinted in the moonshine.

'*I'll hold him off! I found the slipper. I know you were deceived.*'

I tried my legs, but they refused to obey me.

'RUN!'

How could I run? Leave George? Leave him?

Instead I clutched my mangled hand to me and tried to shout back, '*I won't leave you Henry. I promised I'd always come to your rescue – I meant it – however hard, however hopeless.*'

'*It's too late!*' screamed Henry.

The finger of moonlight rose up the far wall, reached out towards the crystals. The cave shimmered. I focused on the glinting. The potion bottle! I grabbed George, pointed to it.

Sir Oswald advanced. '*I know you're there …* ' he hissed, his voice growing cavernous. As he spoke, his breath became one long sheet of ice.

The cavern was instantly lit by scores of little frosty pinpricks, tiny mirrors that shone and glinted, like a galaxy of stars. In their glow I saw Henry and Sir Oswald standing in the centre of the cavern.

And as they stood, it seemed their shadows lengthened. Their eyes brightened and their shoulders hunched down until they were all flickering movement. Huge grotesque shapes danced on the walls and grew larger and more terrible by the minute. At what point could I say they stopped being men and became something else that reared up and filled the cavern?

I watched, mesmerised by the flickering lights. Their shadows ran; their shapes writhed and compressed and lengthened, until right before my eyes they became their true dragon selves.

And now Henry looked nothing like the shining crimson dragon I'd ridden to the stars. He looked a terrible demon, with bony claws and leathery wings, like a devil straight out of Hell. He breathed out in a jet of flames which seared across the cave. The flames were not directed at me, or even at Oswald. It didn't seem like they were intended to scorch anything. But as I felt their welcome warmth soaking into me, I understood.

It was just as if in taking on his true form a great relief had come over him, and the very first thing he must do was breathe like a newborn.

And suddenly I knew – he could see through rocks and stone. He could see me crouched behind the stalagmite.

(For he took care that not one cinder of burning ash touched me.) But even as he could see me so could Sir Oswald.

Henry's mind reached out to me. He didn't speak in words, but in some strange way he communicated directly in images and scraps of half-remembered noises. '*Ellie*,' he seemed to utter, in a tone so deep it could have plumbed the oceans. '*I love you.*'

And he breathed again and this time his searing breath was directed at Sir Oswald. Except that it wasn't Sir Oswald any more, it was a gigantic dirty-white winged monster.

I heard George say almost inaudibly, '*That's him; that's the thing that was outside Halfway House.*'

The thing that was Sir Oswald turned towards me. '**Come out Ellie**,' it boomed, as its mind searched behind the rocks of the cave. '*You cannot escape me.*'

A jet of dry ice seared towards us. Particles of moss froze solid in its path. With a crack, the pool we'd run from iced over in an instant.

My heart sank. Even if we retrieved the potion, there would be no way to put it in the pool now.

Then Henry roared. I mean really roared. The world rocked. I clamped my hands to my ears. With my head ringing I reached for George.

Fire filled the cave. In a blinding flash Henry launched

himself on the White Dragon, his razor talons ripping into its side. Images came flooding from Henry: hard fought battles, old wounds, ancient anger, and underneath all that a craving – his own dark unbearable craving for battle, his desire to split the icy white flesh of Oswald, rend it apart, tear, scatter. And at the same moment images came flooding out of Oswald. I could feel his mind reaching out, imagining how he would thrust me on to his crystal, and watch as my blood slowly drained away.

And all the time George gently squeezed my arm and whispered, 'That's it old girl, don't panic, I'm here. Don't give up.'

'Nor you,' I whispered back. 'Let's find a safer place.'

Together we retreated further from the burning debris, out of reach of the flames – until we were right at the very back of the cavern. 'In there,' I whispered.

George squeezed into the alcove and I followed.

And in front of us the dragons fought.

The first blow Henry struck would have killed a thousand men. The cave shook. The floor actually buckled under my feet. If I hadn't been wedged into the crevasse against George, I would have fallen out.

'*Holy Crap!*' said George, 'The hillside's gonna split open if they do any more of that!'

And he was right. Huge chunks of rock cracked loose and crashed down from the ceiling. Stalactites fell like stony swords. One came smashing down right beside our little refuge with such a screech it nearly deafened me. My heart beat so fast, I thought it was going to explode in my chest.

But despite Henry's blow, the White Dragon did not fall. His skin didn't even tear!

His bulk rippled beneath the assault and his huge forelegs shuffled back. He righted himself, swayed and re-aligned his whole body, ready to strike.

The White Dragon of Wessex shook off Henry's blow like a dog shaking off rain drops. Then he slithered towards me.

Henry jumped again, right over it, blocking its progress and struck a second time. He didn't speak, and yet I heard him in the depths of the shrieking that ricocheted around the cave, crying: '*NO! You will not have her!*'

But the White Dragon was much larger, and all the blows that Henry delivered – across the face, the shoulders, the flank and back – made little impact. The White Dragon of Wessex held his ground and shook him off at every turn.

One blow hurt though.

Henry raked a taloned foot across the White Dragon's eyeball. He must have caught a vein or that soft junction of tissue and blood, for suddenly a jet of greyish pink stuff spurted out of the sliced eye and disappeared into the dim vaults of the cave. The White Dragon screamed, blasting ice particles everywhere. Lichen and water vapour flashed in frost, and the whole place glittered and crackled.

I shrank back against the rock and squeezed my eyes tight, fearing I would be frozen too. And I huddled against George, teeth chattering, shivering with the cold.

The White Dragon blundered about. His thoughts, his voice – I am not sure what it was – spilled out of him and, just as his breath had illuminated the air, so his fury filled it. I tried to block my ears. George buried his head in his arms in an effort to muffle the sound.

And all the while beneath the thrum of anger, I felt the clash of their two wills. The one that wanted to seize me, impale me, rip me limb from limb, and the other that wanted to save me.

But wanting to save me put Henry at a disadvantage. In an open space he could have sped and soared and ducked; used all his agility and out-manoeuvred the larger, older Sir Oswald. Here, trapped in the confines of the cavern, with my safety at stake, he couldn't. He dodged, weaved, struck, but the onslaught of the White Dragon took its toll. Sir Oswald was purposely wearing him out.

Henry tried to keep the fight as far from me as possible, but that meant taking blows. And once he flew too close to the stalactites overhead, and I saw a stony dagger spear him. I felt the spray of his dragon's blood burn my face.

And all the time the finger of moonlight slowly rose up the cavern wall towards the crystals.

The White Dragon of Wessex roared. Icy sheets of white bloomed on the rocks. The Red Dragon of Wales roared and the ice melted and the rocks glowed red. Then the White Dragon pounced on Henry, and blew polar breath straight into his face.

Henry coughed and fell back. He opened his maw and shrieked. A huge exhalation of flame lit up everywhere. Stalactites blossomed in white hot silhouette. I turned to see George staring at me. *Henry could not hold the White Dragon off.* Another horrendous blow. Henry fell. I flinched, almost feeling the pain shearing through him.

I looked around. If I could only displace a rock; lob a hunk of something at the White Dragon. Draw him off before he hurt Henry further.

The finger of moonlight rose steadily up the shimmering wall.

I bit my lip. Henry struggled up; flew close to the roof of the cave, close to the glimmering crystals. Oswald followed.

They locked together, their talons sunk deep into scaly hides, tails lashed, wings pounded. A small hurricane seemed to blast inside the cave. One desperate blow from Henry sent a shower of rocks hurtling around us. Then the whole cave shuddered and the White Dragon roared in an explosion of ice – and in its cold light I saw the new danger Henry was in.

He was high in the air with the White Dragon's talons deep in his chest. He could not see that the tail of his enemy was wrapped around a pinnacle of rock. Oswald was dragging Henry ever closer to a point where he would haul the roof of the cave down on top of him.

I saw what would happen: the cavern would collapse, and Henry would be pinned beneath it.

The White Dragon dragged. Henry wrestled. I drew in my breath. I closed my eyes. I screamed out, '*NO*,' so loudly it left my throat rasping.

George tried to turn my face towards his, murmured: 'Easy, Ellie, easy.'

Roughly I pulled away. On an impulse I shot forward, jumped out from the alcove and stood for a split second exposed. Then my brain kicked into action. They were fighting over me, weren't they? So if I fled, if I ran towards the cave mouth, if Oswald thought I was escaping …

I must *make* the White Dragon believe I'd get away, make him chose between burying Henry and losing me.

So I ran.

'*No,*' screamed George. But I broke free.

'*NO!*' screamed Henry.

I faltered.

Sir Oswald dropped Henry. With a sickening crash, Henry fell, twisting in the air like a cat. One huge leathery wing curled under him. He landed heavily on it. I heard it break. I heard his deep exhalation. There was no fire on his breath, no tongues of flame.

And then two things happened simultaneously:

The White Dragon pounced, and George leapt forward.

Twenty-Nine

The finger of moonlight struck the crystals.

The White Dragon shrieked. He twisted. He swooped towards me. But somewhere in his dark dragon's brain he'd forgotten the charms Gran had laid on me, forgotten the herbs of Blodeuwedd. Or else he underestimated the speed at which a girl can move. Whatever the reason, the blow he should have used to fell me missed.

I felt the rush of air against my skin, heard a scream of sinew, but the blow fell short. It raked through my hair, ripped my collar and sliced across my shoulder blade. My head jerked backwards as a hideous talon latched on to the chain around my neck – the silver chain with the sickle moon and the wild flower clasp that Granny had given me. For a brief second, my head swam. I felt a pain shooting down my spine then the chain sprang apart.

The sickle moon spun out and shot towards the White Dragon. The charm hit him full in the face and even though it was only a few ounces of silver, it seemed to hurt him in a way that the horrendous blows from Henry hadn't.

He shrunk away, his head tilted back in agony. He shook himself and must have blinked, because the bulk of his vast body missed me entirely and crashed into the cave wall. A megalithic shudder shook the cave. The ground rocked. I picked myself up and sprinted towards the cave mouth, bursting my lungs to reach it. *Just let me reach it, let me get out – draw Oswald off as far as possible.*

The ground under my feet heaved. Suddenly I was rolling, tripping, sprawling across the dirt.

A low moan came from the back of the cave. I felt Henry's rush of thoughts as if they were tangible. He was saying, *'No! No! Not Ellie!'* The ferocity of them numbed me. I couldn't get back up on my feet. I rolled over and lay there, nursing the pain in my grazed hands, with the taste of blood in my mouth.

Then I saw the White Dragon peel itself back off the wall and re-bunch its muscles. Its bony wings beat a storm in the air. With an ear-splitting screech it sent a plume of dry ice scorching towards me. It gathered up its hideous wings, arched its fearsome neck and, using the wall to counter-lever itself, plunged straight at me.

This was it.

I heard Henry's shout fill the cave. I lay there and breathed in one last breath.

Oswald was only metres from me when out of the depths of the cavern something came whistling.

A shot of silver clove the air. It flashed and turned in the icy breath of the dragon. It split the darkness with its cold steel.

George's axe!

His best axe!

His drop-forged, carbon-steel-head, (hardened and tempered for super strength) hickory-shaft axe.

And it imbedded itself in the face of the White Dragon.

The dragon, thrown off course, nudged the cave wall and coughed, trying to shift the steel embedded in its snout.

But as it coughed – in that instant – it swivelled round to face the new threat.

And George stepped out from behind the stalagmites.

The flames and embers danced in the air around him. There he stood silhouetted in ice and fire.

The White Dragon swirled in a one-hundred-and-eighty-degree turn. It snorted dust and debris and ash. It wrinkled up its foul maw. It meant to blast George and shrivel him to freeze-dried particles. I saw Henry arch out a leathery wing to protect George.

Henry heaved his giant form and dragged himself free from the pile of rubble around him, out into the centre of the cave.

Maybe it was the combination of silver charm, of axe, of Henry trying to save George, of George trying to save me, of me trying to save Henry, of moonlight lighting up ancient crystals – maybe the universe and the stars came together in one great alignment and at that moment our deaths were not meant to be, for the White Dragon – too sure of himself now – stepping out to blast George – placed his foot on the dragging wing of Henry.

The White Dragon skidded, his hooked foot caught on the surface of Henry's wing.

George danced out into plain view.

Oswald shot forward.

Henry levered his wing up and sent out a scorching burst of flame.

The ice on the pool melted.

George raced to the far side, dived to the ground where he had dropped Gran's potion and stood up. In his hand he held the glass bottle. Oswald tried to follow but, caught off balance by Henry, dived too short.

The moonbeam lit up the crystals in one full finger of light.

George poured the potion into the pool.

Oswald opened his mouth to blast George, hit the pool instead and took in a mouthful of its waters.

The crystals trembled and started to shimmer. And, remembering Gran's curse, I shouted, '*Blodau'r deri, y banadl a'r erwain a greuodd Blodeuwedd; ni allwch hela morwyn gyda'r blodau hyn.*'[1]

And Oswald swallowed the water.

Henry sank back, his right wing completely broken.

Instantly the potion worked. And there was the White Dragon of Wessex turning, hitting stone, as his mind and body numbed up.

The hillside shuddered.

Rocks rattled.

It was all over.

And it was all too late.

---

1. 'Oakblossom, broom, and meadowsweet; created Blodeuwedd, you cannot hunt any maiden with these flowers.'

Thirty

I ran to Henry, but his low growling warned me to stay away. I looked up. The boulders overhead hung poised – one careless movement and they would fall.

'Henry!' I cried.

'Don't come any nearer, Ellie,' he said.

'*Change*,' I yelled, 'There's still time.'

The finger of moonshine trembled over the crystals.

'I can't,' said Henry wearily.

'*Why?*' I shrieked.

George sped to my side and put his arm over my shoulder half in support, half in restraint.

'I can't change back into human form,' Henry said.

'*There's still time.*' I pleaded. There *had* to be time. *The crystals were still lit up. The magic would still work.*

'It's not the crystals,' whispered Henry. 'If I change

back now, I'll die. My wounds are too deep, I've lost too much blood. As a dragon I'll heal, in time, but as a man I will not.'

'No,' I cried. I tried to race to him.

George held me back.

'You must go now,' said Henry, his huge dark eyes filled with pain. 'Go quickly. Take her out of the cavern, George. The rocks will fall as soon as the moon-beam fades. *You must! Go now!*'

'*Henry,*' I cried.

'I love you Ellie,' whispered Henry. 'If there had been any other way, I'd have given you my heart.'

'*Come on,*' said George tugging at me.

'*No,*' I cried again, '*I WON'T leave.*'

'We got him, boyo,' said George, pointing at the slumped white shape.

'You did well,' whispered Henry. 'We dragons are not easily defeated.'

Suddenly George took his hand from my shoulder. He sprang to Henry. He pulled out the tiny vial from his pocket. Inside a few drops of potion remained. 'Drink it,' said George, 'It's powerful. It'll numb the pain; you'll wake up feeling better. These few drops alone will knock you out.'

Oh God, was it going to end like this? I looked up at the

roof of the cavern. I prayed to the mountain. *Yr Wyddfa, please save him.*

But Henry, raising his eyes, seemed to say: 'This is how it must be,' and he lifted his poor blood-stained head and opened his mouth. And George poured in the last few drops of the potion.

'*I'll wait for you forever,*' I said racing over to him too, '*I'll break the spell.*' I put my cheek against his huge glittering head and kissed his torn scales. '*I promise I'll find a way.*'

Henry exhaled once and whispered, 'Don't tie yourself to promises that can't be kept.'

'*But I can keep them! I will keep them!*' I cried and threw myself against him, threw my arms around him.

Henry barely moved.

'*I won't leave you,*' I wept.

Henry curled himself into a tight blood-stained ball. His great eyelids hung heavily over his dark eyes. He looked at George: 'Take care of her. Don't leave her,' he said.

'No way,' said George. 'I'LL NEVER LEAVE HER.'

The moonbeam passed over the crystals. The shadows deepened. The earth shifted. George dragged at me. I clung hopelessly to Henry.

'This is what must happen,' whispered Henry hardly awake. 'Trust me.'

I couldn't bear it. Tears burst out. I fell against him sobbing.

As if in a dream, I felt George pick me up, felt George carry me like a child to the mouth of the cave, and I could not hold on to Henry any longer.

The mountain groaned. Then, with a screech that sounded like trucks braking and earthquakes quaking, the stones moved. Boulders tumbled, twisted and fell, covering the body of Oswald, covering the slumped form of Henry.

George put me down, took my hand in his, and hauled me outside. Henry didn't move. His limbs, dark beneath their burden of rock and shale and slate, trembled slightly. He let out a low moan and dragged at himself, and then the whole roof of the lair gave way.

Down toppled the rocks and stalactites, down over the Worms of Dinas Emrys.

Outside the full moon was sinking towards the horizon. George supported me down the mountain and wrapped me in his coat. A few hundred feet away, sharply downhill, hidden by the turn of a mountain spur was the Range Rover.

'The mountain decided,' said George. 'We did our best. Nobody can interfere with the will of Snowdon.'

I said nothing. We struggled past trees, over frozen rocks

and snow-tufted grass. I leant on George as he half carried me to the car.

'Elles?' said George. He turned the engine on. Hot air started to fill the space around us. I still shivered.

'Elles?'

I put my head on his shoulder.

'You owe me a snog, you know.'

I sighed.

'And an axe.'

I didn't even hear him.

'I'll take you home.'

My mind was far away, under the dark cliffs, inside the lair.

'Elles?'

I will save you, Henry. I won't rest until I do.

'I wish you'd say something.'

I brought up my chin and straightened up my shoulders.

'Elles?'

... and in my imagination, I turned to Henry's Heart's Crystal, still shimmering on the cavern wall and etched these words upon it ...

'*I will find you again. Trust me.*'

Fin

So It Will Be

Later that winter ~ 29th February

This morning, the mists were tight around Moel Cynghorion, Mum was out on an early morning mission. Some rocks had fallen over by Clogwyn Du'r Arddu. A ewe and one of our first lambs were trapped, apparently. Before Mum had even got to the Black Cliff, she called me on my mobile to follow her. It's like that sometimes – what at first seems like an easy job turns more complex. 'Meet me up by the Ranger Path,' she said.

I sorted out ice axes, crampons, flares, compass, blizzard bags, thermal mat, space blankets (just in case) and hurried out after her. Since New Year's Eve I'd tried to stay off the mountain –

too many memories, too much sadness — but I guess I was needed today, and anyway, nothing much mattered any more.

I'd climbed up through the top pasture still white with frost.

I think it was as I broke out of the cloud bank above the valleys that I turned to look up towards Garnedd Ugain. I think. I couldn't be sure. Everywhere was thick with morning mist, but through the dawn, standing in the vapour, on that place we call Lovers' Leap, was a figure, a shape blurred by the distance, blurred by the sunrise.

I'm sure I saw a figure.

There in front of Garnedd Ugain on the very rim of the great knife edge, way above the Llanberis Pass. That dangerous place that Mum and I call the Devil's Bridge.

There he was, the figure of a young man poised on the edge of the abyss.

I rubbed my eyes. Was it really? Maybe just a trick of the light? A memory? Rays from the risen sun dazzled me. By the time I'd looked again, new banks of mist had swirled down.

My heart started pounding.

I peered through the mist again.

Nothing.

Maybe.

But then this is Snowdon.

Yr Wyddfa.

The great Snow Den of the Dragons.

Here anything can happen.

When I was done helping Mum, I'd take a detour and check.

Look for footprints in the frost.

Look for a way to keep my promise.

© Roger Bool

Author Biography

Sarah Mussi is an award-winning author of children's and young adults' fiction. Her first novel, *The Door of No Return*, won the Glen Dimplex Children's Book Award and was shortlisted for the Branford Boase Award. Her second novel, *The Last of the Warrior Kings*, was shortlisted for the Lewisham Book Award, inspired a London Walk, and is used as a textbook in Lewisham schools. Her thriller *Siege* was nominated for the CILIP Carnegie Medal (2014) and won the BBUKYA award for contemporary YA fiction. Her thriller *Riot* won the Lancashire Book of the Year award and was longlisted for The Amazing Book Award. Her most recent novel, *Bomb*, was published in 2015 by Hodder Children's Books and featured in *The Guardian's* list of Best New Children's Books for 2015.

Sarah was born and raised in the Cotswolds, attended Pate's Grammar School for Girls, and graduated with a BA in Fine Art from Winchester School of Art and an MA from the Royal College of Art. She spent over fifteen years in West Africa as a teacher and now teaches English in Lewisham, where she is also the current Chair of CWISL (Children's Writers and Illustrators in South London).

Acknowledgements

I'd like to thank:

Jon Barton

Joy Coombes

Susie Day

Matt Dickinson

Ruth Eastham

Sophie Hicks

Jane Howard

Caroline Johnson

Susie Ryder

Bydded i'r Ddraig Goch roi ei bendithion i chi.
May the Red Dragon bestow his blessings on you.